MW01265367

Sacred Gold

Also by Linda Rawlins
The Bench
Fatal Breach

Sacred Gold

Linda Rawlins
with Krista Liotti
Riverbench Publishing, LLC

Sacred Gold
By
Linda Rawlins
With Krista Liotti

Copyright © 2014 by Linda Rawlins
ISBN
EBook 13: 978-0-9914230-8-8
Softcover 13: 978-1494949006

Discover other titles by Linda Rawlins at
www.lindarawlins.com

Riverbench Publishing, LLC
PO Box 1252
West Caldwell, NJ 07007
www.riverbenchpublishing.com

Thou Shall Not Steal

Dedicated
to
All my readers

Acknowledgements

Writing a book is a lot of work, but so rewarding when the final manuscript comes together. Imagine three generations working on one novel. We all contribute and bring different talents to the table. I love working with my children. Their laughter and enthusiasm often balanced my jaded cynicism. I love working with my mom, our cheerleader and initial editor. However, I have many other people to thank for Sacred Gold.

My cowriter, Krista Liotti. With her love of everything Italian, she embodied the voice of Gemma and Willow. She adds the warm and cozy to my clinical being and writing. I am ever grateful she agreed to co-write with me.

My son, Matt Liotti. His invaluable assistance and talent in design, production, research, cover art, and marketing is so appreciated. The book trailer is awesome as well.

My mom, Joyce, for initial edits and content feedback. Known to us as goddess of grammar, defender of commas and apostrophes forever. She's great with term papers too. All omissions and errors are mine alone.

My husband, Joseph, whose vast knowledge of military medicine and religion helps focus content and he supports me with everything else along the way!

Anita – my wonderful personal assistant with research, events, review and fan support and encouragement.

Stephen – who allows me to pick his brilliant mind for information on everything including curators, art and museums.

Ashley – for all her wonderful support and creative input.

Ray – for ethereal support and encouragement.

Helen B – for encouragement and being such a good sport.

Kevin Franz – career Firefighter Irvington Fire Dept, Irvington, NJ for all his enlightening help with fire procedure and protocol.

Kim-Hampton Saul – Former Chief – Hillsdale Volunteer Fire Dept, for all her informative help with proper procedure during nursing home fires.

Paul Marinaccio – Top Shot Season 3 – for help with all things relating to weapons and police procedurals.

Kim O – for helping with specific nursing home admission information.

Aiden King – for great book trailer narration.

First circle readers – Joe L, Joyce R, Carol M, Sandi C, Jennifer M,

Anita U. Your feedback and proofreading have been invaluable. I know I still missed some.

Christine Held - for post-publication revisions.

Peggy Kirchoff, Sister Johnice Thone and St. Francis Residential Center – Denville, NJ – for the wonderful tour and encouragement. What a great place.

Market Street Mission – Morristown, NJ – for the incredible tour and dinner. Thank you for a great opportunity.

To all the dynamic librarians who help promote literacy and are so kind to me.

Especially, to all the readers – your enthusiasm and support are beyond compare and I humbly thank you! Hope you enjoy, Sacred Gold.

Happy Blessed Reading!

Love One Another

Chapter One

Moonlight bathed the icy path as she ran. Panting, she looked back for a mere second before starting to fall. Trying to regain her balance, her feet lost traction causing her arms to swing wildly. Her body pitched forward, slamming into hard stone. Several minutes went by before she stirred, regaining near consciousness from the shock. She tried to remember what happened, crying out as she moved. Torn vessels leaked rivulets of blood which pooled upon the white ground. One hand, caught underneath her body, clutched an object. The other was near her face, fingers sticky and covered in sanguine fluid.

The woman looked up as shifting clouds revealed a full moon. The ground was cold beneath her. Winter had arrived with an icy chill and if she was not already dead, she would be by morning. She was not ready to die. She had a good life, but there was more to do. Her eyes on the moon, she felt the pain begin to subside. Her body relaxed as a feeling of warmth and peace drifted over her. Maybe it would be all right? Or is this what it was like to die?

Had she realized dying was not painful, she would have ignored the anxiety which consumed her entire life. She squeezed the object in her hand and laughed, knowing it was never worth the price. It had always been the chase. As her mind floated toward inky darkness, the moon illuminated the gentle snow which innocently covered her trembling body.

Chapter Two

Two weeks earlier

"Dr. Daniels speaking," Amy said into her chiming cell phone.

"Hi, Amy, it's Ernie. Sorry for the early morning call but you may want to get in here, sooner rather than later."

"I was just leaving," Amy said. "Why? What's going on?"

"We caught a trauma case." Ernie paused.

"And? I get the feeling there's more," Amy said, as her stomach clenched with anxiety.

"Well, I hate to be the one to tell you this, but it's your friend, Helen."

"Helen? Oh no, how bad is she?" Amy pressed.

"She's pretty banged up." Ernie watched the EMT's transfer the elderly woman to the trauma bed. "Broken hip at least, maybe more."

"Is she alert?" Amy asked. "Do you know what happened?"

"I'm not positive, but her neighbor, Harold, went to put his garbage out early this morning. He saw her lying in the driveway and called the police."

"What? It was twenty degrees last night and it snowed this morning."

"I know. Harold has no idea how long she was out there."

"Is she talking?" Amy tried again.

"I'm not sure," Ernie said. "I've got to get in there. I called as soon as I found out. I knew you'd want to know right away."

"That's for sure. Thanks, I'm on my way," Amy said, as she disconnected the call.

Dr. Amy Daniels was the acting medical examiner for Rocky Meadow General Hospital in Rocky Meadow, VT. Trained as a trauma surgeon, she had held a prominent position in Boston, but Amy's world was changed by the life-saving surgery she performed on the perpetrator of a home invasion, as his victims had been her own sister and niece. She was not informed of that fact until after she revived the murderer. Amy's sister had died instantly, but her niece survived and was still in a coma. The realization she had saved the life of the man who had attacked her own family sent Amy into a deep spiral of guilt, anger and despair. Her confidence and spirit were broken and she could not continue at her position in Boston. Making sure her niece was well cared for in a neurologic institute, Amy moved to Vermont looking for answers and a place she could recover from the tragedy. She settled into Rocky Meadow General as an ER physician; then later, acting medical examiner to keep her skills sharp while she healed. Hating calls such as this one and fighting back tears as memories rushed through her mind, she picked up her purse and bolted out the door.

Chapter Three

"Breakfast was great, Katie," Father Michael said, using his napkin to wipe crumbs from his mouth. "Thanks."

"Thank you for saying so. I'm glad you had a good meal before leaving for the conference today. What about you, Father Victor?" Katie smiled as she turned to the visiting priest from Chicago.

"Oh Katie, you know the only reason I haven't gone back to my parish is your cooking." Father Victor beamed at her.

"Oh, go on," Katie laughed, clearing the plates off the table. "I'm sorry Sister Maggie couldn't make it for breakfast. I hope she eats something before you leave."

"I'm sure she'll grab something on the way, but it won't be as excellent as this was," Father Michael said, as he pushed back his chair and stood up from the table.

"I hope so," Katie said. "It's a busy day and there are a lot of lectures scheduled."

"With any luck, all good ones," Father Michael said. "We're trying to plan ways for the archdiocese to serve the community more effectively. There should be a lot of discussion on modern social issues and the needs of the congregation."

"You should mention the soup kitchen while you're there," Katie said. "Sue does a great job running the one in Burlington, but there's a growing need in this part of Vermont."

"It's true. The economy is not good and we have more homeless veterans living in the area," Father Michael agreed.

"Rocky Meadow General has done a great job with the medical clinic so there's improved healthcare for those in need," Father Victor said with a nod. "Dr. Amy still volunteers every Saturday in the clinic. I usually see her when I make spiritual rounds for the patients."

"Well, it is Saturday, so I'm sure she'll be at the hospital most of the day," Katie said, clearing the table. "Instead of the clinic, Willow agreed to spend the day with me at St. Francis, so we're finishing the church decorations for tonight's Advent mass."

"That's great," Father Michael said. "She's come a long way this year."

"Thanks to Dr. Amy," Katie said with a nod.

"And I'm sure Dr. Amy would say thanks to us," Father Victor replied with a huge grin. "So now we're all happy. Let's find Sister Maggie, go to the conference and get this over with."

"You behave yourself, Father Victor," Katie said. "Otherwise, I'll get after you with my broom."

Laughing, the two priests left the kitchen to collect their things and Sister Maggie.

Chapter Four

Ernie donned his vinyl gloves, blue-green hat and gown, and walked into the trauma room toward the bedside. "What do we know?" Not waiting for an answer, the attending physician at Rocky Meadow General Hospital ER started examining the small, white-haired woman lying in front of him. She was restlessly moving her arms and had a cervical collar around her neck. Fully clothed, except for a jacket, an IV ran into her right hand as her left was bloodied and swollen. A cut in her pants, made by medical personnel in an attempt to check for wounds and bleeding, showcased her fragile right leg dressed in a splint.

"Let's see," the EMT said, looking at a flip chart. "Helen Coyle, ninety-two year old, white female, lives alone in a house on Boulder Ridge. She was found lying in her driveway by a neighbor this morning. Minimally responsive except for tactile stimuli. Right leg was at an unnatural angle, probable hip fracture. She was fully dressed, but we removed her coat so we could start intravenous. She was covered with warming blankets in the rig.

"She's a repeat visitor. Been here a few times this year. Helen? Can you hear me?" Ernie asked, raising his voice.

The elderly patient looked toward the doctor, but said nothing. Confused, she moaned as he gently prodded and examined her.

"Anything else?" Ernie asked the EMT.

"The front door was open and the police checked inside. All seemed in order. There was no medication list and they didn't find prescription bottles. There was a trash can lying on its side near her body, so we assumed she was taking out the garbage and fell."

Turning to Brenda, an ER nurse, Ernie said, "I'm familiar with this patient. She's a close friend of Dr. Amy Daniels, and this isn't the first time she's fallen. She was here for a head injury several months ago. Let's get an x-ray of that right hip and pelvis, a CT scan of her brain, and x-rays of her cervical and lumbosacral spine. Keep the collar on for now and pull some lab to make sure she's not bleeding internally." Ernie carefully placed his stethoscope on her chest. "Her heart sounds irregular. Do we have an EKG yet?"

"We got a rhythm strip in the ambulance – it looks like she's in A. Fib," the EMT offered, looking at the chart. "But I don't know if that's new onset or chronic."

Turning back to Brenda, Ernie said, "Okay, get a graph and call Dr. Lou Applebaum for a cardiology consult. Also, make sure they pull the record from her last admission. I can get her medication list and medical history from there. I already called Dr. Daniels and she's on her way in."

"Consider it done," Brenda said, with her usual efficiency.

"Thanks guys," Ernie said to the EMT team. "We'll take it from here."

An hour later, Ernie was back at the front desk making notations on Helen's medical chart.

"How is she?" Amy asked, upon her hurried arrival at the

ER.

"Stable at the moment," Ernie said, leaning over to grab a silver clipboard from the desk. "Hold on, I've got some results for you."

"Is she conscious?"

"She's in and out," Ernie said. "The good news is the CT scan of her brain was normal. No bleeding, no mass."

"And the bad news?" Amy asked, with wide eyes.

"Well, she definitely has a broken hip. Looks pretty nasty too. She's out of it because we gave her a painkiller to keep her comfortable. I called Dr. Weber. He's covering orthopedic emergencies today."

"She has to go to the operating room?" Amy asked.

"Oh yeah," Ernie said, nodding his head. "Wait until you see the film. Weber can try to pin it, but it won't be easy. He may have to do a partial replacement."

"I know she has osteoporosis and her bones are fairly thin, which may pose a problem. The poor woman," Amy said. "Did anything else show up?"

"She's anemic. Her hemoglobin is nine. They're typing and crossing her for a couple of units tonight."

"That makes sense, she'll probably bleed for a while."

"She had some A. Fib on her graph," Ernie said, skimming the chart.

"That must be new," Amy said. "Good thing she wasn't on a blood thinner, but she may have to start one. Is she talking? Was she able to tell you anything?"

"I haven't been able to get a full story from her yet," Ernie said, with a shrug. "You know her better than any of us. What do you think she was doing?"

"Probably taking her garbage out, like Harold was," Amy said, with a wry smile. "I know she doesn't like to leave it out the night before. She hates when raccoons get into it."

"Amy, there you are," Lou Applebaum said, as he crossed the ER, flashing a large smile.

A smirk appeared on Ernie's lips as he whispered under his breath, "Ah, your cardiologist in shining armor is coming to bask in your presence. Thank goodness I have more patients to see. I'll see you later."

"Ernie, don't leave me," Amy pleaded.

"Sorry Babe, gotta go." Ernie thrust the silver chart into Amy's hands and walked toward the triage room. Smiling shyly, Amy turned toward Lou and waited until he reached her side.

"Good morning," Lou said, with a glowing smile. "You're looking lovely today."

"Hi, Lou," Amy said sheepishly. "It's nice to see you."

"I got the call about Helen and ran right over," Lou said. "I'm sorry to hear she fell."

"Thanks, I haven't seen the x-rays yet, but Ernie says it looks bad enough to send her to the OR."

"That's how I found out. They called me to do a cardiology clearance," Lou said, genuinely concerned. "Does she have any history of heart disease?"

"Not that I know of. She had an echocardiogram last time she was in the hospital and it looked okay for her age. It should be in her records. But apparently, the graph is showing A. Fib. I think it may be new, but we'll have to check."

"That'll be easy to pull up," Lou said.

"She's a strong, ninety-two year old woman, who exercises every day," Amy said. "This should not have happened."

"Unfortunately, everyone has a weakness. It would seem Helen's is icy weather."

"Apparently," Amy said, shaking her head. "I'm sure she only wanted to take her garbage out. The problem is we don't know if she simply slipped and fell or if there was a medical issue first."

"Has she ever passed out before?"

"I don't think so," Amy said. "She was in here with head trauma a couple months ago after falling off a step stool. She was trying to fill the bird feeder in the back yard with a twenty pound bag of bird seed."

"I remember." Lou chuckled. "She's a spit fire."

"She sure is," Amy said, nodding her head in agreement. "And we're back to the chicken and the egg thing. Did her hip snap and cause her to fall or did it break when she hit the ground? She has been complaining of increased hip pain recently and I know she had some degenerative disease there to begin with."

"Well, Weber will have to deal with that end of it," Lou said kindly.

"I know," Amy said. "I want to try to see her, but Ernie medicated her for pain so I don't know if she's alert enough to talk."

"I'll see her with you," Lou reached out and touched her arm.

A moment passed as the two exchanged glances. Attempting to break the silence, Lou said, "Listen, Amy, I know this isn't the best place to ask, but if I've learned anything from working in a hospital, it's that I should seize the moment. So, I know the last time we went out was a little crazy, but I'd really like to go out with you again…now that things have calmed down a bit, I mean."

Amy smiled at Lou. He was a handsome cardiologist, compassionate, well dressed and very single. She knew he was attracted to her. They both had experience working in an intense medical environment and, for different reasons, had relocated to Rocky Meadow, VT. Amy was the first woman he could relate to medically and intellectually. He had convinced her to have dinner several months ago, in a fancy restaurant near Lake George, NY. The date was wonderful except they were almost run down by a ruthless killer. Since then, Amy had refused his advances.

"I don't know, Lou. You know I'm not ready for a relationship right now," Amy said, embarrassed. The only man she looked forward to spending time with, at the end of the day, was her good friend, a local priest.

"Hey, I didn't propose. I just want to eat," Lou laughed. "And have conversation with someone who can stay awake when I bore them with quotes from cardiology journals."

Amy giggled at his honesty. "Maybe dinner is a little much. How about we start with a coffee date?"

"That sounds perfect," Lou agreed readily. "Have you been to the Cider Mill?"

The Cider Mill was an independent book store which moved

into space left behind by a closed apple cider mill in Rocky Meadow, Vermont. Besides stacks of books, new and old, as well as a table devoted to local authors, it boasted one of the best coffee bars in the area. The new owners had designed a large area for comfy cedar wood chairs, near walls lined with electric outlets for clients to plug in their laptops, all for the price of one cup of java. They defrayed the cost of electric by using freshly installed solar panels on the roof of the building.   Extra funds went to display various artifacts, found across Vermont, around the store. The cold weather, during the autumn and winter tourist seasons, not only helped book sales but coffee sales as well. "How about this weekend?"

"I'm told they make a Mocha Cappuccino to die for but I can't promise this weekend," Amy said. "I still have to see what's going on with Helen and there are patients to see at the clinic and…"

Lou interrupted Amy with a tingling kiss on the cheek. "I completely understand. Just promise we'll go soon, okay?" Lou asked, raising his eyebrows. "It doesn't have to be the weekend. Mid-week is probably less crowded anyway."

Amy tried to fight the redness that flooded her cheeks, "I promise. I've wanted to spend some time there anyway. I hear it's a perfect literary getaway."

"I can't wait." Lou looked delighted. "Well, I guess we'd better get Helen ready to go to the OR. After you," he said, as he stepped aside for Amy to pass.

Chapter Five

"The advent wreath looks lovely, dear," Katie said to Willow, as she admired the greens perched on a pedestal near the altar of St. Francis Church.

"Thanks, Katie," Willow said shyly, twisting her mouth in a small grin. "I worked really hard on the velvet bows. I wanted it to look pretty for Advent."

"Well, it's beautiful. You're a natural when it comes to decorating. First those Christmas tree decorations and now these bows. I'm sure Father Michael will love it when he gets back from the conference. Goodness, they should be here soon. They'll bless the wreath and light the first candle at tonight's mass." Katie stood back to take in the whole view of the altar. "Advent is such a special time, full of hope and love."

"Purple is my favorite color," Willow said, looking at the candles in the wreath. "I like to watch them light the candles. My grandmother used to take me to church, but I haven't been to an Advent mass since she died."

"I'm so glad you've been coming to mass with Amy for the last few months, dear," Katie said with a smile. "It's been good for both of you."

"I'll second that," Father Michael said, walking into the church with Father Victor and Sister Maggie at his side.

"My stars." Katie jumped and held her hand to her chest. "Don't sneak up on an old woman that way."

"Katie, you'll outlive us all," Father Michael said, grinning ear to ear.

"Not if you keep sneaking up on me," Katie said, as she looked at the three of them and laughed. "Well, did you all enjoy the conference?"

"Yes, Katie, very much," Sister Maggie said, as a smile lit up her eyes.

"I'll tell you one thing, the food couldn't touch anything you make here," Father Victor said. "I couldn't wait to come back for dinner."

"Oh Father, your appetite astounds me."

Father Michael stood still, wearing a smug grin on his face.

"Well, don't you look like the cat that ate the canary," Katie said, frowning at the priest.

"Katie, I have some exciting news," Father Michael smiled. Sister Maggie beamed and excitedly nodded her head behind him.

Father Michael was the pastor of St. Francis Church and Rocky Meadow Retreat House, which were located in a beautiful remote woodsy area in Vermont. The church had been named after St. Francis of Assisi, and used for years as a sanctuary by various religious clergy and laypeople in need of spiritual respite. Initially, priests and dignitaries would visit to meditate and relax while immersed in the beauty of nature. Over the years, the Retreat House became a well-known sanctum for anyone seeking inner calm.

As the town grew, the archdiocese needed to turn St. Francis into a full time community parish. St. Francis now offered routine mass, religious education, and a beautiful landscape for self-reflection. The miles of natural hiking paths and running trails were only surpassed by the astounding peace and beauty, offered by the prayer walk. Several years ago, Father Michael Lauretta had been assigned to the church per special request from the Bishop. Trained in counseling, Father Michael had a special ability to help overwhelmed clergy, and was a perfect fit to serve as the new pastor and counselor to those who sought the healing presence of St. Francis and the Rocky Meadow Retreat House.

"Out with it then," Katie said, with a disapproving look and hands on hips. "You've gone this far, you can't leave us in suspense." Willow shook her head in agreement.

Katie Novak began working as the parish housekeeper when her husband passed away from cancer. At the suggestion of Father Michael, she sold their farm and moved into the rectory to care for the priests and Retreat House guests.

"Do you know the restaurant on Main Street? The one down the street from Hasco's?" Father Michael asked.

"You mean the place that's been closed for the last six months?" Katie asked, as she tilted her head.

"Yes, exactly."

"Of course, I've often driven past and thought it would be a perfect place….Oh dear," Katie said, after realizing what Father Michael was hinting at. With a small rise in her voice, she asked, "You don't think it could possibly work out?"

"That's what I'm trying to tell you." Father Michael grinned.

"While we were at the conference, I got a phone call; the bank has put it up for auction. Next week, as a matter of fact. We missed it in the newspaper, but we still have a shot. Thankfully, the bank manager, Mr. Owen, knew we were looking for a place."

"Oh my." Katie's hand flew to her throat and her eyes started tearing. "I'm afraid to dream. It would be such a blessing. What do you think, Sister?"

"It would be wonderful, Katie. But, I think the Lord has his plan and we'll be given an answer when he's ready." Sister Maggie was from a convent located near Rocky Meadow which supported the church when needed.

"Miracles can come true, Katie" Father Michael said. "Just have faith. The Lord may have a different vision than you, but things usually work out in the end."

"I know, but I don't want to get my hopes up. Opening a soup kitchen in Rocky Meadow has been my dream for a while now. The place would be perfect. It also has several apartments above the restaurant," Katie said. "We've had a homeless person or two who could use a warm place to sleep on occasion."

"You know the Retreat House always offered a place to sleep, especially on a cold Vermont night," Father Michael reminded her.

"Of course, Father. But St. Francis is so full of visitors, some of our homeless guests feel uncomfortable. And now, we have an occasional tour group stopping by."

"You mean, we would have a soup kitchen right here in Rocky Meadow?" Willow asked.

"Yes, just like the one in Burlington, where we helped several months ago," Katie answered.

"I hope nothing bad happens, like it did there," Willow said, as she shuddered.

"That was an isolated circumstance, Willow," Father Michael said as he tried to comfort her. "It could have happened anywhere. Someone was in the wrong place at the wrong time, and there was a case of mistaken identity as well."

Father Michael referred to a situation which occurred at the soup kitchen in Burlington, VT, several months ago. The group had volunteered to help for the day. One of the guests went outside to smoke and was accidentally shot and killed by an assassin.

"Soup kitchens help so many people," Willow said. "I'd definitely work there. Especially after everything you've all done for me."

Willow was a sixteen year old girl who spent a lot of time at St. Francis Church. She was abandoned by her parents at birth and raised by her wealthy grandmother who was recently murdered. Willow had instantly become a teenaged millionaire. The estate was controlled by a lawyer who had been chosen to protect her assets until she was educated and of age to manage her own investments. At the request of the estate, Willow was assigned a guardian. She was home schooled and volunteered at Rocky Meadow General Hospital, as well as St. Francis Church and the Retreat House. Despite all her legal protection, she remained a lonely, frightened girl until she was befriended by Dr. Amy Daniels. Now with a strong circle of friends and support, she continued to volunteer but was surrounded by loved ones.

After being threatened several months ago, she formally moved into the Retreat House instead of living in a large farmhouse with a disinterested guardian as her only human companion. "My mother still needs to connect with community service after she gets out of rehab. It would be good for her to work there too."

"And we would need the help, believe me," Katie said with a nod.

"The Lord will provide," Sister Maggie said, in her soft sweet voice.

"I'm sure we would all help out," Father Michael said happily. "Your dreams are close Katie, very close."

"Oh, I'm so nervous," Katie blustered.

"And I will volunteer to be the official food taster," Father Victor offered with a small bow and wave of his hand.

Father Victor Cerulli had come to Rocky Meadow Retreat House for formal counseling, as advised by his archbishop in Chicago. He was a large priest who loved to box in his free time. After his mandatory therapy, he opted to stay at St. Francis and help with parish duties while he continued to work on anger management. Katie often wondered if his self-imposed reflection was really a ploy for good home cooking. Even if it was, Katie was thrilled.

As Willow laughed, Katie frowned. "Father Victor, you'll be helping all right, but you won't eat until all our guests have been served."

As Father Victor's face registered total shock, Katie continued. "Okay, one plate before we serve and the rest after our guests have eaten. Otherwise, we may not have any food left."

"Agreed," Father Victor laughed. "As long as I get to choose the plate."

Grinning, Katie clasped her hands together, almost in prayer. "It would be wonderful to have our own soup kitchen. Lord knows, with the downturn in the economy, so many people are in need."

"Well, we've got a shot at a great location next week," Father Michael said. "Monday morning, we'll make some phone calls and see what we need to do to bid on that closed restaurant."

"Do we have the money?" Katie asked, with a worried frown on her face.

"St. Francis has some assets put aside for community programs. We could always appeal to the archbishop for some assistance as well." Father Michael shrugged. "The worst thing he can say is 'no' and we keep looking for another facility. But he sounds rather agreeable lately. Something will come up – I believe in the Lord. Remember Proverbs 3:5,"

"Trust in the Lord with all your heart."

"I do," said Katie and Sister Maggie simultaneously.

"And me," said Willow.

"Count me in," Father Victor said, rubbing his belly.

"Oh Lord, well don't just stand there." Katie handed Victor a decoration of evergreens. "We finished everything except the garland. You're the only person tall enough to hang this." Turning to the group, she said, "If you all want a hot dinner, you'd better get to work."

Delightedly, the group spent the next hour draping the church in streams of velvet and evergreen, displaying signs of hope and joy that immersed the Advent season.

Chapter Six

The icy amber Italian liquor burned as it slid down the yearning throat of Gemma Montanari. She sat in a posh, Manhattan lounge, poised at a small table. An array of modern art enveloped the dark room in tasteful fashion as colored lights were directed up the walls in a montage of graceful pastels. Highlighted frosted glass, etched with wistful roses and wine bottles dotted the wall behind the bar. An instrumental of Verdi's best flew from the fingertips of a professional pianist amid the fragrant rose scented air. La Vita Rossa had a reputation for fresh air long before smoking was prohibited. Gemma timidly raised her hand as the male server glanced toward her table. He was dressed in a formal suit, complete with a silk pocket square, and emitted more style than some of Gemma's recent male companions. She looked up as he quietly approached the table.

"Madame? May I be of service?" He asked, as he flashed his most charming smile.

"Another drink, and make it a double." Gemma said sweetly, smiling in return.

"Of course." He removed her empty glass and bowed his head. Using the linen napkin that was carefully folded over his left arm, he dried the miniscule liquid which had collected on the table from the ice in her first drink.

Gemma took a moment to survey the room. She realized her

next drink would add forty dollars to the tab, but Paolo was late. Next time he asked for a meeting, he'd make it a point to be on time. It was his tab, his problem. He was a jerk anyway. She loved her job when she first started working for the acquisition broker. It was exciting and she was damn good. She managed to secure more art and rare items than his last three representatives combined. Everyone was thrilled with her work. She loved the challenge of hunting down a special artifact and closing the deal. The seller got his money, she and Paolo got a percentage, and the buyer was ecstatic. Then Paolo got greedy. He pushed harder and encouraged her to become devious. Paolo realized underground acquisitions were worth a lot of money and garnered far more power, but to what end? The consequences were more serious. Let him play his little game. She refused to be pulled in any further.

Standing at the doorway, Paolo Sartori stood watching Gemma. Paolo was a small man. He wore expensive clothes and cologne to match, but he was not attractive. Tonight he had chosen his favorite Calvin Klein pinstripe suit and dress shoes by Hugo. His hair was lighter than most Italians, but he slicked it back to make it appear dark, which matched his ugly personality.

Gemma was beautiful by any standard. Silky jet black hair framed an ivory face ablaze with intense blue eyes. She looked even more beautiful in her Roberto Cavalli dress and Christian Louboutin heels. Gemma had been referred to Paolo by her father back in Italy. Not knowing Paolo's depravity, he asked Paolo to teach his daughter about the world of acquisitions. And Paolo complied, partly because she was the most beautiful woman he had ever seen, and partly because he was obligated to her father for his own career. Paolo not only taught her the business, he introduced her to his associates as well. She was assured instant success and did not need his connections. Using her beauty, Gemma charmed rare artifacts from owners who vowed never to let go.

As a youth, Paolo was interested in being a curator. He always wanted to work independently so he would have the freedom to pursue the acquisitions and exhibitions which interested him most. Paolo held non-profit exhibitions for several prestigious universities from the private collections of his friends, which provided extraordinary education to the students, while establishing his reputation as curator. Fund raising and grant proposals were always aggravating, but it was part of the job.

Hoping that Gemma would be more suited to financial management, he agreed to teach Gemma how to be a curator. It was not long before they both realized her specialty was in acquisitions. She established her own network, researched the internet, followed other exhibitions, especially private ones, and went after her goal. Within a few years, she had a reputation as a leading acquisition specialist for all types of fine art and artifacts. She collected rare and amazing pieces, and did so legally.

Gemma could have started her own business, with outstanding success, but out of respect for her father, and partially Paolo, she remained part of his company. She was not aware requests for art had come to Paolo from less than proper channels. Paolo would simply start Gemma on the chase, and most times she would succeed. But when the owners were not willing to part with their treasures, Paolo sent a cleanup crew who would convince them otherwise. It did not take Gemma long to realize what was happening, and she wanted no part of it. Paolo offered her money, prestige and her own company. He also asked her to marry him several times. Due to her beauty, allure and rare talent, Gemma was the greatest treasure he could ever acquire, but she turned him down repeatedly. It was her culture to pursue love and success, and Paolo offered neither. Yet, she stayed with him for now. He was determined to have her, if not as a wife, then as a prized piece in his personal collection.

Paolo walked to the table, with a smile on his face, and kissed the back of her hand. "*Bella, che piaecer*! I've missed you."

"*Oh la feccia finalmente e arrivata! Ho aspettato per un'ora. Così il piacere è completamente tuo.*" Gemma spat at him while gesturing with her hand. "The scum has finally arrived. I've waited for an hour so the pleasure is entirely yours."

"*Mi scusi, Bella*, I had a meeting," Paolo lied smoothly, as he pulled out a chair at the table, sat down, and crossed his legs.

"You had a meeting with me," Gemma said leaning toward him. "This is your request, not mine."

"Don't hate me," Paolo said, while making a puppy face. He knew she was waiting. He loved the fact he controlled her for at least an hour, and he used the time to watch her, fantasize about her. He even liked how the other men in the bar stared at her, as long as they didn't touch. "You enjoyed your drink?"

"Paolo, what do you want?" Gemma asked, thinking the sight of him made her sick.

"I have to talk business. You will not talk about love, *mio amore*."

"Don't call me that," she hissed through clenched teeth.

"I want you to get ready to travel. Perhaps back to Italy."

"Why Paolo? What are you up to now?"

"I have a feeling we are going to have a great opportunity soon and I want us to be ready for the acquisition."

Gemma stared at him without speaking. Finally, she asked, "Who is the contributor?"

"Not yet, my love. I'll tell you when I'm sure," Paolo said, with a small smile. He knew there was no opportunity, but he wanted her to run when he called. He picked up her hand to caress the smooth skin and Gemma barely contained herself from slapping him.

"Paolo, next time you call me, you'd better have some real information. I don't have time to waste on scum like you," Gemma said, as she grabbed her purse and left the table.

Paolo debated following her for a few moments but decided against it, not wanting to make a scene. He sat at the table, a wolfish grin on his face, as he watched her body move toward the door.

Chapter Seven

Dr. Amy Daniels opened the door to her modern two story log cabin in Rocky Meadow, VT. She was stunned the first time she viewed the beautiful home, with its wall of glass, overlooking a serene lake, a large deck with an outdoor fireplace, and granite and marble accents throughout the interior. As predicted in November, the deck was covered with a foot or two of snow which would remain until she had time to do something about it. It was her first winter in Vermont and she lacked experience stocking firewood and food. As she placed her coat and bag on the closest chair, she reached for the ringing telephone, hoping Helen didn't have a post-surgical complication.

"Dr. Amy Daniels."

"Amy, I'm glad I caught you," Father Michael said, when he heard her voice.

"Hi, I just got home. Really bad day," Amy said, relieved it wasn't bad news from the hospital.

"I was worried about you driving in the dark with all this snow. I know you're not use to it."

"Thank goodness the moon was out. The reflection on the snow actually helped to light up part of the road, but I was still nervous about going over the side. I hope Willow didn't try to drive in this," Amy said.

"She was with Katie for most of the day decorating the church. She told us you wanted to be with her the first time she drove in snow. She's so excited about having her new license, I'm sure she'll want to be on the roads tomorrow."

"Well, sit on her until I have time to get there," Amy said, with a laugh.

"It's good to hear you laugh," Michael said softly. "You said it was a bad day. Want to talk about it?" Father Michael and Amy had met when she moved to Vermont after her family tragedy. Regularly seeing her sitting on a bench, near part of the river which flowed through St. Francis property, he stopped one day to talk to her. As a psychologist and priest, he did his best to reach out to people who were obviously upset. He and Amy had become fast friends after helping solve a murder over the summer, and remained very close.

"It's Helen," Amy said with a sigh.

"Is she all right?" Michael asked.

"No, she really isn't. She fell early this morning and fractured her hip. It was a complicated fracture."

"She's in the hospital?"

"Yes, we spent most of the day doing pre-op work. She needed a transfusion and then we had to wait for the surgical team. The repair was finally done a couple of hours ago, and she was stable when I left the hospital. I waited until she got out of recovery."

"You must be exhausted," Michael said. "I'm glad the surgery went well."

"I am tired," Amy said. "I examined clinic patients and ran back and forth to the OR in between. Thankfully, Helen's out of it for now, exhausted from surgery and painkillers. She'll be uncomfortable when she wakes up, though."

"But, she'll be okay? Would you like me to see her in the hospital tomorrow?"

"That would be great if you have time after mass," Amy said. "She's got a difficult road ahead of her. Treatment in the hospital for a few days and then she'll be transferred to the sub-acute facility down the road for further therapy and rehab. Healing could take a while."

"Doesn't sound pleasant," Michael said.

"Therapy can be painful, especially after breaking a hip," Amy said. "They'll push her as much as they can, otherwise she runs the risk of becoming bedbound. It's a challenge for someone who's ninety-two years old."

"Does she have family to help her?" Michael asked.

"Actually, no. We had a long talk about family over the summer. Her only close friend was Harold and he's been shying away from her now that she's starting to have some difficulties. So, she asked me to look after her. I promised I would help her on a medical and personal level as best I could."

"Wow, sounds like you both have a challenge to face."

"Yeah, but she's tough. She exercises every day so I'm hoping she'll come through with minimum difficulty."

"I'm sure she'll be happy to have you by her side. Can we see her together?"

"That would be nice, Michael. I'd like that," Amy said, as she smiled.

"I'll pray for her and for you, too," Michael said. "You know I always do."

"I know that," Amy said softly. "And by the way, I really appreciate having you as a friend. It's been quite a year."

"You know I'll always be there for you, Amy." Michael said.

"Me too," Amy said, suddenly feeling shy.

"Well, I'd better let you get some rest. I'll try to call you after mass so we can go to the hospital. Unless I see you at church?"

"I'll try, but it depends on whether any emergencies come up. I could be anywhere. You know that," Amy said quietly.

"Good night then, Amy," Michael said. "Sweet dreams."

"Good night," Amy said, as she hung up the phone and hoped his wish came true.

Chapter Eight

"Hi, how did it go last night with Helen's surgery?" Amy asked Dr. Weber when she saw him amidst hospital rounds the next morning. "I didn't get a chance to speak with you in recovery." Amy had waited until Helen was out of surgery, but Dr. Weber was unable to do the same, as a car accident was newly admitted to the OR. Needless to say, Amy was curious about the details of the fracture.

"Better than I'd hoped." Dr. Weber nodded. "She's amazing. I have patients who are half her age who don't do as well with a complicated procedure like that."

"Trust me, she's a strong woman," Amy agreed, with a laugh.

"I guess you don't make it to ninety-two if you're not," Dr. Weber said.

"So true. What do you think about post-op?"

"She'll be in pain for a while, but I think she'll do great in therapy," Weber said, with a shrug. "After that, it's her choice where she goes. She may be safer in a monitored situation."

"Possibly," Amy said thoughtfully.

"Amy, there you are."

Both doctors turned to see Father Michael standing at the entrance of the nursing station on the surgical floor.

"Hi, Michael how are you?" Amy said, as she beckoned him

over.

"Hi, how are you today? I didn't see you at church so I rode over to the hospital with Father Victor."

"I'm sorry, but I had to get here early for a patient," Amy said apologetically. "Do you know Dr. Weber? He's the orthopedist who operated on Helen last night."

"How are you, Father?" Dr. Weber asked pleasantly. "Nice to meet you."

"You too, I didn't mean to interrupt but I wanted to ask about Helen," Father Michael said. Looking at Amy he asked, "Maybe we can go see her together."

"I'm sure she would like that. She always feels better when she sees you...and Ernie for that matter," Amy smiled coyly, remembering Helen's infatuation with the ER physician.

Dr. Weber watched the pair with interest. "I take it you're all close friends?"

Amy didn't speak for a moment and felt her face turning red. "Yes, we are. We both take care of Helen and Willow. You know, the candy striper who lost her grandmother last year."

"Yes, sadly, I heard about her." Turning to Father Michael, Dr. Weber said, "Thank goodness, you're a priest. Otherwise Lou Applebaum would have a fit."

"Oh?" Father Michael replied, with a raised eyebrow.

"Well, he's a bit enamored with Dr. Amy, so we've been warned off," Dr. Weber said with a laugh.

"Are you kidding me?" Amy asked sharply as she turned to Dr. Weber.

Realizing they were both looking at him expectantly, Dr. Weber cleared his throat and began to shift his feet. Turning to Amy, he said, "You were asking about Helen."

"Yes," Amy said slowly. "How long do you think she'll be in the hospital?'

"If her post-op labs come back normal, she may transfer to the sub-acute facility soon. But things would change if she needs another transfusion or anything else shows up."

"That's seems pretty quick," Father Michael said softly.

"Well, we like to get them up and around as soon as possible, Father. It helps prevent complications. It all depends on how much pain the patient has and what their other medical conditions are." Turning to Amy, Dr. Weber said, "As a matter of fact, I already wrote for the case manager to start discharge planning for when she's ready."

"Good, she's strong and fairly stoic," Amy said. "I'm sure she'll want to start therapy as soon as she can."

Closing his iPad, Dr. Weber looked up and said, "Well, I've seen all the post-op patients scheduled for today, so I'm going to run home before anything else pops up." Shaking the priest's hand, he said, "Father, enjoy the rest of your Sunday."

"Nice to meet you doctor," Michael replied.

"Amy, keep an eye on your friend," Dr. Weber said as he turned. "Even if Helen moves to sub-acute, she'll need repeat x-rays and blood work. Make sure they forward everything to my office. If she develops any kind of a fever, call me immediately."

"Thanks, I will." Amy smiled. "I don't know if I'll be

following her. I'm not sure I have privileges there."

"If not, you better get them. Mercy Manor is one of the only nursing home sub-acute facilities in the area."

"Thanks, I'll look into it," Amy said, shaking his hand. "Thank you for taking care of Helen. I appreciate it."

"My pleasure, she's a wonderful patient," Dr. Weber said. With a wave and a smile, the orthopedist turned and quickly walked toward the elevator.

Chapter Nine

"Well, that was awkward, but I take it she's doing well?" Michael asked, as he turned toward Amy.

"As well as can be expected." Amy shrugged. "She was dozing when I went in earlier, but she may be up now." After a minute, she blushed and added, "Michael, I don't know what his comment was about. I'm sorry."

"Technically, it's none of my business, so don't worry about it," Michael said woodenly. He was surprised by the amount of jealousy and guilt he felt since he knew his devotion must be elsewhere. "Is it still all right for me to go with you?"

"Of course. I'm sure Helen will be thrilled to see you."

"Good," Father Michael said. "I'd like to give her a blessing." The two silently walked through the hall of the hospital as they made their way to Helen's room. They waited while an aide helped Helen get comfortable in the hospital bed. When the blankets were readjusted and the call bell back in place, Amy and Michael walked to opposite sides of the feeble woman's bedside.

"Amy, is that you dear?" Helen asked weakly.

"Yes, it's me and Father Michael too." Amy took in Helen's appearance in the hospital bed and her heart broke realizing how weak and fragile the woman appeared, lying back against the rigid pillows. The paleness of her face was accentuated by the ghostly white sheet pulled up to her chin. "How are you feeling?"

"It hurts, a lot," Helen said, as she took Amy's hand. "I'm not going to lie, but the medicine does take the edge off."

"I'm so sorry," Amy said.

"I don't know what happened," Helen said, starting to tear up. "One minute I was taking the garbage out and then I was lying on the ground in terrible pain."

"Thank goodness Harold saw you and called the police," Amy said. "It was twenty degrees outside."

"I know, but I had to take the trash out," Helen said. "I didn't realize it was so icy."

"You know you fractured your hip, right?" Amy asked. She wasn't sure what had been explained to Helen.

"They told me I broke it and I had surgery to fix it," Helen said, as she squeezed Amy's hand harder. "Now I have to have therapy."

"Yes, but not forever. Just until you're healed and can walk by yourself again," Amy said, trying to reassure her.

"The lady who was in here made it sound like forever," Helen complained, as her voice became weaker.

"You look so tired. Father Michael wants to bless you and then maybe we should go," Amy said kindly.

"No, not yet. I have to tell you something," Helen said. "My mind is getting all mixed up with the medicine."

"Okay, relax Helen. We have plenty of time," Amy said, looking at Michael over the bed. He gave her a nod of encouragement and she went on. "We're here for you, whatever you need."

"Well, I'll need those prayers, but first I want to tell you about the lady who was here," Helen said.

"What lady?" Amy asked, afraid that Helen might be hallucinating from the pain medicine. "Was she floating?"

"What? Are you nuts? Did you take some of the medicine?" Helen asked.

"No," Amy said, feeling embarrassed. "I was wondering about the lady you saw."

"She was from the nursing home. I think it's Mercy Manor. I remember Ethel went there and she said the food was disgusting."

Amy burst out laughing. "I'm sorry Helen. How long ago was Ethel there?"

"Maybe about five years ago. I don't know. I can't ask her now because she died. I'm all mixed up," she said, shaking her head. "But anyway, I want to tell you about the lady."

"Helen," Amy said patiently. "Slow down, take your time. We're ready when you are."

"If I take too long, I'm gonna be out cold from my last shot," Helen complained.

"Okay, so tell us. We're listening," Amy encouraged her.

"The lady said I need a whole bunch of papers. She wants my social security card, my license and my birth certificate, I think. Then she asked for my living will and she wants details about my funeral. Good Lord, does she think I'm checking out today?" Helen asked, in that small, frail voice.

"No, of course not. She has to collect those papers to get your chart ready, that's all," Amy tried to explain. Father Michael placed his hand on Helen's other arm.

"Thank goodness. I got scared when I saw the good Father here. I thought he was giving me last rites," Helen said, with a little laugh.

"No, Helen," Father Michael said. "I wanted to share a prayer to make you healthy again."

"In a minute Father, okay?" Helen asked.

"Whenever you're ready." Father Michael smiled.

"Dr. Amy," Helen said, as she turned to face her. "Will you please be a dear and do me a big favor?"

"Of course, what can I do for you?" Amy pressed closer to the bedside.

"I need you to go to my house and get those papers for me. I have a lot of important things there. I don't want anything to get lost and I don't want anyone else in my house. I only trust the two of you. Will you get them for me?"

"Yes, but how will we get in the house?" Amy asked, hoping the police would have locked the door.

"Do you know where the bird bath is? The one in the back yard?" Helen asked, looking at Amy through drooping eyelids.

"Yes, I can find it," Amy said.

"Underneath the bird bath is a key to the house. Tilt it over and you'll find a metal box in the hollow section of the pedestal. The key is in that box."

"Okay, we can do that," Amy said, while making a worried face at Father Michael.

"Good," Helen said, coughing and trying to catch her breath. "Can I have a sip of water, please?"

Father Michael picked up the yellow plastic water pitcher which sat near him on the bedside table. He poured some ice water into a disposable cup and handed it to Amy.

"Here you go," Amy said, as she held the cup to her lips. "Sip it slowly. I don't want you to choke."

"My, that's good," Helen said, sighing after swallowing the cold water.

"Helen, don't go to sleep yet. Where do I go when I get in the house?" Amy asked quickly.

"What?"

"Your house, Helen, where do I find the papers?" Amy asked.

"Oh yeah. Go to my bedroom and in the corner, you'll see a closet. Go in there and in the back you should find a wooden box that my father carved for me when I was a little girl. It's about the size of a bread box. I drew flowers on it when I was young," Helen said weakly. Amy realized the medicine was kicking in and she would be asleep within minutes.

"Helen, is everything in the box?" Amy asked.

"Everything you need and other special things," Helen said. "Find the box, it's important, especially for you, Father."

"Helen, don't go to sleep yet," Amy said, closer to her ear.

"I have no control over this, you know that. Amy, listen to me and remember, trust no one but each other." Helen said, her voice a faint whisper. "Father, I think you'd better say those prayers now."

"Of course," Father Michael said, reaching out to hold Helen's hand. Placing his other hand over his heart he said,

"Dear Father, please bring strength to Helen, your loving servant. May you have compassion for her pain and suffering and let your healing touch bring her comfort. Restore her to full health so she may dwell in your house with joy. And from Jeremiah 30:17, 'I will restore you to health, and heal your wounds, says the Lord'. Amen."

"Amen, Brother," Helen said, as her head dropped and she started to snore.

Father Michael looked over at Amy, who had crossed herself. She looked at him and said, "That was beautiful. The poor dear, I feel so sorry for her."

"She's a strong woman," Michael said.

"I know, but I worry about her," Amy said, as she adjusted her blanket.

"What do you think she was talking about?"

"I have no clue, but it was weird. Maybe it was just the medicine. I guess we'll know more when we get there." Amy felt uneasy as they left the room and walked down the corridor.

Chapter Ten

Gemma was still in bed, late Sunday afternoon. She had not slept well after her meeting with Paolo the night before, rendering her exhausted. Lately, he was more demanding and less friendly. Gemma loved acquisitions and there were so many beautiful objects waiting to be admired and cherished. Most people had no idea of the beautiful craftsmanship and art which currently existed in the world. Elegant exhibits and education should be arranged for the public to appreciate and share. But Paolo wasn't interested in beauty anymore. He was more concerned with power and money. As a result of Paolo's greed, her original, idealistic enthusiasm for exquisite items was eroding.

Gemma rolled over in bed, while a tear trickled down her cheek. She had no significant other, no one she could talk to and she was lonely. Feeling despondent, she barely moved when the phone rang. She didn't want to answer in case it was Paolo again. But if she didn't, he would show up at her apartment, banging on the door. She was sure there were nights she had seen him standing across the street watching her window. Finally, having no other choice, she rolled to the side of the bed and picked up the phone. "Hello?"

"*Gemmella, come va?*"

"Papa? Papa, is that you?" Gemma heart soared.

"*Si, mia Gemmella.* How are you? Your mother and I were

having dinner and we couldn't stop thinking of you," Marco Montanari said.

"Oh, papa," Gemma said, her voice choking. If there was one thing her Italian family had mastered, it was the art of guilt.

"*Gemmella, Gemmella,* what's wrong?"

"Nothing papa, *ti manco.* I miss you," Gemma sniffed into the phone.

"*Ti manca la madre.* Your mother misses you, *Gemmella,*" Marco Montanari said with strain evident in his voice. "I can tell you are crying. Tell me why, *bambina.* What's wrong?"

Gemma hesitated to tell her thoughts to her father. He was a wealthy powerful man in Italy, respected by politicians and criminals alike. He would solve a problem if she asked him to, without sharing the details. Perhaps she was being too sensitive or blowing the situation out of proportion. His strong voice interrupted her thoughts, "*Gemmella,* I'm waiting. Talk to your papa."

"It's Paolo," Gemma said haltingly.

"Has he hurt you?" Marco asked sharply, his tone all business.

"No, papa. He hasn't hurt me, but he's very different lately," Gemma said softly. "He's spending a lot of time with wealthy businessmen."

"Go on, Gemma," Marco said.

"He's asked me to find a few artifacts and then do nothing," Gemma said.

"Perhaps he has his reasons," Marco said, trying to be fair.

"Yes papa, but two of the artifacts were reported stolen

several weeks after I found them and one of the owners was murdered."

"*Che peccato*. That does not sound good," Marco mused to himself.

"He's also very concerned with money and he's throwing it around. I'm afraid, papa. What if it was discovered I was the person who located the objects? They may think I had something to do with it."

"My *bambina* could never be involved in something like that," Marco Montanari said.

"I know, papa, but I'm afraid he is using me for something greater. Something criminal."

"This is serious," Marco said quietly. "*Non stai in piena piccolina*. Don't worry. But also, don't tell Paolo we spoke so I can look into this. For now, go about your business, but be safe, little girl. If anything is wrong, you call me immediately. I have friends in America and they can be at your side in minutes."

"*Papa, posso venire a casa per Natale*? Can I come home for Christmas?"

"Of course, *bambina*. Your mother and I want you here. This is your home. It's only twenty-eight days to Christmas. You should be here when the *prescepe veivent* starts in two weeks. I will send a plane for you soon. Do you have an assignment now?"

"Not yet, but Paolo is looking into something. He said I may have to go to Italy."

"Even better. Find out what he wants from you and call me," Marco said. "Once you are in Italy, we can take care of him. But first, I need to collect some information. *Gemmella,* listen to your papa. If anything seems wrong, you call me immediately. You understand?"

"Yes papa, *ti manco,*"Gemma whispered.

"I miss you too, *bambina* and it's time for you to come home, for good I think," Marco Montanari said. "*Ti amo.*"

"I love you too, papa." Gemma said softly, hanging up the phone. Grabbing the hand-knit pillow her mother had given her for her third birthday, she thought of her family in Italy and began to cry. The thought of Christmas at home, mama's *sette pesci* Christmas Eve dinner and freshly filled cannoli's eased her mind. She couldn't wait to see them.

Chapter Eleven

"I guess they didn't plow this area," Amy said, as she cautiously drove along the snow covered roads leading to Boulder Ridge. Having left Father Victor at the rectory, Amy and Father Michael continued towards Helen's house. It would take more than a snowstorm to prevent them from retrieving the documents Helen requested.

"Take it slow," Michael said. "There may be ruts underneath the snow and the last thing we need is to lose a tire."

"I'm trying," Amy said, her knuckles white, as she gripped the wheel. "Thank you for coming with me, Michael. Who knows what we'll find there?"

"Helen said we're the only two people she trusted. I thought that was strange considering how cryptic she acted while telling us about her papers."

"Yeah, she's normally very open with people, so it strikes me odd that she'd be so protective. I know the nursing home will insist on seeing her documents when she gets transferred, but aside from that, I don't know what other papers she could be referring to. To be honest, I feel bad for her. She'll be in rehab for a while, healing from this hip fracture, so it could be some time before she goes home again." Amy tightened her grip on the steering wheel as the car fishtailed on an icy patch. "Whoa."

"These roads are bad. Let's hope we don't wind up in the bed next to her," Michael said. "You may want to invest in an SUV soon. Vermont winters can be tough on sedans."

Amy froze as she processed Michael's assumption she was staying in Vermont. She rented her cabin for a year, as she needed some time to sort things out. She did have an option to buy, but always expected to return to Boston. Amy didn't come to Vermont to grow roots. She came to cut the dead ones loose.

"I guess I'll have to think about it," she said hesitantly.

Michael noticed the change in her tone and decided not to press. The late afternoon sun filtered through her hair and backlit her profile, making her appear almost angelic. She'd been living in Vermont for nine months now, and while her smile had returned, the ghost of sleep and grief still haunted her eyes. He was surprised he felt so close to her. He wanted to comfort her and to assure her everything would work out, but he needed to get his priorities straight.

As they rounded a bend in the road, a small line of three homes opened up in front of them. Each was a simple two-story farmhouse, with a wraparound porch, stacked with wood. Only one home had a cloud of smoke billowing from the chimney.

"Which house is hers?" Michael asked, as the car slowed down.

"The one in the middle." Amy pointed. "Harold lives in the house on the left and it looks like he's home. I didn't realize there was another house. Helen never mentioned other neighbors."

"Maybe it's a rental," Michael suggested. "I don't see any

lights on."

"Maybe, but I would think if she had another neighbor, Helen wouldn't need as much help from poor Harold."

"I guess we'll have to ask Helen," Father Michael said.

"At least these properties are all plowed. Maybe they worked something out with the town considering Helen and Harold are getting on in years," Amy said, driving as far as she could up the long, plowed driveway next to Helen's house. Helen's walkway had been cleared, which was a godsend, considering there were no streetlights or lights on inside her house. "We should probably leave a light on when we go," Amy said.

Turning off the ignition, Amy followed Michael toward the house. "It must be very dark here at night. It's a wonder Harold saw her lying in the driveway," Michael said.

"Very quiet too. But I'm sure they can sense when something is off," Amy said. "After living in one place for most of your life, you get used to the typical ambience."

"Where do we start?" Michael asked, adjusting his gloves.

Pulling her designer coat tighter, Amy said, "We're supposed to look under the concrete bird bath in the back yard. The key is hidden in a box tucked inside the pedestal."

Michael smiled, as he watched Amy trudge through the snow in a pair of sneakers. "You may want to update your winter clothing too. Snow in Vermont is a bit different than Boston."

"Apparently, but the forecast indicated it'll warm up next week. Besides, winter can't last forever," Amy said, with frosted breath. The two stepped into the backyard and rounded a patch of boxwoods. The bird bath sat dead center in the yard and Amy wasted no time nearing it. "This must be it. Helen said to tip it forward and we'd find a box in the base."

"Ok, I'll tip and you search," Michael laughed as he crossed to the other side of the bird bath. "Ready?"

"On the count of three,,..one..two..three!"

Michael pulled the concrete bird bath toward him and pulled downward. After a few forceful tugs, the base lifted and pulled out of the snow. "Either Helen is a bodybuilder or she hasn't used this key in years," Michael grunted. Snow from the top fell over his coat and shoes.

"I'm sure the base wasn't covered in a few feet of snow when she hid this," Amy pointed out, laughing. Squatting down, she looked into the pedestal and found a small metal box, wrapped in plastic. Amy grabbed the box and stood up. "Done, you can let go."

Michael pushed the bird bath back into place, but it wouldn't sit level in the uneven snow. "Let's hope this melts before Helen gets home. She won't be happy with a crooked bird bath."

"I'm sure she'll have something to say about it," Amy said with a grin. "If we're lucky, Harold will come over and straighten it before Helen sees it." Amy unwrapped the plastic from the metal box. Opening the lid, she retrieved the small key hidden inside. "Got it. I feel like I'm on a treasure hunt."

"Unless we find the crown jewel, I doubt this is the most exciting treasure ever found." Michael teased as they walked toward the front of the house.

Turning the corner, they walked up the wooden steps and

onto the front porch. Looking around, Amy noticed the firewood had been stacked about ten feet from the door. It was a short walk for someone to grab logs for a fire, but far enough away to ensure safety going in and out of the house. The remainder of the porch was decorated by antique rocking chairs, aged with thin cobwebs. Amy turned away from the house. Her gasp caused Michael to turn around.

"It's breathtaking, isn't it?" Amy asked in awe.

Michael looked at the sight before him. Now fully dark, the lights in the valley twinkled below, like fallen stars. The evening sky traced the edge of the valley, becoming darker the further up it went, until it blended into a starry night sky, dotted with a moon, masked by innocent gray clouds.

"The view from this porch is absolutely magnificent," Amy said. "Now I can understand why someone would brave the climate to live here. I almost feel like I'm floating in space."

"It really is beautiful," Michael agreed. "A little piece of Heaven in the mountains. I'll bet the view, during the day, is equally amazing."

"I can't believe Helen never mentioned this. I imagined her house being surrounded by a forest," Amy said.

"She's either a very private person or didn't want to share," Michael pointed out. "How many of us look at our daily surroundings as if it were the first time? When we see something every day, we take its existence and beauty for granted. I think that's one reason why people get so excited about Christmas trees. They're beautiful examples of nature, especially when fully decorated, but only to be enjoyed for a short time. Even so, after the holiday is over, we don't notice the allure anymore."

"For some, their daily view may not be as beautiful," Amy said sadly, thinking of those stuck in hospital rooms and nursing homes.

"True, but that's why we need to appreciate who and what we have before it's gone," Michael said. "Even sadder, when something goes missing and we don't notice at all."

Amy felt herself choking up. She realized how much she missed her sister. The grief threatened to overwhelm her as tears dropped down her cheek. She swallowed and took the pressed handkerchief Michael offered for her tears. "It's okay, Amy. It's good to let it out."

Amy used the handkerchief to dry her face as she cleared her throat. "Sorry. Sometimes, I get overwhelmed. I miss her so much." Amy started crying again and buried her face in his scarf.

Michael hugged her tightly and whispered in her ear, *"Weeping may last for the night, but rejoicing comes in the morning." Psalm 30:5.*

Chapter Twelve

Helen went still in the hospital bed. The call bell was beyond reach of her fingertips. She wanted to see the nurse, but instead steeled herself as another wave of intense pain surged down her leg from her hip. Beads of sweat popped out on her forehead. She hated the pain medication. Her head felt fuzzy when she took narcotics, and they made her more tired than her ninety-two years. The pain was excruciating, and she could not stand it any longer. She already refused a dose or two of her medicine, but now she wanted the pills desperately, especially before she had to go to the bathroom.

Helen realized she had been a fool to take the garbage out in the snow. What else could she do? She refused to slow down or wait for someone to help her. Dr. Amy warned her to be careful, but Helen wanted to prove her wrong and obviously failed. Now she was in agony and the damn call bell had dropped to the side of the bed. Not that someone would come if she pushed it anyway, but she could not get close enough to try. She closed her eyes and tried to be still. Maybe the pain would fade a little.

The knock on the door made her jump and sent a fresh bolt of pain through her hip.

"Helen? Are you in there?" A male voice sang cheerily from the open door.

"I'm here," she said, weakly.

"Hello," he said, as he walked from the door to her bedside. A young female assistant was at his side taking notes. "I'm Dr. Weber. May I call you Helen?"

"Who?" Helen asked, as she squinted and peered closer at the pair.

"Dr. Weber, your orthopedist. I'm the doctor who fixes broken bones," he said, with a smile. "How are you today?"

"In pain," Helen complained. "It's my fault because I refused the medicine, but now I can't stand it. Could you call my nurse for me?"

Dr. Weber turned to his assistant, Marcy. "Can you please find Mrs. Coyle's nurse?"

"Of course, doctor," she replied and left the room.

"Helen, you'll be okay. We have plenty of medicine to make you comfortable. I know you don't like the side effects, but you should try to take it, at least for the next couple of weeks."

"Why?" Helen asked, looking up at him.

"Because you're going to need it for rehab. The good news is that your blood count and temperature are stable. I'm going to check your incision today."

"And the bad news?" Helen asked directly.

"There is no bad news," Dr. Weber replied. "You broke your hip, but we fixed it. Medically you're stable. That means you're graduating from this hospital and being transferred to the sub-acute facility."

"Does Dr. Amy know about this?" Helen asked, frowning.

"I haven't told her yet, but she does know rehab is the next step. They will help you out of bed and with your physical therapy each day. That's why it would be a good idea to take some of the pain medicine. It will help you get moving again."

"How long will I be there?" Helen asked.

"That all depends on the progress you make," Dr. Weber explained. "At least three weeks, maybe longer, depending on how quickly you heal."

"The case manager woman asked if I wanted to stay there forever," Helen complained. "I've got my own house. I don't want to be stuck in some old age home."

Dr. Weber smiled. "Helen, it's a rehab facility. They give you active physical therapy and make you as independent as possible. The senior center also has regular festivities."

"You're not fooling me," Helen said stonily. "It's a nursing home. I'm getting out of there as soon as I can."

"Of course you will. It's not a prison. We just want you to be as safe as possible," Dr. Weber said.

"I'll discuss this with Dr. Amy," Helen said. "I trust her."

Dr. Weber chuckled when he realized the implication she did not trust him. "I expect you to do nothing less. But they're getting ready to move you soon, so the next time you speak to her will probably be at Mercy Manor."

"I don't have my papers," Helen said nervously. "I can't go yet."

"We have all we need for today, Helen," Dr. Weber explained. "And Marcy is back with your nurse."

"Oh, I need to talk to her," Helen said. Pain shot through her leg as she squirmed with agitation.

"We've got you covered," the nurse said. She picked up Helen's intravenous line and inserted a needle. "Doc says you need something for pain. This will make you feel much better." Pressing the plunger, she injected the medicine and adjusted the intravenous flow.

Before Helen could respond, she felt the cold medicine course through her veins, reaching her head and making her weak and dizzy. She tried to say something but her voice was faint and the words wouldn't come. She stared up at the doctor with worried eyes. Dr. Weber took her hand and reassured her. "It's okay, Helen. Just try to relax. Get some sleep and build your strength. You'll be back home in no time."

Helen heard his words but maintained her doubt as she slipped into the darkness.

Chapter Thirteen

After composing herself, Amy jiggled the rusty key in the front door lock before she heard it move. As the bolt slid back, she turned the knob and gently pushed the door open. The house was dark and smelled musty. Amy ran her hand along the wall, to the right of the door, until her fingers came across a light switch. A dim light appeared from a lamp on the opposite wall as Amy flicked the switch.

Crossing the threshold, Amy closed the door once Michael had stepped onto the creaky floor boards. As they moved further into the room, Michael turned on a few other lamps, allowing Amy to look around. On the left side, a floral printed fabric sofa was draped with a homemade afghan. Oak end tables were adorned with white lace doilies that prevented the wood from being tarnished by the thin lamps that stood upon them. The painted wall was covered with framed handmade landscapes and an etching that read, *Home is where the heart is,* which rested peacefully above a Queen Ann chair. A bag of wool dangled from its side. A small television teetered on a splintered TV tray, on the right side of the room.

Directly in front of Amy was a stone fireplace, most likely original to the house, with cold, burnt logs resting in the hearth. A slate mantel framed the stout fireplace, and was bashfully decorated with two black and white photographs and ceramic bric-a-brac. As

Amy and Michael approached the photos, a young girl with pigtails, standing next to a couple in front of an old barn, came into view. She held a tiger striped cat against her overalls.

"Do you think that's Helen as a child?" Amy asked.

"The time frame looks right," Michael said. "They may be her parents."

"As much as I think I know about her, I've never heard her mention family. I assume she didn't marry."

The second photograph had a larger frame that showed the same girl and the same couple standing next to an older couple, a young boy and a priest. "What do you think?" Michael asked, as they studied the photo.

"I'm not sure. It could be a set of grandparents. Helen never mentioned siblings, so I have no clue who the boy is," Amy said. "What about the priest? Do you think he was one of the original pastors?"

Michael shook his head. "I wouldn't know, but there are some old photos of the previous clergy at St. Francis. I could look and see if he's there."

As Michael continued to talk, Amy took out her smart phone and snapped a new photo of the group. "I'll show this to Helen. Hopefully, she won't be upset I took this picture, but she may be able to explain who these people are and help you get a better idea of the original clergy of St. Francis."

"Good idea," Michael said.

Amy gingerly placed the frame back on the mantel and they both turned to continue their quest for Helen's documents. The first doorway they entered led to the kitchen. Michael turned on the light, by pulling a cord hanging from the overhead fixture, with a small ceramic ear of corn attached to the end. A wooden table with four chairs sat in the middle of the room, decorated with a vase of plastic daisies and placemats, with images of birds. Amy opened the door of the antiquated refrigerator and immediately wrinkled her nose at the scent of spoiled milk. "I thought the mothball smell in the living room was unpleasant, but this is worse, and Helen's not going to be back here for a long time." Amy dumped the milk in the sink and then ran the water until the drain had completely cleared. She put the carton, as well as some other spoiled food, in an old shopping bag. "I'll take that with us and dump it at home. I'd hate for all of this tainted fare to attract unwanted friends, while she's gone."

They left the kitchen and walked down a small carpeted hall which led to rooms on either side. Entering the first room, Michael finally found another overhead light with a pull cord. This time, a ceramic chicken was clipped on the end of the chain. They found various plastic bins filled with doilies, embroidered tablecloths, mothball scented clothes, aprons and floral curtains. In the middle of the room, stood a statuesque ironing board carrying the weight of an ancient twenty pound iron, complimented, on the side, by an indoor drying rack garnished with lemon-scented underwear. "No wonder she's strong," Amy said. "This iron weighs a ton." Amy put the heavy iron back on the board and looked into a bin. "I wonder if Helen did all this needlepoint. It's difficult to find quality handiwork like this. You can barely find wool in Boston."

"If it's her work, she's very talented," Michael said, as he looked at the pieces.

"They're beautiful," Amy said. "I never imagined her making things as dainty as this." Feeling guilty for invading Helen's space, Amy placed the material back in the bin and said, "We better move on." Amy turned to leave the room, as Michael pulled the chicken cord and turned out the light. Across the hall, they entered another room that had a light switch on the wall. A floor lamp, in the shape of a hay silo, revealed the mass of Helen's bedroom. Amy jumped when she saw a pair of eyes looking at her. "Oh," she yelled, jumping backward into Michael's side. The eyes stayed fixated on Amy, staring straight ahead. Holding her hand to her chest, Amy laughed. "It's a doll. I don't believe it. It's just a doll. For a minute, I thought there was a body in the bed."

"I know what you thought," Michael said, as he rubbed his arm.

"Sorry about that. I'm a little on edge lately," Amy said, approaching the small twin bed, covered in a lovely granny square afghan. At the head of the bed, near the pillow, sat an old fashioned china doll with ceramic legs straight out in front of her. The doll was approximately three feet tall, with piercing blue glass eyes. "I guess Helen made the bed before she took the garbage out."

"She's very neat," Michael said. "I"ll give her credit for that."

Turning toward Michael, Amy said, "Being in an empty house like this is creepy to me. I can't thank you enough for coming along."

"You're very welcome. I know what you mean. I get the

same feeling, when I walk over a grave."

Amy looked up at him and made a face. "Well that sure helped."

Michael grinned and shrugged. "Sorry, it's all I could think of."

"Let's get this over with so we can leave." Turning around, Amy spied a small closet by the corner of the wall. "That must be it." Walking to the door, she turned the old fashioned glass knob and opened it. The space was narrow, but long, and smelled strongly of mothballs. "Whew, I don't know how she can stand that smell," Amy said, as she fanned her nose. There was an overhead light, with a chain pull cord that ended in a ceramic shoe. Amy pulled the cord and the light bulb came alive. On the left hung organized blouses and slacks, followed by a few outdated dresses and sweaters. Six pairs of shoes were lined up neatly, on the floor, and shelves on the right, held a good number of old boxes.

"Do we have to go through all of this?" Michael asked.

"I don't think so," Amy said. "Helen said the documents were in a wooden box her father carved for her. Come to think of it, that's the only time she mentioned family. She said she drew flowers on it." Walking to the back of the narrow closet, Amy was able to eye the box. She tried to pick it up and turn around, but it was a tight turn. "Michael, can you help me with this?"

"Of course," he said as he walked up to her. Amy held the box near her shoulder and Michael easily reached over to retrieve it. She could feel his warm breath against her cheek and his body heat, warm on her back, as he leaned forward. Her heart skipped a beat or two as she waited for him to back out of the closet. Amy immediately attributed her irregular heartbeat to her claustrophobia. Michael's nearness couldn't have made her feel that way, could it? She shook off her thoughts, paused to take a deep breath, and ducked under the wooden clothes rack to leave the closet.

Michael placed the box on the bed and turned to face Amy, as she awkwardly approached him. "Are you okay?" Michael asked.

"Yeah, fine," Amy said quickly, as she looked down at the box. "This is just strange, that's all. Let's open it and get out of here."

"You got it," Michael said, raising the lid. They both noticed a small stack of documents nestled inside, as well as a very old fashioned key. Lifting the pile out, they sorted the papers.

"There's her social security card," Amy said. "I see her insurance cards too, although the hospital must have a copy of these, by now."

"And she has a living will," Michael said, as he examined the next folded paper.

"I wonder if she has a copy on file at the hospital," Amy said, looking toward Michael before she pulled the next document. "Here's her birth certificate. Now this is interesting. Helen Elizabeth Coyle, born September 20th, 1921, in Rocky Meadow, Vermont. Wow, that's impressive, isn't it? She's seen a lot of changes over the years."

"That's how you develop wisdom," Michael said with a smile.

"We should all be so wise," Amy scoffed, as she turned over

the document. "Birth certificates were so different then. I wonder if there will be paper certificates ten years from now. Everything is converting to digital."

"We'll just have to wait and see," Michael said, continuing with the pile. "She has some old letters here," Michael said. "Maybe she'll want to read them."

"We'll ask her when we show her this stuff. Hey, Michael, look at this." Amy was holding a small, yellowed journal. On the cover, was a round symbol and the name, James Alex Coyle. "That must be her relative. Isn't that the same symbol I saw on the wall, in the basement of St. Francis?" Amy asked. "It was on the tapestry, as well."

"Sure looks like it to me," Michael said.

"The symbol looks like a crown. Do you know what it represents?" Amy asked. "I don't recognize it."

"I have no idea," Michael said.

"Let's open the journal and find out. Helen said there were special papers in here for us."

"I've seen the symbol around the church a few times," Michael said. "Now I'm very curious."

Amy opened the first page. The paper was crisp and fragile, breaking into small fragments as she touched it. "Look at the date, 1878. This journal is 135 years old."

"Wow," Michael said, looking over her shoulder. "James Alex Coyle. That name is written on the next page again. Do you think that's Helen's grandfather?"

"I don't know," Amy said, as she continued to turn the pages.

"But I doubt it. Helen was born in 1921. Assuming her grandfather was around fifty at the time, he would have been born in 1870. This journal is dated 1878 and it doesn't look like the writing of a child."

Counting backward, Michael said, "So her great grandfather would have been born somewhere around 1850. What do you think?"

"That sounds more likely," Amy agreed, as she continued to carefully turn the pages. "Apparently, he was quite involved in building the church. This journal is all about the early days at St. Francis and the Rocky Meadow Retreat House, but it's hard to read in this light. The ink is so faded."

"And the penmanship looks difficult."

"It's certainly different from the modern world," Amy said, as she turned to the last page. "The journal stops here. The rest of the pages are blank."

"Maybe he became ill?"

"I don't know," Amy said softly. "Wow, Michael, listen to this –

April 23, 1878 – At last it is done. The sacred gift is safely ensconced in a place that should remain hidden. Only the pastor, the Italian carver and I know the truth, but I fear we shall go to our graves without sharing the wonder of its glory. Perhaps, it can be better protected, yet cherished, in the future. We have left instructions and its magnificent story in the antechamber. When the time comes for the wall to be breached, our predecessors will guide us. Only the humble will discover its passage and a righteous soul will find its key. God Bless us all."

-   James Alex Coyle –

"This journal has to be what she wanted us to find," Michael said. "The sacred gift?"

"Are there any church papers that reference something similar?" Amy asked, looking up at the priest.

"Not that I'm aware of, but I haven't read through all the papers in the church archives."

"Well, I guess it's time you did," Amy said kindly. "In the meantime, let's ask Helen if she knows what this is all about. She kept the journal with her things for a reason. We don't know if this key is important or if the journal was referring to something else. It's interesting and obviously connected to the church. Helen doesn't have any children that I'm aware of, so maybe that's why she wanted you to have the journal. She has no one to pass it down to."

"That's very possible," Michael said. "I hope she can tell us the secret."

"This is an amazing find," Amy said, as she started collecting the papers and the key. "Let's straighten up. It's getting late and we should leave. Tomorrow, we'll show this to Helen and see if she has any more information."

"I agree," Michael said as they left the room. "And we'll see what secrets are hidden in those archives."

Chapter Fourteen

"Oh dear," Katie said, as a fork clattered to the floor.

"Calm down," Father Victor said, sipping his coffee. "That's the third piece of silverware you've dropped this morning."

"I can't help it." Katie put down the dishcloth she was using to dry dishes. "I'm so nervous. I'm afraid we won't get the property for the soup kitchen. The auction started thirty minutes ago. It would be perfect."

"It will happen if it's meant to be," Father Victor said. "Do you want me to dry the dishes?"

"Not on your life," Katie said. "Once you get a fork in your hand, you're impossible to stop."

"What's going on?" Willow asked, bouncing into the kitchen.

"Good morning, Willow," Katie said. "How did you sleep?"

"Great," Willow chimed.

"I'm glad to hear that," Katie said. "Sit down, dear, and have yourself a nice hot breakfast. After all, it's the most important meal of the day and those winter winds are already kicking up."

"Awesome. I'm starving. Oh, and isn't today the auction for the soup kitchen?"

"Why, yes it is, dear. The bank is auctioning the property for the closed restaurant. It would make a lovely soup kitchen for us. Father Michael put a bid in for the church. Now we have to wait."

"I really hope we get it." Willow smiled, as she poured herself a large glass of orange juice. "How does the auction work?"

"Well, when someone buys property, they usually have to take a mortgage," Katie explained. "In other words, the bank loans the money and the owner has to make monthly payments to pay them back."

"With interest, of course," Father Victor scoffed, pouring himself some juice.

"Well, yes," Katie said. "That way, the bank makes a profit in the end, dear. Would you like some eggs?"

"Yes please. Ok, so how does it get to auction then?" Willow asked.

"Well, if the owner can't make the payments, the bank will try to come to an arrangement," Katie explained, as she filled a plate and handed it to Willow.

"You hope," Father Victor mumbled into his juice.

"Father, please," Katie said, while shooting him a warning glance, and handing Willow a bottle of ketchup.

Father Victor gave a small chuckle as Katie continued. "Anyway, dear, if the owner cannot come up with the money, by any means, the bank takes over the property, because they don't want to lose their investment."

"Then what happens?" Willow asked, now wide-eyed. "Can you please pass the toast?"

"The bank will sell the property to recoup their investment," Father Victor said, as he handed over the plate of lightly browned toast and Katie's homemade jam.

"That's right. Sometimes, it stays on the market for a while, or they hold a one-day auction and take the highest bid."

"So what happens to the original owners?" Willow asked.

"They lose out. They have no right to the property. Many times, they've declared bankruptcy. They have to settle whatever financial obligations they can before their credit and name can be cleared."

"Wow, that's terrible," Willow said, as she took a gulp of her juice.

"Yes, it can be very stressful for the owners who have to vacate," Katie said, clucking her tongue pitifully.

"Do we have a chance to get it, Katie?" Willow looked up hopefully, as she swiftly spread jam across a piece of toast.

"It's possible, dear. It depends on how many people submit bids and how much money they offer. Usually, the first offers are low. The bank may take anything to get the property off their hands."

"But you may have a bidding war," Father Victor added. "If a lot of people are interested, the bank will contact everyone and tell them to put in their absolute best offer. The highest bid usually wins."

"Whoa." Willow sighed, blowing hair out of her face. "Maybe I'll have to study accounting before I get my inheritance."

"There's a lot to learn." Katie wiped her hands on another dishrag. "We'll have to wait and see what happens."

"I'll keep my fingers crossed for you." Willow smiled, biting into her toast.

"Thank you, dear. Now what else do you have planned for the day?"

Willow looked up after swallowing. "Well, I was hoping to go to the strip mall and do some Christmas shopping."

"After you have your school lessons, of course," Katie pressed, raising her right eyebrow.

"The tutor should be here any minute," Willow said, the despair of school children evident on her face.

"Now Willow, don't look so miserable," Katie said, with a chuckle. "Will you help me start making cookies this afternoon? I have a whole bunch of Christmas music for us to listen to."

"Sure," Willow replied with a half-smile, remembering that she had not had a normal Christmas in a long time.

Realizing Willow's apparent, but timid interest, Katie added, "I'd like to make about ten different varieties this year. We'll start with butter and chocolate chip cookies today."

"That does sound great," Father Victor interjected, mesmerized by the thought of the sugary treats.

"Oh, now don't you get started, Father. I'll have to make extra batches to satisfy you," Katie complained with desperation.

"I think I'm going to like my first winter in Vermont," Father Victor grinned.

"I'm sure you will, Father," Katie said, with a toss of the head. "Now since you're busy doing nothing other than worrying about your stomach, you can look over Willow's college materials with her, when she finishes with her tutor."

Willow started to giggle when she saw Father Victor's face.

After a minute, he turned to Willow. "Have you given any more thought to where you'd like to go?"

"No, I'm too nervous to decide. I've never been to public school. I don't want to look stupid," Willow said, looking down, ashamed.

"Oh, honey." Katie placed her hand on Willow's shoulder. "You'll be fine and we're all here to help you. Especially, Dr. Amy. She knows a lot about schooling. She'll set you straight."

"Yes," Father Victor said, seizing the opportunity. "It would be much better to have her look over your information."

Katie turned to Father Victor and scowled. "All you need to worry about now is making a list of colleges that seem interesting to you. Then we can visit them. We don't have to put in the actual applications until next September. You have plenty of time to decide."

"If you say so," Willow whispered, finishing her plate.

"For now, keep looking at that book about the colleges," Katie said.

"Ok, I will," Willow promised.

"Don't worry, Dr. Amy will help us figure everything out," Katie reassured her.

Realizing he was off the hook, Father Victor smiled and wiped his brow, but couldn't help feeling a pang of guilt upon noticing how anxious Willow looked. "Hey, things will work out in the end. Look at me, I went through all of public school with the nickname, 'Godzilla' and I survived."

The tension broken, Katie, Father Victor and Willow shared

a good laugh. Looking into the retreat house kitchen window, one might have mistook them for a normal family.

Chapter Fifteen

A pair of white French doors swung open and Gemma stepped inside the wonderland that was her wardrobe. The clothes ran along the walls, organized by style, color, and season, and were accented by a series of shoe-shelves, home to a rainbow of casual wear and pumps. In the middle of the closet sat the centerpiece of the arrangement, a table that on one side acted as a professional makeup vanity, and on the other, displayed fifty racks of jewelry and handbags. Behind the center display, the far wall was accented by a three-way mirror that need say no words to inform Gemma she was the fairest of them all.

Gemma hummed a pop tune as she went to her luggage, in the far corner, and began to pack her belongings to be shipped back to Italy. She had been away from home for more than three years and was overjoyed to be moving back to Ponticello with her family. Hopefully, Paolo would be none the wiser until the plane landed, at which point her father could take care of him, if need be.

Gemma looked at her beautiful clothes and her eyes misted over. They were all original designs: Oscar de la Renta gowns, Armani business suits, Stella McCartney daywear. It was unimaginable what one could do with a credit card and an apartment in walking distance to Saks Fifth Avenue. Gemma fingered a Jimmy Choo pump in one hand and a Prada sandal in the other, while throwing a Marc Jacobs bag over her shoulder. She eyed her jewelry display, overrun with Allen Shwartz and Tiffany.

When she first moved to the United States, she was excited to live in Manhattan, a city where time never stopped. She envisioned lush parties and scads of New York loving friends. She imagined herself on the A list for social gatherings and these clothes were designed to get her there. Unfortunately, her work as a curator, took her to places outside of the city. Although her mail was delivered to a luxury apartment in the heart of New York, Gemma was never there long enough to establish herself.

Ponticello was the only place Gemma really knew. It was her home. If she had to give up her job, then so be it, but Gemma would give anything to settle into her home village, meet a loving Italian man and settle down for life. The party scene and designer clothing would never replace the life her mama had envisioned for her, the life she truly wanted. For the first time in a long while, Gemma radiated a genuine smile that relayed her excitement and hope for the future.

Gemma pulled a pair of black skinny jeans and a blue billowing blouse to match her Alexander McQueen ankle boots. To brace the cold, she wrapped herself in a Burberry pea coat and the only item in her closet that wasn't designer, a knitted beanie made by her grandmother, Margharita.

Gemma usually sent presents home for the holidays, but this year was special. She hoped to pick the most beautiful gifts New York had to offer to take back to her family, in time for their Christmas celebration. Supremely focused and determined, she took one last look in the mirror and moved out of the wardrobe room. Grabbing her keys off the cherry wood table by the front door, Gemma left her apartment, rode the elevator to the lobby and carelessly strutted towards Fifth Avenue. She never noticed the tastefully dressed man in the Gucci loafers, following behind her.

Chapter Sixteen

"She's gone," Amy said, as she padded into the foyer of the rectory, holding Michael's chivalrously extended arm.

"Come in…who's gone?" Michael asked, closing the heavy rectory door against the forthcoming snow.

"Helen's gone. Can you believe it?" Amy asked, as she absently unwrapped her freshly knit scarf, unknowingly showering the rug in tiny bits of melting ice.

"Hello, Amy," Katie said, as she walked into the foyer. "It looks like Father Michael beat me to the door."

"Hi, Katie. Thank you again for the scarf. It's beautiful and, need I say, extremely useful," Amy said, smiling while twisting the scarf between her fingers. "It smells amazing in here."

"Oh, you are more than welcome, dear. It's an early Christmas present to get you ready for the cold weather. And that will be dinner you smell. Let's hope Father Victor isn't in the pots while I'm out here," Katie said with a laugh.

"Amy, I've missed you," Willow said, her excitement manifesting into a bear hug.

"I've missed you too, honey," Amy said as she squeezed Willow closer. Brushing back the hair from her forehead, she asked. "How are you?"

"Great," Willow said. "I helped Katie make Christmas

cookies today and I started some shopping."

Amy laughed at her enthusiasm. "That's wonderful, Willow. I can't wait to see what you bought."

"You'll have to wait until Christmas for some of it," Willow said with a grin.

"Amy," Father Michael said, as he placed a hand on her arm. "About Helen?"

"Oh Michael, you wouldn't believe it. I walked into her room and it was cleaned and empty," Amy said, looking up at him. "I was so surprised, I ran over to the nursing station."

"And?" Father Michael asked, the air heavy with anticipation.

"I got the standard reply, 'Sorry, Helen is no longer with us'."

Michael somberly crossed himself as Katie pulled Willow into an embrace. "God rest her soul. A funeral near Christmas. What happened?"

"What funeral?" Amy asked, perplexed.

"Helen, you said she was gone," Katie said, clearly distraught.

"Oh," Amy chuckled. "She didn't die. They moved her to Mercy Manor without telling me. I was quite annoyed, I'll tell you that."

"Well that's a relief," Willow said, color once again flushing her cheeks.

"I'm sorry, I didn't mean to scare you like that," Amy said, looking at the three with concern. "How about we check on that dinner?"

Katie jumped first. "Oh, I hope there's some left." After a beat of silence between the group, Katie pulled Willow towards the kitchen, while giving a knowing look in Amy and Michael's direction. "Come along Willow, why don't you help me set the table?"

Amy took off her coat and stepped out of her damp sneakers, the right one giving a feeble squeak upon contact with the wood floor.

"You really need to get some winter clothing," Michael said, hanging her thin polyester coat, on a wooden peg near the door.

"As soon as I get a moment, I'll go to the strip mall," Amy said, while tousling her hair to remove most of the ice. "Maybe I can shop online."

"Perhaps," Michael said, with a smile. "Did you get to talk to Helen today?"

"No, not at all. I had set aside an hour, assuming we would be talking for a while, but I guess the hospital had other plans. By the time I located her, called Mercy Manor and made arrangements, I had to get back to the clinic."

"Maybe tomorrow then?" Michael suggested, with a smile.

"Yes, I hope so. If I drop off copies of my license and malpractice insurance, they'll let me attend her immediately. Plus, it helped that the hospital administrator called and put in a good word," Amy said. "How did you do? Did you find anything interesting in the archives?"

"I didn't have much time, either," Michael said. "But I went through some photos and I think the priest, in Helen's photo, is the third or fourth pastor of St. Francis."

"That makes sense," Amy said. "If the little girl is Helen, that photo had to be taken around 1930."

"The construction on St. Francis Church started around 1875. The Retreat House was recognized long before that, but it was more of a log cabin back then, so it was rebuilt the same year the Church was established. The guest rooms and initial prayer walks were the biggest addition. It's been entirely maintained since its completion, save a few minor improvements," Michael said.

"That's interesting," Amy said. "I wonder if Helen knows what happened to that priest."

"I think I can tell you where he is," Michael said.

Amy watched him questioningly. "Oh, is he buried here? I never thought of the cemetery."

"The previous clergy aren't in the cemetery. They're in the crypt," Michael shrugged.

"St. Francis has a crypt? I didn't know that," Amy said, shock registering on her face.

"Yes, it's below the floor of the church. We don't advertise it," Michael said. "There are six people buried down there. There's more room, but I think modern methods started to prevail and most of the clergy left the area, upon retirement."

"That is so strange," Amy said. "Have you been down there?"

"Not recently but I'm fairly certain I saw the symbol, from the journal, near the crypt," Michael said.

"Does that connect with the part of the cellar I saw when we went down through the kitchen earlier this year?" Amy asked.

"It sure does," Michael said. "You won't believe how many tunnels and rooms are down there."

"That's fascinating. Can we take a look?" Amy asked excitedly.

"Definitely, but I think we better have dinner first or Katie's going to have a fit."

"Okay, as soon as dinner is over."

"Sounds like a plan," Michael said. "But before we go down there, I was hoping you would talk to Katie, about the soup kitchen, with me."

"Of course, Michael. Step by step, we'll get it all done," Amy said, laughing as they started to hear voices calling them from the kitchen.

"Shall we?" Michael asked, as he extended his arm to Amy.

"It would be my pleasure."

Chapter Seventeen

"Nurse, Nurse," Helen yelled, as she pushed the call bell for the twentieth time. "I need to go to the bathroom."

"Don't hold your breath," said a small voice, on the other side of the curtain.

"Who's there?" Helen asked, shifting in her bed.

"My name is Mildred, but you can call me Millie. It might be days before that aide comes to check on you."

"Where am I?" Helen asked, with obvious anxiety in her voice.

"You are now a guest of Mercy Manor," Millie said. "They brought you in here a while ago, but you've been sound asleep."

"I must have passed out with those pain killers," Helen said. "I don't want to be here."

"Trust me, no one wants to be here," Millie said. "What are you in for anyway?"

"I broke my hip. They fixed it in the hospital, but now they said I need therapy. How about you?"

"I had my foot amputated," Millie said. "Damn diabetes. I go to therapy twice a day. Hopefully, I'll be out of here soon. At least they gave me the bed with the window."

"Is this place okay?" Helen asked quietly.

"It's not a wonderland, that's for sure," Millie said. "In the beginning, I thought I was the only patient in the place. The bell would ring and no one would come. Very scary."

"Are we the only patients here?" Helen asked, fear pinching at her stomach.

"Not even close. Once I started going to therapy, I met other patients and realized the facility isn't bad, from what they told me anyway. They only have a few aides to work with all the patients, so you don't get a lot of private attention."

"Well, it seems a far cry from the hospital, so far," Helen said, while pushing her call bell again.

"Before I say this, is there anyone else is in the room?" Millie asked.

"Unfortunately, no one is here except you and me," Helen said, as she privately hoped the disembodied voice of Mildred wasn't a hallucination, from the pain killers.

"Just to let you know, our aide, Susan, is a bit of a slacker. She's not very friendly or caring," Millie said. "The patients, on the other side of the nurses' desk, have a different aide and are very happy with their care. The patients, on this side, are pretty upset. Do you have any family?"

"I have no one," Helen said sadly.

"That's too bad," Millie said. "From what I hear, the families who complain the most are the ones who get attention first. You need to find someone to fight for you."

"What about you?" Helen asked.

"My son comes in every other day, but I'm a little more mobile now," Millie said. "Another couple days and I'm out of here."

An aide appeared in the doorway. "Which one of you is ringing the bell?"

"I have to go to the bathroom," Helen said.

"Oh, you finally woke up," Susan said, scrunching her face. "I thought you were going to sleep all day. You already missed dinner."

"I hope not," Helen said getting upset.

"Don't worry, I'll take you to the bathroom and put you back to bed. We can order a tray for you tonight."

"Okay, if you say so," Helen said feebly, anxiety flooding her voice.

The aide roughly pulled back the blankets and pushed a wheelchair next to the bed. "Now wait until I tell you what to do," Susan said. "We don't want you to go and fall again."

Helen stopped moving and waited for the aide to position the chair. Sensing the quiet, she looked at her and whispered, "Is there anyone else in here?" Susan looked up and saw the closed curtain.

"Millie, are you in bed?" Susan pulled Helen's side rail back up and went over to the other side of the room where she pushed back the curtain, revealing a dark haired woman lying against the sterile pillows. "Are you okay?"

"I'm fine, just fine," Millie said, looking at Helen with big eyes.

Helen smiled back, sensing Millie was not going to talk with the aide in the room. Helen was also thrilled to realize she wasn't hallucinating.

Chapter Eighteen

"Katie, that was delicious," Amy said, as she carefully placed her fork and knife on the porcelain plate that sat empty in front of her. "Stopping over for dinner was a great decision."

"I'm happy to have you whenever you can, dear," Katie said. "I have to admit, a little birdie hinted to me that you might be tired of stale cheese and crackers for every meal."

Amy shot a glare over at Michael, who immediately ducked his head to hide the smile creeping up his face.

"I really appreciate this, Katie. Plus, the more often I come for dinner, the more I can see Willow and help her look at colleges."

"Thank goodness," Willow smiled in sheer relief. "And maybe we could fit a few hours of Christmas shopping in, sometime? Amy, do you want to help me clear the table?"

Michael cleared his throat. "Actually, I was hoping Father Victor could help you Willow, so I could talk to Dr. Amy and Katie in my office. Is that all right with everyone?"

"Not likely, Father," Katie said, as she stood up. "I don't like being called into the office. Nothing good ever gets discussed in the office."

"Now Katie, it'll be all right," Father Victor said, as he tried to soothe her. "I'm sure this is simply a secret ploy to make sure I take my turn doing the dishes."

"We'll see," Katie said, untying her apron and placing it over the back of her chair. "All right, Father. I'm ready."

The sound of Father Michael and Dr. Amy both pushing back their chairs seemed to soften the tension in the air. Katie looked over at Amy for support, but Amy shrugged her shoulders to show she had no idea what was happening. The trio left the kitchen and walked single file to Michael's office, at the end of the hall. Father Victor and Willow watched them go and upon clearing the doorway, Father Victor turned to Willow. "Katie's right. I'm glad I don't have to go in there." Willow's expression remained thoughtful, her face impassive.

Father Michael flipped the light switch, next to the door, and stepped back to hold the door open for his guests.

Katie nervously settled herself into a chair near Father Michael's impeccable desk, with Amy at her side. "Does this have to do with the auction, Father?"

"Why, yes it does, Katie."

"Then it can't be good news," she said. "If it was, you would have blurted something out the moment you saw me."

"No, I'm afraid it's not good news. We lost the bid," Father Michael said, as he watched her face fall.

"For just a moment, I was hoping you were going to surprise me with good news," Katie said, searching his face.

"I really wish I could. But I thought it fair to share exactly how things at the auction played out today," he gently explained.

"Did we ever have a chance?" Katie asked. Many times, in Michael's life, people had come to him seeking truth, this being an instance in which he wished he didn't have to share it. Amy placed an arm around Katie's shoulders and squeezed, now realizing her purpose in the meeting.

"We put in a nice bid, Katie, but there was another company that came in with a higher offer. The bank is not allowed to give us actual numbers, but Mr. Owen, the bank manager, really tried to help us out. He called and encouraged me to raise the bid, above the other company. After some calls and relenting on the Bishop's part, I was able to do so," Father Michael explained.

"Okay, so what happened?" Katie asked, as quiet tears rolled down her face.

"Legally, the bank has to give everyone a fair chance, so they called the other bidder, who offered more money than we did."

"And we don't know who it was, I'll bet," Katie said.

"No Katie, they can't tell us that," Michael said. "But, it doesn't end there. The bank manager called back to encourage me to make a higher offer, but we didn't have enough money. I'm sorry."

"Is it too late?" Amy asked. "I have some savings. Why didn't you ask me?"

"Oh, I would never ask you to do that, dear," Katie said, turning to Amy. "It was just a dream of mine and we were so close."

"Unfortunately, we were never that close," Michael said, as he handed her a tissue. "I received one final call, from the bank. They had been getting inquiries, throughout the day, from other parties. They told me neither the church nor the other company won the bid. Apparently, a third party swooped in, at the end, and outbid us all. We would never have been able to match half that price, much less beat it."

Katie looked at the floor, as her tears fell. "That's okay, Father. I thank you for trying."

"Katie, we might have lost that building, but we're not giving up the soup kitchen. We'll still hold our Christmas Day meal, right here in the all-purpose room," Father Michael said, as Katie looked up at him with red eyes.

"That's fine, Father," Katie said softly. "But my dream was to make sure meals were offered daily to those who need it. We can't do that in the all-purpose room."

"Maybe, we can use the back room at Hasco's Bar and Grill," Amy said, realizing the fault in the plan, the moment it left her lips. Hasco's Bar was run by Tony Noce, a former NYPD detective who inherited the place, after it was left to him, in the will of his deceased partner's dad. Tony was also dating Willow's mother, Marty Davis, and was responsible for encouraging her to start rehab.

"Some of these people are homeless because of alcohol," Katie said. "I don't think the bar would work out. I suppose we'll have to continue to pray."

"The Lord has his ways, Katie," Michael said. "Just have faith."

"I do, Father. I do. Well, I best be getting back to the kitchen," Katie said, as she wiped invisible lint off her pants. "Father Victor has probably broken at least half of the dishes by now."

"Don't be discouraged, Katie. Things will work out," Michael said again.

"Thank you," Katie said, as she turned and left the room, with a broken spirit, and slumped shoulders.

"I feel terrible, Michael. There's so much good she can do with that soup kitchen. All she wants is to feed the homeless," Amy said, increasingly frustrated. "Isn't there something we can do?"

"Not with this particular piece of property," he explained. "Maybe I'll call a real estate agent and see if there's anything else available."

"That's a start," Amy said dejectedly, glancing at her watch. "It's getting late. I don't think I'm in the mood to visit any crypts tonight. I'll visit with Willow for a bit and then go home."

"I'm sorry I had to break Katie's heart," Michael said. "I tried the best I could."

"I'm sure you did," Amy said. "I should be going. Please call me in the morning to see if we can find time to see Helen together?"

"Of course," Michael said with a nod. "That would be great."

Amy stepped out of the office and closed the door behind her. Michael, now alone with his thoughts, leaned back in his chair and tapped a pen on the desk. He didn't quite understand why things happened as they did, but he did believe this turned out to be a bad day all around.

Chapter Nineteen

Marco Montanari sat calmly in his study, his eyes fixated on his much younger associate, Luca. The grandfather clock, hung on the far wall, chimed, signaling it was 2:00 am in Italy. Marco's wife, Eloisa, had long ago retired for the evening. It had always been Marco's custom to escape to his study after dark, in an attempt to complete the business he was unable to conduct while people milled about during the day. Usually, after a peaceful and productive sixty minutes, he would join his wife in bed, and sleep comfortably, knowing the day's goals had been accomplished. Tonight had required more time.

"Giancarlo called," Marco said to Luca. "He's been watching Gemma since I spoke to her. She had a beautiful day and went shopping on Fifth Avenue."

"Maybe she's oversensitive to Paolo," Luca gently suggested.

"*Ma che* oversensitive," Marco said. "Gemma is a strong-willed girl and doesn't get upset easily. Besides, my inquiries about Paolo have turned up some questionable business deals he better not be involving my *piccolo* Gemma in."

"Do we need to have a talk with Paolo?" Luca asked, as he sat stoically in his wing-backed chair waiting for Marco's decision.

"*Non ancora*," Marco said. "Giancarlo is having someone

watch every move Paolo Sartori makes, as we speak. I don't want to do anything until I have more information. I've spent my life making sure my reputation and business stayed honest. If Paolo is up to no good, I don't want to be associated with him and if I find out he's hurt Gemma or tarnished our reputation, Paolo will hear from me. *Crederlo!*"

"I do believe it, Marco," Luca said, crossing his legs. "Gemma is coming home regardless of what happens. Is that correct?"

"Yes, Luca, she is," Marco said slyly, looking at the younger man with a smile. "I imagine you are very happy to hear that."

Luca looked away, embarrassed, but not before Marco noticed the red in his cheeks. "Luca, I know how you feel about my Gemma. *Chissa*, maybe she's ready to settle down. I have trusted you with my deepest secrets, over the past years, so you can imagine I already consider you a part of *mia famiglia*. I would love nothing more than to have you as my son-in- law. But, Luca, I am not the one who needs convincing."

Luca stood and squeezed Marco's hand in appreciation. "*Mille Grazie, Signore Montanari.*"

Marco smiled back at him. "Let's bring my Gemma home and have a beautiful *celebrazione* for the holiday so she can readjust to our culture. And then, if her heart allows, she may be ready."

"Of course," Luca said timidly.

"But first, we take care of Paolo."

Chapter Twenty

On Wednesday morning, Susan, painstakingly helped Millie into her wheelchair. As the two left the room, Susan noticed Helen was sound asleep from the pain medication she received the night before. After delivering Millie to her daily workout at physical therapy, Susan slipped back into their room and silently moved around to Millie's nightstand. Millie often wore two expensive gold rings that weren't on her fingers when she went to therapy. Susan was desperate for some extra cash and now would be a perfect time to collect the rings. She slowly opened the top drawer next to Millie's bed and pushed aside some used tissues only to find an open bottle of baby powder. In the bottom drawer, Susan rummaged through a basin, some carelessly written notes in red ink, and a pair of dirty socks. Exasperated, she closed the drawer and turned her attention toward the slim closet across the room. Having dressed Millie herself, Susan knew those rings could not have been hidden in her clothing. She made a mental note to prolong Millie's waiting time when she rang the bell for help, as punishment for making this search so difficult.

Susan quietly crossed the room and began to open the slim closet door, only to be startled by voices approaching the room. Already having two strikes from administration, she would be immediately dismissed if she got caught stealing personal items from a patient. In a panic, Susan hurried back to Millie's bed and hid behind the curtain. As the voices drew near, it became clear they were visitors for Helen. With nowhere else to run, Susan covered herself up with the stained white sheet and jumped into Millie's bed.

"I hope Helen is not too upset," Amy said, as she rounded the corner. "I feel terrible she's been here for two days without visitors."

"Not to worry, I'm sure she'll be delighted to see us," Michael reassured her. "Who's been writing her orders, if not you?"

"The nursing staff automatically called the house doctor," Amy explained. "Starting today, I'll be her attending physician again." Amy stepped toward the sleeping woman, in front of her, and delicately touched her arm. "Helen? Are you awake?" A soft moan emanated from the blanket prompting Amy to push a little harder. "Helen? Please wake up. It's Dr. Amy and Father Michael."

Helen feebly rolled over onto her back, and watched her two visitors for a few minutes before her vision focused. "Amy? What time is it?"

"It's after eleven. Haven't they gotten you up today?" Amy turned to Father Michael, her guarded expression mirroring his concern.

"I don't think so," Helen said. "They made me take a pain pill last night and that's the last thing I can remember."

Visibly upset, Amy turned to Michael and said, "This is unacceptable. I need to talk to the administrator about this."

Under Millie's smelly sheet, Susan mentally cursed the pair, on the other side of the curtain.

After blinking her eyes to focus, Helen began to sit up. "I

haven't been able to keep track of time since I got here. How long have I been here?"

"It's Wednesday, Helen. You've been here for two nights now. How are you?" Amy asked, with a smile.

"Learning the ropes, I guess. I was out of bed for a little bit yesterday. I'm supposed to start therapy today."

"Are you having any problems? Any pain other than your hip?"

"No, not really. I hate it here," Helen said, with some strength returning to her voice.

"I'm sorry, Helen. I'm going to try to get you healthy as quickly as possible so we can get you back home. Until then, I'll be having a serious discussion with the administration, so it won't be as bad here. Father Michael is here to see how you're doing."

Helen looked up at the handsome priest. "Yes, I can see that," she said with a smile. "Were the two of you able to get my papers?"

"I think so," Amy said, as she started to look around the curtain. "Are we alone, here?"

"We should be," Helen said. "Millie usually has physical therapy in the mornings and is gone for a few hours. I think I remember her leaving."

Amy turned back to Helen. "Ok, we brought the paperwork with us, but you may be too tired to talk about it now."

"Not on your life," Helen grinned. "Father, did you find the journal?"

"Yes, Helen, we did," Michael said softly. "Tell me, who is

James Alex Coyle?

Helen paused for a moment before answering. "He was my great grandfather. I learned a lot about him from my grandfather. He used to talk about him all the time."

"Would you like to talk about your family?" Father Michael asked. "We found some photos on your mantel."

"No, thank you, Father. Talking about my family reminds me of how lonely I am. My grandfather passed when I was twenty, my brother a few years after that and my parents have both been gone for over forty years."

"Oh, Helen, I'm so sorry," Amy said, touching her arm.

"I've tried to forget it," Helen said. "Back then, we didn't use funeral parlors. Grandfather was laid out in the living room, for three days, surrounded by white carnations to hide the smell. To this day, I can't stand the smell of fresh flowers because of that experience." Helen turned her head to the side as she valiantly held back tears.

"We don't want to upset you, Helen," Father Michael said, squeezing her arm. "We can talk about this another time."

"No, Father," Helen said. "I want you to have the journal. You read through it, right?"

"Yes, we read it together," Father Michael said. "But it's a mystery. Helen, what is the sacred gift? And do you know where it is?"

"When I was a little girl, my grandfather made me promise to never lose that journal. He said, 'Helen, there is a solid gold crucifix hidden within St. Francis Church and it's worth a fortune. One day, the world will be ready to receive it, but for now, promise to hold onto this journal and keep the secret safe. You'll know when it's time to use it.' That was all he ever told me, so I never found out where it was or why it was there. But, I know I'm not going to be around forever, so it's time the secret goes back to the rightful owners," Helen said, feeling freed.

"I don't know what to say, Helen," Father Michael said. "All my days at St. Francis, I've never known about this."

"It's not exactly something to be excited about. Some will see it as a blessing, and others, a source of greed. My mother always use to quote the Bible to me.

– *For the love of money is a root of all kind of evil* –
1, Peter 6:10.

"Something as rare and valuable as that needs to be hidden or protected, Father, but I didn't want to bury the secret with me. So now, it's in your hands."

"Helen, do you know where the crucifix came from?" Amy asked.

"I only know what the journal says. If you find the cross, you'll find the story, but be careful," Helen said, turning to Amy. "Did you find my other papers?"

"Yes, we found the insurance cards and living will, and I turned copies of those over to the business office. There was also some old letters and a skeleton key. Do you know anything about those?"

"Put the letters back," Helen said, seriously. "When I was but eighteen, I stepped out with a man who wanted to marry me, a salesman. Sadly, my father wouldn't allow it, but that boy continued to write to me from each town he visited, vowing to come back when he had enough money, but he never did."

Shifting uncomfortably, Amy asked, "Helen, what should I do with the key? Do you know what it unlocks?"

"Oh, the key. Yes, you better keep that handy. It unlocks the gate to the Coyle mausoleum in the graveyard," Helen said sadly. "You may need it soon, Amy, for me."

"Helen, stop that," Amy said with scorn. "You're going to be out of here in no time. You'll have to work a little in therapy, but there is no need to think like that."

"Are you sure?" Helen asked, looking up at Amy.

"Yes, I'm sure," Amy said. "You're a strong woman and you are going home."

"Okay," Helen said, with a small smile. "I like that. But while you have the key, you better see if you can get that gate open. It's been years since I've gone inside there. I don't like remembering any of my family that way. It hurts too much."

"I don't want to make you upset, but I need to ask if you have any other family. Is there anyone we can call?" Amy asked.

"Not that I know of," Helen said. "I never had children and my brother died in an accident, at the quarry. Once I die, the Coyle line will cease to exist."

"Helen, your presence on earth will never be forgotten," Father Michael said. "We all have a purpose. Our lives do make a difference."

Helen looked up at the two of them. As her eyes misted over, her stomach let out a large growl. "I appreciate that wholeheartedly,

Father. But unless I get some lunch, I'll be making that trip to the Coyle mausoleum sooner than you think."

Laughing, Amy said, "I'm going to the nurses' station and find your aide. The administrator will be hearing from me, as well. I want you out of bed, cleaned up and fed within fifteen minutes. We've been here twenty minutes and your aide hasn't shown up once."

"I'm told she's not the best aide, in the facility," Helen said with a sigh.

"We're going to work on that," Amy said. "In the meantime, try to get strong as quickly as you can. I'll be back to check on you later."

"Thank you, I appreciate that," Helen said, as she smiled at the pair. Michael placed his hand on Helen's forehead and said a special blessing, for healing, before he and Dr. Amy left the room.

In the next bed, Susan was already texting her cousin, in New York. She had information about a fortune in gold, and she would be willing to reveal the location, for a sizeable finder's fee. Susan then went onto social media and proclaimed to the world, that her proverbial ship was finally coming in.

Chapter Twenty One

Paolo rapped on the ornate laminate door until an annoyed Gemma had no choice but to open it. "It's about time," he said, as he angrily stalked into the apartment.

"What do you want?"

"What are you doing?" Paolo asked, as he looked around and saw suitcases and boxes, ready to be packed.

Gemma flashed a guilty look, away from Paolo. "You said I should be ready, that I was going on a trip soon. Possibly to Italy. Remember Paolo? So, I am packing."

Paolo calmed, as he remembered telling her to be ready, when they were in La Vita Rossa. He was bluffing then, but now they had an assignment. As Paolo's voice lowered, Giancarlo shifted his position, in the hall, to be closer to the front door. His hand on his Beretta 92fs, he strained to hear the conversation behind the door so he could report back to Mr. Montanari.

"I'm glad you're packing. You're leaving today," Paolo said matter-of-factly.

"To Italy? Paolo, I can't be ready that soon," Gemma said, while tossing her head.

"No, *bella. Andrei* in Vermont."

"Vermont? What is in Vermont that is so important?" Gemma asked.

"A client of mine has just learned of a great treasure, made of solid gold, which may be located in a church up there," Paolo explained.

Gemma paused for a few seconds, irate because she did not want her return to Italy to be interrupted, but intrigued the lifelong rumor of a missing solid gold crucifix may actually be true. "Do you think it could be the sacred treasure?"

"*È possible*. But either way, we're going to take the chance and find out. As of now, I believe we're the only ones who know of this," Paolo explained. "My source will let me know who to get in touch with upon your arrival in Vermont. I want you to start searching immediately. Hurry up and get packed. You drive up there and call me if I need to get involved."

"It will take an hour to pack for Vermont," Gemma hissed. "Why don't you go get my car from the garage? And where am I supposed to be going?"

"To a little town by the name of Rocky Meadow. I'll get your car and program your GPS. The drive will be about five hours. *Fai in fretta*, Gemma. Now!" Paolo turned on the balls of his feet, and slammed the door behind him. Cursing to himself as he strode to the elevator, he did not see Giancarlo slip behind a statue. Within minutes, both Gemma and Giancarlo were on the phone with Marco Montanari.

Chapter Twenty Two

Thursday morning dawned bright in Vermont and was sure to offer an excellent day of winter bliss to pink-cheeked tourists, save one. Dr. Amy pushed through the gray pair of doors leading to the Emergency Room of Rocky Meadow General. Ernie sat statuesque at the front desk, fatigue etched into his face. "Ok, I'm here, what happened?" Amy asked, as she dropped her overflowing leather purse on the counter.

"A couple of college kids decided to have a few drinks, to warm up, before skiing down Mount Chione," Ernie said, noticing Amy's confusion. "Mount Chione is the biggest slope. It's named after the Greek goddess of snow and winter winds. Anyway, male, age twenty, hit a tree on the way down. I'm certain his neck snapped instantly."

"Confirmed with film?" Amy asked, her stomach churning.

"Yes, I got a plain film, as well as a CT scan, to define the injury," Ernie said. "Parents are already on their way up and I'm sure they're going to have a lot of questions."

"So tragic." Amy released a defeated sigh. "I always feel terrible speaking to parents about trauma cases. I hate being the one to extinguish the last spark of hope in their eyes."

"That's the fun of being the medical examiner," Ernie said, with a compassionate face. "Look at the films before you go to autopsy."

"I wish this hospital would find someone else qualified to fill this position," Amy said.

"Good luck with that," Ernie said with a laugh. "They would find someone faster if better pay were involved."

"Ha-ha," Amy said, frowning.

"Speaking of laughs, here comes Dr. Applebaum," Ernie said. "Does he have Amy radar or what?"

"You're kidding, right?"

"I wouldn't turn around right now, if I were you," Ernie said, smirking as he looked down at the desk.

"Hey Amy, how are you?" Lou asked, as he approached the desk.

Amy turned when she heard his voice. "Lou, how are you?"

"Fine, I'm just about finished with patient rounds for the day. Want to get some coffee?" Lou asked, hope burning bright in his eyes.

"Actually," Amy hesitated. "I only have a few minutes. We had a tragedy on the slopes, this morning, and I'm here to do the post."

"Oh, I'm so sorry to hear that," Lou said. "Those skiing accidents are always sad."

"I know," Amy said. "I have to meet the parents today."

"Well, I'll keep them in my thoughts. It may be a bad time to ask, but are we still on for the Cider Mill?"

Remembering how kind Lou was on their last date, Amy felt bad putting him off again. "Yes, we're definitely on, for coffee and lunch, at the Cider Mill. How does Monday sound? Most of the weekend crowd will be gone by then," Amy pointed out.

"Perfect for me," Lou said. "I'll come in and finish rounds early, so we'll have a couple hours."

"I'm looking forward to it," Amy said with a smile. "Meet me here at noon and we can ride over together."

Lou smiled, from ear to ear as he walked away. "You got it. I'll be here at noon, sharp."

Amy smiled, as she waved goodbye. The minute he was through the door, Amy turned and threw a paperclip at Ernie, who was snickering, on the other side of the counter. "You are now on my list and I don't mean Christmas."

Still laughing, Ernie walked away, with his hands in the air. "Don't be mad at me. I didn't invite him."

Chapter Twenty Three

"Gemma, *non capisco*. What are you saying?" Paolo said, into his cellphone, while raising his hand to shield the Vermont sun from his dark eyes. He had been speeding down Route 4, when Gemma called, and pulled onto the shoulder to answer.

"I said, I had to stay in a little motel on Route 4 last night," Gemma screamed into the receiver. "All of the rooms at the nicer places, were filled with *touristi*."

"*Va bene*, Gemma. Need I remind you that this isn't a vacation? Did you speak with that nursing home aide yet? Do you have more information for me?"

"Yes and no," Gemma said, aggravated Paolo did not seemed concerned with her uncomfortable night.

"What the hell does that mean?" Paolo demanded.

"I went to Mercy Manor and sat in the front lobby, for an hour, until the woman, Susan, finally had a break to see me. She told me there is a patient, in the nursing home, with knowledge of a solid gold crucifix and it's worth a fortune."

"*È vero?*" Paolo asked. "It's true?"

"I don't know, for sure, if it's true or not," Gemma said. "She wouldn't talk after that, gave me no more information and refused to meet with me again, unless I brought a check for a million dollars."

"That's not the way Paolo Sartori does business," Paolo

scoffed.

"Well, she's not talking. So I tried something else," Gemma said.

"And what might that be?" Paolo asked, the disgust evident in his voice.

"I checked the yellow pages and there is only one Catholic Church, in this town. I made an appointment to speak with the pastor, a Father Michael Lauretta, tomorrow morning," Gemma said matter-of-factly.

"And what do you think he's going to say? Yes, I do know where the solid gold crucifix is. Would you like to borrow it?"

"Paolo, non *prendermi in giro*," Gemma said. "The priest doesn't know we want it, so the least I can do is confirm it exists. Just that fact would be worth something in the acquisitions circuit. I doubt they would let us do an exhibition, but the interviews and photos would be good publicity. You know the church will never give up a sacred treasure, so I don't understand your goal here."

"Don't worry about my goals, Gemma. Do your job and find out more information. I can get to Vermont, in minutes, if I have to."

"Okay, Paolo. I'll call you once I meet with him," Gemma said, wincing as she heard the phone click in her ear. "So much for *ciao*."

Paolo clicked off his phone and violently threw it on the console, freeing his hands to punch the steering wheel with his fists. He turned to the other men in the vehicle. "We have nothing, zilch on where this treasure is. *Che merda!*" Pointing toward the silent man in the passenger seat, he said, "Gemma has no idea I followed her here and I want it to stay that way. We're going to eat, find a place to sleep and tomorrow morning, we visit that nursing home and make someone talk." Shoving the key in the ignition and twisting the steering wheel, Paolo started back on the road toward Rocky Meadow.

Chapter Twenty Four

After finishing the autopsy on the young skier and speaking with the grieving parents, Amy trudged out of Rocky Meadow General and drove to the Retreat House. After her promise to enjoy a wonderful dinner, at the hands of Katie, and her visit with Willow was fulfilled, Amy and Michael planned to do some sleuthing in the basement, in search of the strange symbol from Helen's journal. Amy pulled up to the icicle covered rectory and crunched across a few inches of snow. No sooner than she knocked on the door, Amy was invited in by Katie, but kept out of the kitchen, as she was early. With Willow still focusing on homework in her room, Amy took a seat in Michael's office, as they began to trade stories about their hectic day. One look at Amy's facial expression upon opening the front door, had prompted Katie to slip into Michael's office with a full pot of cinnamon spice tea, which she poured into delicate china cups. Before she tiptoed out of the room, she made sure to uncover a homemade batch of hazelnut biscotti. The combination of the two flooded the room with scents of the season.

Amy massaged her temples as she finished telling Michael about the trials of her day. "I haven't missed being away from trauma surgery in Boston. Days like this one remind me why I left. It wasn't healthy to live every day like this."

"Let me get your mind off medicine, for a moment," Michael said, hopefully. "I received a very interesting call today that resulted in a meeting, for tomorrow morning. I was hoping you could be here."

"About what and with whom?" Amy asked, with a sardonic smile.

"A young woman, who called about a rumored historical treasure here at St. Francis," Michael said.

"What's that supposed to mean?" Amy asked, with a small laugh.

Michael shrugged. "That's all she would say, over the phone. I can't help but feel that it's related to the journal. Do you think Helen told anyone else about the crucifix?"

"I seriously doubt it. She's kept the journal and the secret for so many years, I don't think she would tell anyone now. Besides, Helen has been nothing but cryptic since we found the journal, unless it's the pain medicines talking."

"It was a very odd phone call," Michael said, as he looked down at his desk. "Her name is Gemma Montanari. She said she is a museum curator from Italy."

"That doesn't sound right. How could someone from Italy have heard of the treasure?"

"I doubt she decided to call, out of the blue, unless she heard of my good looks," Michael teased.

Laughing, Amy said, "I'm sure that's the reason, but to be safe, we should look her up."

"How are we supposed to do that?" Michael asked, confused.

"Turn on your computer. Put her name in the search bar and see what pops up," Amy said. "You can't hide in the digital age."

Michael did as he was told, and entered Gemma's name into a professionally sponsored search engine. Amy came around the desk and pulled a chair up alongside his. As various links popped onto the screen, the two leaned forward, to get a closer look at the information. Michael turned to ask what link he should click and stopped when he realized how close his cheek came to brushing Amy's. Clearing his throat, Michael sat back and said, "Maybe you should take the reins here. I'm not very technologically savvy."

Holding her breath, Amy leaned closer to the computer monitor and picked a link, realizing she had to reach over Michael to work the keyboard. She felt his warm breath, against the back of her neck, as she tried to read the display. Happy he couldn't see her cheeks color, or hear her heart racing, she tried to sound as nonchalant as possible, as she read the results of the first article. "Well, it certainly appears Gemma Montanari is a curator from Italy. She works for Sartori Enterprises and appears to be quite successful, in international acquisitions. How would she know about the crucifix?"

Michael didn't immediately respond and Amy was hesitant to turn and look at him, considering their proximity.

"Dinner is ....oh," Katie said, as she burst through the door and spied the two at the desk. Chuckling, she picked up the tray. "It certainly looks like the tea relaxed everyone. Am I interrupting something?"

Amy and Michael flew back in their seats, like two guilty

grade school children, caught passing notes under their desk. Katie looked at their flushed faces, waiting for an answer.

Michael recovered first and said, "Katie, have you received any other calls, today, from a woman by the name of Gemma?"

"Or someone from Sartori Enterprises?" Amy chimed in.

"No, none at all except for the call you took earlier, Father," Katie reminded him. "Why, is there a problem?"

Realizing the growing fascination with a treasure at St. Francis had yet to reach the populous of Rocky Meadow, Michael said, "No problem at all, Katie. We've recently learned St. Francis may be part of an important historic find. Gemma Montanari made an appointment to discuss it with Amy and me, tomorrow morning."

Shrewdly looking at the two of them, behind the desk, Katie said, "My goodness, how wonderful for our little parish. I know this must be important, but now might be a good time to break away and have some dinner. Then you can have a fresh start afterward. I expect to see you both, in the kitchen." Giving one last knowing look toward Amy and Michael, she turned and hurried away from the door.

Amy and Michael looked at each other, with eyes wide, and burst out laughing. "I think I'm in trouble," Michael said.

"Both of us. We better tell them something during dinner," Amy said. "Everyone is bound to start asking questions when we go down to the crypt."

"I agree," Michael said, still grinning. "We should explain."

"Okay, but let's leave the gold crucifix out of it. Just simple details for now. The less they know, the better for all of us."

"Sounds like a great start," Michael said, as he reached over and squeezed Amy's hand.

Pulling her chair back to the other side of the desk, they turned off the computer and hurried to the kitchen for dinner.

Chapter Twenty Five

Tony Noce stood behind the mahogany bar and dried glasses with a clean towel, which had been draped over his right shoulder. Scanning the room, he took in the sights of a nice crowd at Hasco's Bar and Grill, for a Thursday night. The customers were laughing, playing games of pool, and the juke box sang a holiday tune. It was only three weeks to Christmas and Hasco's customers were already merry.

Ten years ago, Tony's partner in the NYPD, Jim Hasco, was killed in the thick of an undercover operation. Tony was the one who broke the news to Jim's father. The devastation continued, but Tony became like a son to Mr. Hasco, which helped them both to move on. When Tony had vacation, he took time to help Mr. Hasco run his business, a bar in Vermont, named Hasco's Bar and Grill. When Mr. Hasco died two years later, having no other family, he left the bar to Tony.

Throwing caution to the wind, Tony took a leave from the force, left the city, and had been tending bar in Vermont ever since. Hasco's was a comfortable place, and Tony looked after the local clientele as his own family. In Mr. Hasco's tradition, Tony called cabs when needed, and stopped arguments long before they started.

After a day of skiing and riding gondola's, exhausted tourists usually spent their money at one of the fancy ski lodge bars complete with comfy lounge chairs and roaring fireplaces. They weren't interested in an old bar like Hasco's.

The three men entering the bar caught Tony's attention immediately. He realized they were not locals and certainly not tourists. His police training kicked in as he watched them saunter to one of the booths in a dark back corner. Quietly, they piled in either side of the scarred, varnished, wooden table and looked around. A middle-aged waitress stood near the bar, but Tony stopped her with a cautious glance, and shake of his head. He checked to make sure his baseball bat and .9mm were in place, before he left the bar and went over to take their order.

"What'll you have?" Tony asked, as he stood and looked over the men. Noticing their clothes and shoes, he immediately recognized the vestiges of the city. The obvious leader was dressed in a business suit, with a blue button up shirt, Italian silk tie and black buckled dress shoes. The others wore day clothes, dark tee shirts and cargo pants, with boots. It was obvious they had guns under bulky jackets. They weren't relaxed and Tony seriously doubted they carried permits.

"Do you have a menu, in this fine establishment?" Paolo asked, with a sneer.

"Barfood," Tony said, with a practiced glare, he learned while on duty in Manhattan. "Hamburgers, cheeseburgers, fries. You know the drill."

Paolo looked up to say something sarcastic, but stopped when he saw Tony's face. Tony was a tall, muscular, beefy man, with salt and pepper hair. Paolo didn't know Tony spent a lot of time in the gym down the street, boxing with a large priest named Victor, but he realized Tony was strong and could crush him, with little effort.

"Cheeseburgers, for everyone, with the works," Paolo said, with disdain. He ordered beer for the men, and scotch, for himself. He had not had a greasy cheeseburger, since he and his father visited New York City, when he was a teenager. He hoped that eating common food would not make him sick.

Tony went back to the bar and pushed a small slip of paper through a window into the kitchen. He drew beer from the tap, poured the scotch and silently delivered the drinks to the table. Once the men were served, he went back to the bar and continued to dry glasses as he watched the crowd in the large mirror behind the bar. It was then he spotted the other man, sitting alone, in a small booth in the opposite corner. He was not a tourist, and was better dressed than the regulars. The waitress called over to Tony. "Guy in the corner is looking for Campari, or whatever vermouth you have. Get this, he's in Vermont, in winter, and he's still wearing Gucci loafers. Guess he isn't here to ski, either."

"Apparently not," Tony said, gathering the food after a bell rang at the window. "Stay away from the group over there. I'll take care of them. Loafers looks okay. Any trouble, walk away and give me the signal."

"You got it, Tony. I don't need any problems," the waitress said, as she snapped her bubblegum and scribbled on her order pad.

Chapter Twenty Six

"I don't know how you two do it," Amy said. "Dinner was delicious and these cookies look wonderful."

"We had a blast making gingerbread men today," Willow said, with a big smile.

"When do we get to try some?" Amy asked, with a mischievous glance.

Flattered, Katie pushed back her chair and said, "Maybe we'll put a few out with Sunday dinner."

"I'll make sure I run an extra mile, or two, that day," Father Michael said, as he rubbed his full stomach. "I might need two cookies to get a feel for the taste."

"Amen to that," Father Victor said, pushing away from the table.

"You'll have to work for your cookies, Father Victor," Katie said, with a stern tone.

"Why me?"

"Because you'll eat us out of house and home, otherwise." Katie said, holding up her chin. "If you expect me to do all this cooking, you can help me with some chores. You can start with putting out the garbage tonight."

Father Victor let out a hearty laugh. "For you, Katie, anything. I'll even clear the table."

"Oh, my heart," Katie said, as she feigned weakness. Laughing, they started collecting the utensils and dishes.

"Katie, after we're done with the dishes, Amy and I would like to open the door, to the basement," Father Michael said quietly, passing his plate to the end of the table.

"Good Lord, why would you want to go down there?" Katie asked, her hands planted firmly on her hips. "Father, I don't mean any disrespect, but if you have to go down there, you might need Father Victor's help moving the hutch. What's this all about?"

Glancing knowingly at Amy, Father Michael hesitated before saying, "Katie, you know Helen broke her hip?"

"Yes, Willow and I are bringing her some homemade butternut squash soup tomorrow, isn't that right, dear?" Katie said, as she looked over at the young girl.

"Yes and we also have a few Christmas cookies wrapped up for her. Sister Maggie is coming too," Willow said, with a smile.

Father Michael turned to Amy. "Maybe you should take it from here."

"Thanks," Amy said sarcastically, as she turned to the others. "When Helen was hurt, she asked Father Michael and me to collect some papers, from her house. She told us, in confidence, her great grandfather had a part in the original planning and rebuilding of the church and retreat house. He was one of the earliest trusted members of the parish."

"Yes, I recognize the name Coyle," Katie said slowly. "You know, I've seen that name attached to several things in the church, but never put it together until you mentioned it."

"James Alex Coyle," Father Michael said, "was Helen's great grandfather. I've been going through the archives, looking up any information I can find on him."

"Anyway," Amy continued. "Helen mentioned that in 1878, a sacred gift was bestowed upon the church and hidden somewhere, on the grounds, to protect its wellbeing. The secret has been passed down for generations, and being the only remaining Coyle, Helen wants Father Michael to be the one to decide what happens from here. The only problem is, we have to find it first," Amy said, with a shrug.

"That sounds so cool." Willow looked back and forth at the group. "It must be some kind of treasure."

"Fascinating," Katie said, slowly putting the dishes in the sink. "Do you know what it is?"

"We're not completely sure yet." Amy looked at Father Michael. "That's what we have to find out."

"Very interesting," Katie said, as she turned to get Father Victor's attention. "You're drying the dishes, so don't go anywhere."

"Stung again." Father Victor held a hand to his heart and made his way over to the sink. "So what does the basement and the hutch have to do with it?"

"The only clue we have at the moment, is the symbol on the wall, near the basement steps," Father Michael said.

"I remember that symbol from when we ran down there during the FBI raid," Willow said.

"Willow, it wasn't an FBI raid," Amy said with a laugh. "Well, I guess it was a sting to start catching those awful people from Shepherd Force."

"So what does this have to do with the woman coming here tomorrow?" Katie asked, as she turned to face them.

"We have no idea," Father Michael said. "We don't know why she wants to see us, or where she got her information. I guess we'll find out tomorrow."

"It's very important this information goes no further, but we thought you should know because we may be searching in some strange places," Amy said. "Please do not say anything to anyone for now, especially Helen."

"Our lips are sealed, and search all you want," Katie said with a shudder. "You won't get me back down in that basement."

"Why not?" Amy asked, suddenly concerned.

"Oh, it's filled with passages, tunnels, and plenty of cobwebs," Katie said. "It's dark and creepy."

"It's true, it's a bit daunting down there," Michael explained. "Especially at night."

"That's why I had the hutch put in front of the door," Katie said, as she shook her head. "I don't need anything sneaking up behind me when I'm cooking."

Father Michael grinned as he looked at Amy. "I don't think it's that bad. Still feel like going down there?"

"I guess so," Amy said, although somewhat less excited. "We really need to know what's going on before Ms. Montanari arrives tomorrow."

"Well, since you're doing this for St. Francis, I suppose I'll let you off dish duty. Have fun, but be careful," Katie said, while handing Father Victor a dry towel. "Willow and I are going to a meeting, with the food committee. Tony was kind enough to let us use the back room at Hasco's tonight. We're getting together to firm up our menu for Christmas and see what supplies we'll need for the gathering."

"And I graciously offered to drive them," Father Victor said, with a wicked smile. "I can spend time telling Tony how weak he is in the ring."

"Hasco's? Katie, there are plenty of rooms in the church you can use for the meeting," Michael said.

"Thank you, Father, but I can't imagine heating the entire church for one room," Katie said. "And there isn't a room large enough for all the committee members in the retreat house. Besides, they're more agreeable to meeting if some of their husbands can hang out by the bar for a while."

"I understand, Katie. After all, you are the head of the committee," Michael said.

Katie suddenly turned from the sink, grief lining her face. "Speaking of feeding the homeless, do you know I got a call from Florence today? Can you believe the new owners are already cleaning out the restaurant and starting to rebuild? They have a dumpster and everything. It makes me so sad we can't use that property for the soup kitchen."

Father Michael went over to Katie and gave her a large hug. "Keep the faith, Katie. The Lord doesn't answer our prayers when he has a better idea in mind. It'll work out."

"I hope so," Katie said, as she sniffed and took the dishtowel back from Father Victor. She rapidly turned back to the sink and said, "Father Victor, they'll be needing you to help get the door open."

Chapter Twenty Seven

It was dark when Katie, Willow and Father Victor left the Retreat House, the scent of lavender dish detergent still looming in the air. Willow wanted to stay and explore with Amy and Michael, but Katie would not entertain any thoughts of Willow in the dark basement. Properly equipped with flashlights and jackets, Father Michael and Amy avoided the hutch Father Victor had put aside, and pulled open the heavy basement door. After descending the basement steps, Michael tugged the rusty chain, attached to an overhead bulb, at the base of the stairs. The surrounding cinderblock was covered in cobwebs, and their line of vision was filled with three dark tunnels, leading in different directions. Each tunnel was populated with heavy, wooden doors that were dark and closed.

"It's freezing down here, and smells musty," Amy whispered, as she pulled her jacket tighter. "When was the last time you were down here?"

"I've had no reason to come down since the FBI incident over the summer," Michael said, as he looked around the base of the stairs. "Why are we whispering?"

"I don't know," Amy laughed. "I didn't want anyone to hear us."

"The only one able to hear us down here, is the Lord himself," Michael laughed. "We don't have to whisper. Look, the candles are still here from summer. It doesn't look like anything has been touched."

"I would hope not. If something was moved, I'd be seriously concerned. Anyway, when I was down here last, I saw that tapestry hanging on the wall," Amy said, shuffling to her left, a mixture of stone and dirt beneath her feet. "Do you see the symbol on the fabric? It's also on the wall behind the tapestry and written in Helen's journal."

"I've seen the symbol inside the crypt," Michael said as he studied the wall, noting the symbol appeared to be a crown sitting on top of a shield. Michael pushed and prodded the stone to no avail. "I feel cold air flowing through this crack, but it won't budge."

"It's more of a groove," Amy said, as she felt along the cold wall. "Whatever it is, it looks like it was purposefully made."

"There must be a chamber or a room back there, but I have no idea how to reach it," Michael said, as he continued to search. "I don't know anything about the tunnels and rooms down here."

"There has to be a record or some blueprints, in the archives," Amy said, as she looked around. "It looks like you've had maintenance done at some point. The water pipes seem to be rather new."

"I haven't found any information yet, but I'll go back and look in the more secured sections of the archives," Michael said, inspecting the ceiling. "I do know, before the previous pastor, Father O'Connor, retired, he gave me a tour of the crypt and I'm sure I saw the symbol there."

"The journal said, *'our predecessors would show us the way'*.

Maybe, they meant it literally. There must be another clue in the crypt."

"Well, it's worth a shot," Michael said. "We're not getting anywhere down here, and I have no clue where these tunnels lead."

"It looks like we have a lot more exploring to do tomorrow. We should really follow these tunnels in daylight," Amy said, as she fiddled with the key, from Helen's closet, in her pocket. "And I still have to open the Coyle Mausoleum with this key."

"Also a chore for the daylight," Michael said. "Let's head upstairs and look around the church. Maybe there's another way to get behind the wall from there."

"I'll gladly go first," Amy said, as she started climbing the thick wooden steps which led her through the basement door and into the pleasant warmth of the kitchen.

"Right behind you," Michael said, hurrying up the steps. As he struggled to firmly close the chestnut basement door, Amy pulled a kitchen chair in front of it. Laughing, Michael asked, "What are you doing?"

"Don't laugh at me. I want to make sure the door isn't opened while we're gone," Amy said in a confident tone. "But I also don't want anything too heavy there, in case we find ourselves back at these stairs."

"Very clever, Dr. Daniels," Michael said, with a smile.

Amy playfully punched his arm. "Stop it. Come on, let's go to the crypt and see what we can stumble upon."

"You got it," Michael said, as he checked his pocket for his key ring. "We'll have to go through the main chapel."

"You said the crypt is under the church?" Amy asked.

"Yes, the door is in one of the transepts," Michael said. "We have a table with a statue of St. Francis on it so no one is tempted to go inside."

"Okay, now you lost me," Amy said. "I'm not sure what a transept is."

"I'll explain it on the way," Michael said as they opened the front door of the retreat house and braced themselves against the cold. They talked while making their way across the icy, snow covered lawn, toward the church. "I'll bet one of those tunnels was built so the original clergy didn't have to trudge through the snow to celebrate mass. To think, I've been walking through heavy snow, every winter, when I didn't have to."

"If we find this tunnel, you'll still have a few months of winter left to use it," Amy said cheerfully. "Anyway, what is a transept?"

"Okay, the body of a large church is called the nave," Michael said. "The transept is the section that crosses the main body. Some churches were actually built in the shape of a cross. Anyway, at each end of the transept there can be a stained glass window, like St. Francis has. We have candles and religious statues there as well, like the one hiding the door to the crypt."

"Oh, I see," Amy said, as she watched her warm breath fog up in billows against the cold. "Tell me about the crypt. Is it creepy?"

Michael laughed at her question. "A crypt can be a chamber in the floor, or in a mausoleum, but it can also be a room under a church in which people are buried."

"What does St. Francis have?" Amy asked, eyes wide.

"It has several rooms," Michael said. "It's completely underground, but they have natural windows built near the top to let light come in during the day. At night, there is some electric lighting one can use. The walls are made of a whitish marble, with gray streaks through it. Some crypts are made with cinderblock, but marble was easily accessible in Vermont."

"I suppose so," Amy said as she digested the architectural information.

Michael jiggled his key in the front lock of the church, and swung the vast door open with added effort. A series of dim sconces lined the walls, and brazen winter moonlight filtered through the stained glass windows. He carefully closed and locked the door behind them, and together they walked toward the front of the church.

When they reached the transept, Michael dragged the walnut table across the marble floor, while Amy cradled the statue of St. Francis, so it would not fall. When the table was repositioned, she replaced the statue, while Michael opened the partially hidden door, with an oxidized skeleton key. Flipping a switch on the inside of the doorway, a weak light flickered at the bottom of the marble steps, as the two inched their way down.

Amy was surprised to find the air cool and peculiarly fresh. The walls of the small room were also finished in marble, with two archways built into each side. The archways were closed off with a black wrought iron gate. Beyond the gates, Amy could see each section housed three burial chambers.

Inscriptions of names and dates were chiseled into the stone, fronting the chambers in the first two archways. The other burial chambers were blank. Statuesque marble benches, with impressive molding, sat in the center of the room, as metal vases, overrun with cobwebs, and long stemmed religious candles enveloped the room in an eerie embrace.

"It's definitely more polished than I expected," Amy said nervously. "It's still spooky in here, at night."

"I don't think anyone has been down here, for a long time," Michael said. "I have one of the only keys, and no one has ever asked to borrow it."

"Michael, who's buried down here?" Amy asked, struggling to read the name plates.

"The first three vaults on the right, hold the remains of the original pastors of St. Francis," Michael said. "I'm not sure who the other three are, but they may be patrons who helped establish the church. It was expensive to build a church a hundred years ago, much more so than now."

"You really need to dig into those archives. I'll bet this place has some interesting history behind it," Amy said.

"I've already started. I'm sure St. Francis holds a few secrets. Unfortunately, when I arrived here, a two day tour was the extent of my orientation as pastor of St. Francis."

"I'd hate to push you after that thought, but do you have any idea where you saw the symbol?" Amy asked, while feeling the cool smoothness of the marble walls.

"It would have been near the back," Michael said. "You'll need your flashlight. At some point, one of the pastors tried to have modern lighting installed, but the marble was too thick to puncture. It's still very dark back there."

"Okay, let's do it," Amy said, as she switched on her powerful flashlight.

The pair slowly crept forward, flashlight beams weaving back and forth on the walls. They found the symbol at the back of the chamber, near a small hall which led off to the right. Continuing their quest, they followed the marble wall until they located a duplicate symbol at the very end of the corridor.

"Here it is," Michael said. "I knew I remembered seeing it here, because it seemed so out of place."

"It does match the clue about the predecessors," Amy said. "So now what?"

"I don't know. Let's see if we can find an opening," Michael said. The two thoroughly examined the wall, in front and to the sides of the symbol, but found nothing unusual; not a groove or crack, as they did in the basement of the retreat house.

"Michael, even if we were to find an opening, this marble would be much harder to move," Amy said as she reasoned with herself. "We must be missing something important. Maybe there's another clue back in the journal."

"I agree with you, but what?" Michael said.

"Let's think. Do you remember what James Coyle wrote in that last entry?" Amy asked.

Michael slowly repeated the last words of the entry. *"We*

have left instructions and its magnificent story in the antechamber. When the time comes for the wall to be breached, our predecessors will guide us. Only the humble will discover its passage, and a righteous soul will find its key. God Bless us all."

"The antechamber? Is the crypt the antechamber, or is the next room the antechamber?" Amy asked.

"I don't know," Michael said. "The wall to be breached is either this one, or the one in the basement. I can't help but feel we're in the right spot."

"Well, what about, *'only the humble will discover its passage?'* Amy asked. "What does the humble person do that others don't?"

"Pray? Bow their head?" Michael asked with a shrug.

At the same moment, they both looked down at the floor. "Are those holes?" Amy asked.

Three recessed wells, each about four inches in diameter, were sculpted in the floor. "Is there anything in there? Are they for flowers or candles?" Amy asked excitedly while trying to shine her flashlight directly into one of the wells.

"Don't know," Michael said as he gently prodded the cavities. He felt the surrounding area, and came away empty. He tentatively put his finger in one of the wells, and pulled back when he touched liquid. "There's something in there." He rubbed the fluid across his first two fingers with his thumb and brought his hand to his nose. "It's oily, and it smells a bit strong as well."

"Clean your hand, Michael," Amy demanded, a bit flustered. "We have no idea what that is. It could be acid or even a poison. Dry your hand on your pants."

"Then what are we going to do?" Michael asked.

"I can get a pipette from the hospital to sample it, but for now, please don't touch it."

"Maybe that's what we use to open the door," Michael said eagerly, as he wiped his hand. "I don't feel any burning or tingling."

"Or it could be some weird sort of booby trap," Amy said. "Why don't we get out of here and go back to the archives? There must be a document that explains what to do."

"I guess you're right. We made decent progress tonight. We can restart tomorrow, and we'll keep searching until we figure it out."

"Good, let's go," Amy shivered. "It's too dark to be down here. Daylight may make a difference."

Michael let out a little laugh and could not resist pulling Amy into a hug, and planting a kiss on top of her head. "We're fine. There are no creatures, but I agree, let's get out of here. If we're lucky, we can make it back to the kitchen and taste some of those Christmas cookies before Katie comes back."

"You do know, if we get caught, we would've been better off taking our chances down here," Amy chided jokingly.

As they hurried up the marble staircase, the sound of Michael's laughter and receding footsteps resounded in the chamber, until the door at the top of the steps was closed, and stiffening silence flooded back in.

Chapter Twenty Eight

Father Victor stalked into Hasco's, and sat on a slightly frayed, green pleather bar stool. When Tony looked up and noticed him, Father Victor gave a friendly head nod and smile. After a few minutes, the bartender sauntered over. Lifting his chin, he said, "Hey, what can I get you, Father?"

"How about a root beer?"

"The hard stuff, huh?" Tony teased, pouring a cold, frosted mug of soda, and placing it in front of the priest.

"I'm still wearing my clericals and I need to keep in shape for boxing," Father Victor said, hiding his laughter. "By the way, when can you meet me in the ring, for some one on one?"

"Any time you can work up the courage," Tony laughed. The two men enjoyed sparring, outside of the ring, almost as much as inside. "What brings you to Hasco's on a Thursday night?"

"As you know, the food committee for the soup kitchen is meeting in the back, and I was given the position of chauffeur," Father Victor said.

"Ah, I see," Tony said distractedly.

"What's wrong, Tony? You're not your usual jovial self. Unless, of course, you realize meeting me in the ring is just a fruitless exercise for you."

"Ha, you wish," Tony grinned. "No, I have my eye on a

couple of shady guys. Don't look now, but the group in the back to your right, may be looking for trouble, and I'm certain the man to your left, is tailing them."

"Are you sure?" Father Victor asked.

"Tony Noce is always sure. The guys in the corner are packing weapons. The single guy on the left, is wearing Gucci loafers, in Vermont, in the snow. He must be armed as well."

"That is suspicious. I hope it doesn't turn into a problem," Father Victor said as he drained his glass.

"Do me a favor," Tony reasoned. "If it does become a problem, and all hell, oh, excuse me Father, if all *heck* breaks loose and they come running this way, turn around and stick your leg out."

Father Victor let out a hearty laugh. "You got it. Don't forget, I am from Chicago. Hey, I notice the pool table is empty and it happens to be near them. I could sharpen my skills, if you want."

"I wouldn't want you to do anything that might put you in danger," Tony said. "Honestly, there hasn't been a problem yet, but I don't like the look of them."

"Fine, the jukebox is over there too. I'll pick a song and come right back," Victor said, fishing for loose change in the pockets of his black slacks.

"Father Victor, the jukebox is digital," Tony laughed. "You don't need change anymore."

"Whew," Victor said, as he left the change on the bar. "For a minute, I was worried you weren't getting a tip tonight."

Drying a glass, Tony stifled a laugh as he moved down the bar. Father Victor stood up and strolled over to the jukebox, mere feet from where Paolo and his men sat. Victor pretended to look over the song list and stalled as long as he could, before he landed on a cover of an old Elvis tune, made his selection and walked back towards his seat.

After a few minutes, Tony returned with a fresh frosty mug of root beer and asked, "How did it go?"

"They were talking, with a strong Italian accent. The only words I understood were Starlight Motel, Route 4, and nursing home," Father Victor said.

"I guess you were listening harder than you were reading."

"Oh, why is that?" Father Victor asked as he looked at the bartender.

"Because the song you choose was *Devil in Disguise*." Tony chuckled as Father Victor blanched, while he reached up to straighten his white, plastic cleric collar.

"Glad you are so amused," Victor said.

"Not really, but it broke the tension," Tony said with a smile. Looking up, Tony tensed as the four men stood up and Paolo reached inside his jacket. Tony wrapped his hand around his .9mm and watched as Paolo withdrew a handful of bills and threw them on the table in disgust. Grabbing their jackets, the men left the bar, without further incident. Seconds later, Giancarlo, known to Tony as "Loafers," meandered through the door after them.

"I'm glad they're out of here, but I'm calling the police chief," Tony said. "He may want to keep a close eye on the Starlight tonight." He turned to Father Victor as he waited for the call to go through. "Father, if I were still on the force, you might've done well as my partner."

Chapter Twenty Nine

Friday morning dawned cold and gray, as forecasted flurries fell upon Rocky Meadow. Amy pulled her car into the snow covered parking lot of St. Francis, but kept the motor running. She waited for Michael to come outside and replayed last evening's events in her head as she watched the flurries coalesce into powder on the ground.

Leaving the door to the crypt, secured and obstructed, Amy and Michael locked the main door of the church, and upon returning to the retreat house kitchen, were relieved to find the chair in front of the basement door untouched. In a short while, Katie, Willow and Father Victor returned from Hasco's and joined them in the glowing kitchen after a ceremonious shaking of their coat and shoes, to remove any icy residue.

Katie pulled a hidden batch of cookies from the cupboard, and discussed the meeting over a steaming pot of hot chocolate, decorated with clouds of marshmallows. Father Victor voiced Tony's concerns about the men at Hasco's, whereas Katie and Willow talked excitedly about the menu for the Parish Christmas dinner. Katie had secretly hoped to learn information about the new owners of the closed restaurant, and everyone commented on the construction, but no one knew what the renovation would bring.

When asked, Father Michael and Amy shared a very limited view of what they found in the basement and the crypt. After Amy wiped remnants of hot chocolate from her lips, Michael walked her to the door. She wanted to go home for a hot shower and some much needed sleep.

Amy agreed to drive the pair to the cemetery early on, to avoid any visitors with wandering eyes seeing them unlock the Coyle Mausoleum. She hoped they would find another clue, a symbol that would lead them closer to the sacred treasure.

Amy was deep in thought when she was startled by a knock on the car window. With a jolt, she turned to find Michael's face reflecting hers, separated by the glass of the car window. His cheeks were red from the cold, and his breath undulating in clouds of fog. Amy unlocked the doors and invited him in to warm up.

"Good morning," Michael said with a sheepish grin.

"Good morning, yourself," Amy replied. "Sleep well?"

"Yes, I did," Michael said. "Must have been the hot chocolate and cookies. How about you?"

"I've had better nights," Amy said wearily.

"Maybe you can get a nap in, being it's Friday. We'll check the cemetery, and hopefully the meeting with Ms. Montanari will be over long before lunch."

"At least I didn't have to work in the clinic today," Amy said. "It's been a hectic week."

"Well, let's go see if we can find something at the mausoleum. Maybe we'll get back in time for coffee before the meeting," Michael suggested. "If you drive over to the edge of the parking lot, you'll find a small road next to the Divide, which will lead you to the cemetery. I assume your car is okay on snow and ice?"

"Under normal winter conditions," Amy said. "It's probably not the best car to use during a blizzard."

"Fortunately, the snow isn't too heavy yet, so we should be okay. We don't usually allow anyone to drive back here during spring, let alone winter. A lot of cars have gotten stuck in the mud and had to be towed. You'd be amazed at the damage it's done to the grounds."

Amy shifted the car into drive and carefully nudged the vehicle across the icy lot. When she reached the curb, she swerved between two wooden posts which marked the edges of the lane. After a few terrifying moments of skidding and sliding, they made progress rounding the church and the cemetery came into sight.

It sat on five acres of land, and neighbored the church. It was encircled with an elegant, black, wrought iron fence, topped with gold finial spires. A row of mausoleums stood off to the right, while the remaining sections of land were decorated with ornamental headstones.

Father Michael directed Amy to a gate in the side of the fence, which he opened with ease once the car was stopped. Although there had been enough snow to make the Vermont slopes ripe for skiing, the amount on the ground was still easily manageable, for December. After climbing back into the car, he explained this gate was the same one used by the groundskeepers for maintenance and grave preparation. Pointing straight ahead, he guided Amy towards the succession of monuments.

"The mausoleums are to the side of the graveyard. Not many

people build them anymore," Michael said as they made their way through the cemetery. "During summer, this might be a pleasant walk, but winter always makes things look bleak."

"Do you know which one belongs to Helen's family?" Amy asked, as the car skidded slightly to the right. "Oh, that was close. I don't know what I'd do if I hit someone's headstone."

"You're fine," Michael said. "The Coyle Mausoleum is the big one over there. There are steps leading up to the front door. The others are flat to the ground."

"That's pretty fancy," Amy said.

"Apparently, James Alex Coyle was one of the original founders of the church. I found some history in the church archives. He helped to have the church built, and was instrumental in many of the decisions surrounding the original plans."

"Was he born in Vermont?"

"I'm not sure. We'll have to ask Helen about her great grandfather. According to the archives, there were a few Irish immigrants, in Vermont, in the early 1800's, but the Potato Famine, forty years later, increased the number by quite a bit. Those who settled in Vermont, chose railroad towns, like Rutland and Burlington. Vermont started to thrive on industry back then."

"That's interesting. It seems we're finally getting somewhere," Amy said, as the car crept toward the Coyle Mausoleum.

"Some were penniless, but I don't know Mr. Coyle's story. Either he was quite rich, or he was given this mausoleum as a gift, from the church, for all his efforts," Michael said.

"Very intriguing," Amy said. They got out of the car and clamored up the ice-laden steps, to the front of the small building. The gate, made of green patina covered brass, protected a glass door leading into the mausoleum. Looking beyond the gate, they saw several white marble crypts, inscribed with names and dates of loved ones laid to rest. "There are eight crypts in there."

"I can't read the names from here, can you?" Michael asked.

"No, not in this light. Maybe, if there was some sun," Amy said, as she peered into the winter sky. A lone bird sailed overhead, on his way to the forest. "It's very quiet here."

"That's the point. It is easier to lend reverence that way." Michael reached out and gingerly rattled the gate. "The cemetery primarily has visitors in the warm weather, except for the Christmas season, of course. Many of the graves are decorated with evergreen blankets, for the holidays. This gate is solid. Let's try the key."

Amy took off her glove and fished the old fashioned key out of her coat pocket. She was able to place it in the keyhole without difficulty, but could not get the tumblers to turn. "Do you think the cold weather is a problem?"

"It could be rusty. Helen said she hasn't opened it for years," Michael said.

"Here, you try it," Amy proposed as she handed him the key and moved to the side.

Michael moved closer to the gate and reinserted the key. The tumblers moved slightly and then stopped. "The doors looked partially shifted. Let me try something." Michael took the door and lifted one side a small fraction. After moving the gate, he tried the key again. Metal groaned as he applied force, and the latch suddenly opened. "I got it."

"Thank goodness," Amy said. "I was beginning to worry."

The gate creaked as he wrenched back one side to allow them to slip through and open the glass door. "Let's go," he said softly, as they walked down the small corridor. "You take that side, and I'll look over here."

Each wall of the mausoleum held four horizontal crypts. Reading the names and dates, Amy and Michael were able to identify Helen's great grandmother, grandparents, parents and her brother. Continuing on, Amy finally laid eyes upon that of Helen's great grandfather, James Alex Coyle.

"Here it is," Amy said with expectation. "The inscription reads, *Church founder and gentle soul. Grant him eternal rest.'* I don't know why, but I was expecting something more elaborate."

"He sounds like he was a humble man," Michael said. "I'm sure he didn't want a lot of fanciful writing on his crypt."

"I guess you're right." Looking down, Amy said, "There's one empty crypt left. Helen told me to open the gate thinking she may need it soon, so I assume she's planning to be the eighth member of the family who resides here."

"I assume so. She would be buried with her husband, if she had married," Michael said. "Do you see the symbol anywhere?"

For the next fifteen minutes, the pair inspected the walls of the mausoleum, but their efforts proved unsuccessful. On the wall, opposite the gate, was a stained glass window, fronted by a small table, topped with religious candles and rosary beads. A worn kneeler, with faded pads, was placed in front of the table. "Someone spent many hours here, in prayer," Amy said as she looked at the tattered piece of furniture.

"It seems this was a close family," Michael said.

Continuing to search, Amy noticed there was a strange alcove, to the right of the table. "Michael, why do you think they left this space here?" Amy asked in a whisper, as she hugged herself to warm up.

"I don't know," Michael frowned. "I've never seen a mausoleum with this type of configuration before."

"The floor looks normal," Amy said as she stared down at the tile. "I don't visit mausoleums often, but it doesn't seem unusual."

"I agree," Michael said, as he glanced at his watch. "Ms. Montanari will be arriving soon. We'd better get back to the rectory."

"I hope Katie has a hot breakfast and strong coffee waiting," Amy said, as she turned to find Michael's head bent in prayer, her curious eyes finding his. He looked up to Amy's moved expression.

"I wanted to ask for peace, for their departed souls. I'd hate to think we trudged over their place of repose, without respect, but it was necessary, and Helen asked us to open the gate."

"I know, but now we should go," Amy said as she slipped back through the gate, toward the steps. Michael followed behind her and turned back toward the gate.

"I don't think it's going to close again," Michael said, trying to click the latch.

"Leave it unlocked, for now," Amy said. "We may have to

come back if we find another clue."

"You're right," Michael said. "Let's go."

Together, they walked down the steps of the mausoleum, holding each other's arm for support. As they climbed into the car, Amy started the engine and turned the heat on high. She shivered for a few seconds before putting the car in drive.

"I hope the treasure hunt doesn't lead us back here. But if so, I'll bring a big floral piece to ask for forgiveness," Amy said.

"James Coyle created the hunt, so I don't think he would be upset," Michael laughed. "We're just following instructions. Anyway, I'd be shocked if Katie didn't have a hot breakfast and strong coffee waiting."

"Well, then, what are we waiting for?" Amy asked, as she put the car in gear and drove off toward the retreat house.

Chapter Thirty

Paolo awoke and ran his fingers through his greasy hair. He crawled out of the slim bed, threw the blankets aside in disgust, and rechecked the linen for bed bugs. Being accustomed to sheets with silk, satin and eight hundred thread counts, Paolo found the Starlight Motel to be lacking for a man of his esteem. Stretching his stiff back, he limped to the dirty window and separated the mini-blinds with his fingers. The morning sky was a swirl of gray clouds, and snow already covered the parking lot. His ever present agitation intensified when he laid eyes upon the snow, dirt and salt covering his precious BMW.

It was too early to go to Mercy Manor, but he was anxious to talk to the aide. He briefly considered skipping out on the actual mission, but knew his entire organization would fall apart without him in the field. He needed to get this job done in a hurry, starting with the insufferable nursing home.

Across the parking lot, an officer was stationed in his patrol car sipping a large, freshly brewed cup of coffee. Scoffing, Paolo began to feel as if this job was beneath him. The incompetent patrolman was not aware Paolo was surveying him, from a mere twenty feet away. The officer was probably waiting for the snow report, so he could decide if more salt was needed on the roads. Some hero, if he only realized the things Paolo had seen and done to acquire the beautiful treasures he possessed, the officer would not be sipping coffee, oblivious to the world.

Paolo spun around when his room phone began to ring. He gingerly picked up the receiver and said, "*Pronto?*"

"*Padrino*, we're ready to go. Vincenzo was wondering if we're getting coffee and breakfast first. I'm not interested myself, but I promised I'd ask."

"*Porca miseria!* We'll get something on the way," Paolo said.

"Great. I mean, uh, I'll tell Vincenzo. Paolo, I'm just saying, did you happen to see Gemma's car in the parking lot?"

"Of course, but I don't want her to know that, obviously. She has a very important meeting today, while we take care of business at the nursing home. Once I have more information, I'll show her I remain the head of this operation. *Prometto*, she will not forget the lesson."

"*Certo. Assolutamente.*"

"Be in the car, five minutes," Paolo practically screamed. "Nothing funny. There's an officer outside."

"Got it."

Paolo slammed down the receiver. If he didn't hate getting his hands and finely pressed suits dirty, he would do everything himself. He collected his wallet and cell phone, peeked out the window and smiled when he noticed the patrol car was gone. Paolo did not know the officer had taken down the license plate numbers of all the cars in the parking lot. He had started with New York plates, as Tony reported the men were probably from Manhattan, and sent them directly to the station to be analyzed.

Chapter Thirty One

Katie stood in the kitchen when Amy and Michael arrived back from the cemetery. As she whipped up a batch of buttermilk pancakes, she poured each of them a steaming cup of chocolate almond coffee. In typical teenage fashion, Willow groggily trudged into the kitchen, but brightened at the smell of Katie's cooking. Father Victor was on his way back from the church, having celebrated morning mass. Christmas hymns merrily played from the aged boom box Katie had positioned in the corner of the room.

"As soon as breakfast is finished, Willow and I will be heading over to the nursing home to bring homemade soup and cookies to Helen," Katie said, as she refilled their coffee mugs.

Willow slumped in her seat. "I wanted to drive, but Father Victor offered to go and bless some of the patients."

Amy looked at her and smiled. "You'll have plenty of time to practice driving, when the roads aren't so icy. My car slid all over the road this morning." Amy purposely did not mention her loss of control occurred in the cemetery.

"I guess," Willow relented. "But once spring comes, there's no excuse."

"I promise, I will go with you," Amy said. "I just wish we didn't live on top of a mountain."

"How was mass this morning?" Father Michael asked,

turning the attention to a shivering Father Victor, who stood in the doorway.

"It went well," Victor said, walking to the table and heaping pancakes and maple bacon onto his plate. After smothering his breakfast in strawberry syrup, he picked up his fork. "Everyone seems so happy. It's a shame we can't hang onto this feeling all year."

"I know," Michael said. "How hard is it to be nice, to share good faith?"

"In this day and age? Very hard," Amy said, with a cynical tone. "There are a lot of people hurting out there."

Michael turned to look at her. "If we all practiced, Love *your neighbor as yourself,* we might hurt a little less.

Amy sipped her coffee and returned the cup to the table in a swift blasé motion. "I wish it were that easy, Michael. I really do."

Katie shuffled around the table, and landed behind Amy and Michael. "You two better finish up and get to the library. Ms. Montanari should be here soon." She then turned to Willow, "Would you be a dear and help me pack Helen's goodies in the cooler bag, on the counter? As soon as Father Victor is finished eating, we'll head right over. I'll deal with the dishes when we get back."

"Sure thing, Katie," Willow readily agreed as she got up from the table. Michael and Amy followed, gingerly placing their dishes in the sink. As the two began to walk toward the library, they heard Katie switch off her Christmas hymns.

After lighting the fireplace, Michael led Amy to a round table, in the corner. "While we have a minute, let me show you some of the documents I found in the archives. I've been looking for anything that mentions the crypt, the symbol, or those strange wells we found in the floor."

"Did you find anything?" Amy asked, working through the disarray of yellowed books and papers. "There's a lot to go through here."

"I did find a post in our inaugural pastor's journal, which mentions an Italian carver, hired by the Archdiocese, to help design parts of the church. He was sent from Italy to St. Francis, to complete the design called for by the blueprints. I believe his name was Nicolo Pietra."

"Well, that's progress," Amy said. "Have you found anything else?"

"Not yet. There are so many documents here, I haven't had time to review all of them."

"You know, it might be a nice idea if the church could afford to pay Willow to digitalize these records for you. Keep the originals of course, but if she scanned or copied them, you would have a lot more information, at your fingertips, regarding St. Francis. Not to mention, she would be able to gain some work experience before college."

"Excellent idea," Michael agreed. "In the meantime, I'll keep reading."

A sudden knock on the front door interrupted them, as Katie ushered Gemma Montanari into the retreat house. Straightening the table, Amy and Michael reviewed their plan to uncover how she heard about the treasure. At Michael's indication, Katie escorted

Gemma into the library, discreetly leaving a tray of hot coffee and biscuits, in her wake. Father Michael stepped forward to greet the sharply dressed young woman.

"Good morning, I am Father Michael, and this is Dr. Amy Daniels," he said, as he shook her hand.

"Good morning, Father," Gemma said brightly, handing over her business card. "Thank you again for meeting with me." Looking at Amy, she paused for a moment and said, "I'm sorry, but I thought we were going to have a private meeting. Some of my questions may be rather sensitive."

"You mentioned you wanted to talk about a possible historical find," Father Michael said. "I've asked Dr. Amy to join us, as she occasionally serves as a consultant to St. Francis for secular issues. Anything you say will be kept in the highest confidence, I assure you."

"If you insist," Gemma said, obviously unhappy with the arrangements.

"Come, please have a seat." Father Michael pulled a desk chair aside for her. "Let's all get comfortable, and you can tell us what has brought you to our lovely parish." Michael moved around the desk and settled in his chair, as Amy positioned hers to face Gemma.

"Of course," Gemma said, clearly thrown off guard. "I work for Paolo Sartori. Are you familiar with him?"

"No, Ms. Montanari. I can't say that I am," Michael said, with Amy shaking her head in agreement. "What type of company does he have?"

"Acquisitions," Gemma said. "For museums and collectors. I also have an impressive list of personal acquisitions, and am a practiced curator, trained in Italy."

"That sounds exciting," Father Michael said. "How can we help you?"

"My employer has asked me to speak with you, about some information he recently received, regarding a historical treasure, which may be in your possession," Gemma said.

"That's wonderful, but I am unaware of any treasure here at St. Francis," Father Michael said.

"It's only been a rumor, among certain circles, in Southern Italy. There is no evidence the treasure even exists, but if the rumor were true, the historical significance would be of the greatest magnitude," Gemma said as she cautiously glanced at Amy.

"Please continue," Father Michael said, looking at her expectantly.

Swallowing nervously, Gemma shifted in her seat. "Over a hundred years ago, a crucifix made of solid gold, nearly three feet tall, was commissioned by none other than Victor Emmanuel II, and sent to a parish in America."

Father Michael leaned back in his chair. His hands were folded across his chest and he took a moment, before he spoke. "Ms. Montanari, if that is true, what could possibly be the reason for treasure, of that value, being commissioned and sent to Rocky Meadow?"

"As you may know, in 1860, Victor Emmanuel II sent his forces to fight the papal army, and drove the Pope into Vatican City.

For his actions, he was excommunicated from the Catholic Church. It was only after he betrayed his faith, he was established as leader of the Kingdom of Italy."

"I remember the story," Father Michael recalled with a small smile.

"Then you know, Victor Emmanuel II died in January 1878," she continued. "It is said the King was always troubled by his differences with the Catholic Church and the Pontiff. He had corresponded with the Pope for years, hoping to reconcile their differences and his excommunication."

"I do recall reading that history as well," Father Michael said nodding. "What does that have to do with the crucifix?"

"The undocumented rumor was, Victor Emmanuel II commissioned a gold crucifix, to be sent to a Catholic church, in America, as a symbol of his love of religious life in the new world. St. Francis of Assisi is one of two patron saints of Italy. Choosing a church by his name would be most logical."

"Yes, but there must be thousands of churches with the same name in America," Amy chimed in. "Why do you think it's our St. Francis?"

"Other than the information afforded by my employer, I would not have a clue," Gemma admitted as she stared at Amy. "That was the purpose of this meeting. I wanted to see if Father Michael had any knowledge of the treasure, and if so, whether he would be willing to share the information."

"If the rumor were true, and if this were the correct parish, the decision would have to be made by the Archdiocese, not me,"

Father Michael said. "What would be their gain if they did decide to share? Surely, they would not let a treasure of such magnitude out of their sight."

"Not physically, but the revelation of such would mean photos, interviews, tours, and quite a stir in the media for religious and historical purposes," Gemma said.

"I'm not sure St. Francis would welcome that type of attention," Father Michael said, as his desk phone began to ring. When it stopped, he continued. "If a golden crucifix landed on my desk today, I still would have to discuss everything with the Bishop."

"I am not asking you to give me the crucifix. My intentions are strictly innocent, Father Michael," Gemma said as the desk phone began to ring again.

Amy began to question Gemma, but stopped upon hearing her emergency cell phone chime. "Something is happening. We'd better answer these calls. Excuse me." Amy grabbed her phone, crossed to the far side of the room, and answered, "Dr. Amy Daniels."

Father Michael answered his land line at the same moment. He was quiet, as he listened to the voice on the other end of the phone. Finally, he broke into the rant. "Katie, calm down. You're speaking so fast, I can't understand you."

On the other side of the room, Gemma heard Amy say, "Mercy Manor? What? How did this happen?"

Gemma started to tremble, as she realized the crisis could not be a coincidence. Trouble had immediately presented itself after she made an inquiry visit. The same pattern as her last two acquisition queries, and she instinctively knew the person responsible was Paolo. As she listened to the priest and the doctor try to elicit more details from their callers, she sat quietly as her heart raced. Gemma's hands shook, and she balled her fists to steady them. As a dizzy haze engulfed her, she began to tilt to the side.

Amy hung up the phone and noticed Gemma was leaning sideways. Running to Gemma's chair, Amy caught her, just as she lost consciousness and fell to the floor.

When Gemma awoke, she was lying on the fabric couch, with Amy and Michael's eyes upon her. Amy raised Gemma's legs and rested them on a cushion, as Father Michael fashioned a cool rag from his handkerchief and placed it on her forehead.

Raising her hand to her face, she asked, "What happened?"

"I'm afraid you fainted, Ms. Montanari," Amy said as she carefully examined her features.

"How long was I out?"

"A matter of seconds," Father Michael said. "Dr. Amy caught you before you fell, and we placed you on the couch so we could raise your legs."

"What happened at the nursing home?" Gemma asked, as she looked at Dr. Amy. "I heard you say Mercy Manor."

"I did, but first, how are you feeling, and then how do you know it's a nursing home?"

"Scared and very frightened right now," Gemma said, clutching Father Michael's jacket. "Please, I need to know what happened."

Michael looked at Amy, who shrugged. "Apparently, there was a fire at Mercy Manor this morning. Katie, my housekeeper, was very upset. She was on her way there to visit a parishioner, and they wouldn't let her near the place. I imagine Dr. Daniels's call was more informative, as she is the local trauma surgeon, and acting medical examiner."

Gemma let out a plaintive cry as she turned to Amy. "Please, tell me what happened."

Amy swallowed. She felt her stomach clench as she looked at the distraught woman. "I normally don't share information like this, but I suppose most of it is public by now. As Father Michael said, there was a fire at the nursing home. The only other information I can tell you is that a woman was found dead."

Hearing her words, Michael turned toward Amy sharply. "Do you know who it is?"

"No, they wouldn't give me a name or cause of death," Amy said as her eyes filled. "This is a nightmare, Michael. They're waiting until I get there to move the body. I have to go."

As Amy stood up to leave, Gemma started trembling and said, "It's him, Paolo. He must be responsible for this."

Remembering the information from Father Victor's visit to Hasco's the night before, Amy whipped around and said, "Ms. Montanari, I don't know what is going on here, or what you're up to, but you better start talking. Michael, once we have her story, call the police, and do not let her leave until someone arrives to take an official statement."

With eyes wide open, Gemma anxiously watched them, as

the inquiry unraveled directly around her.

Chapter Thirty Two

Elizabeth was at the peak of her thirtieth year of nursing. She worked grueling hours, six days a week, to care for the sick and elderly, admitted to Mercy Manor. She always attended the recertification seminars for resuscitation, fire and disaster planning, but never needed to enact that information, until now. She was seated at the nurses' desk, carefully taking doctors' orders off the charts, when the first announcement came through. The code was usually masked as a common word or phrase so the residents would not be alarmed. The fictitious names of the practice drills, in fact, usually elicited some excitement among the residents, as in "red heat," a drill in which they believed the thermostat was finally being turned up.

There was no drill scheduled for today and as Elizabeth sat frozen at the desk, she sensed the increasing panic in the receptionist's voice as she announced, *"Code Ember, Kitchen. Code Ember, Kitchen."*

Elizabeth followed the mnemonic she was taught, and immediately made rounds to confirm no patient was in imminent danger. She kept abreast of the information which was broadcasted over the loudspeaker, as all fire doors were closed, and the fire department was to arrive at any moment.

The source of the fire was near the kitchen, but it was

Elizabeth's obligation to assure all her patients were in a safe zone, behind fire doors. She scrutinized her list, accounting for everyone. Everyone except Helen Coyle.

Mercy Manor was built on the side of a small hill. The ground floor held the kitchen, some administrative offices, and an auditorium. Off to the side, was a small morgue and maintenance area. The only entrance, on that level, was the back door, located near the kitchen. The other rooms were built into the hill and accessible through a series of elevators, from the top floors. The interior design was beautiful and one would never realize there were no windows in that part of the facility.

Elizabeth quickly reviewed Helen's schedule and determined she would have been in physical therapy when the fire broke out. Physical therapy was located on the far end of the first floor. Elizabeth could not use the phone per fire protocol. She would have to go check the therapy department to see if she could locate Helen. After ensuring another nurse would watch her patients until they heard the "all clear", Elizabeth ran down the hall to search.

Chapter Thirty Three

Scott Baker was dutifully spreading salt on Route 4, when his pager went off.

Engine 41, 44, Ladder 42. Reported Structure Fire, 852 Cole Road, Mercy Manor Nursing Home. Getting numerous backup calls with reports of smoke from rear, ground floor, near the kitchen, possibly in a utility closet. Reports of people trapped. Cross streets are Brook and Norwich Rds.

Scott halted the stream of salt, and turned his pickup around, in the direction of the firehouse, as quickly as possible. As a volunteer of the Rocky Meadow Fire Department, Scott was on call, while holding his regular town job. The population of Rocky Meadow was slight enough to mandate two fulltime firefighters, along with a number of volunteers, who dropped everything, and risked their lives, each time there was a fire.

Most of the volunteers worked town jobs: construction, maintenance, or retail, but responded instantly when their pagers went off. Despite their different lives, at this moment, they were all doing the same as Scott; running to the firehouse to get their gear.

Winter fires in Vermont, seemed to transpire at night, when people lit their fireplaces for heat and comfort, after embracing a day of tremendous cold. The Christmas season consistently brought increased danger as celebratory trees, placed too close to the hearth, or allowed to dry, were deadly. Summer fires were induced by unruly campfires, which raged out of control or were accelerated with flammable agents. A mid-morning kitchen fire, in a crowded nursing home, could be very deadly.

Scott leaned on the horn, as the car in front of him slowed to 15mph, in response to the emergency light he had thrown on his dashboard. It was correct for drivers to slow down when they heard sirens and saw lights, but if they do not pull to the side of the road, they continue to impede progress. Precious minutes waned as Scott pulled around another car and skidded into the parking lot of the fire station. He jumped from his truck and ran into the firehouse, kicking off his sneakers as he ran. While pulling up his bunker pants, Scott noticed three other volunteers arrive and start the same process. Sam, the only career firefighter on duty at the station when the call came in, was already suited up and in the cab of Engine 41, motor running.

Scott drew up his protective hood and bunker coat. He felt his adrenaline pumping, as his heart began to race. Kissing the photo of his new wife and precious baby girl, he kept tucked in the lining of his helmet for luck, he donned his head gear and gloves. Scott's helmet was scratched and dark, a testament to the number of fires he had challenged, and thankfully, conquered. The dirtier the helmet, the greater the sacrifice, and grateful praise for a safe return.

Scott jumped onto Engine 41. The fire was reported at the rear of the building, on the ground floor, so it was probable the engines might have more of a role today. Fire engines always held the water, while fire trucks carried the ladder. As they drove toward the nursing home, he and the other fighters put on their air bottles and masks.

When they reached Mercy Manor, the police had arrived and started directing traffic, holding up cars, so the firefighters could pass directly into the parking lot. A band of volunteers followed behind, blue lights flashing on their dashboards, while all other vehicles were detoured a safe distance away from the facility.

Sam was advised the scene was a working fire. He drove the engine to the back of the nursing home, and stopped close to the door. Scott and several other volunteers jumped off the engine, while other firefighters gathered around and began to pull hoses and back stretch them to a hydrant on the street. The fire and police chiefs were stationed next to each other, barking orders into their radios. In front of the nursing home, the fire truck had set its stabilizers. A ladder was being raised to check the roof for fire extension. Mutual aid was called in from nearby communities.

When the alarm first sounded, several kitchen workers were able to run out the back door before the smoke made passage impossible. The remainder of the kitchen staff were ushered toward the administrative wing. Realizing the origin of the fire was not in the kitchen, the Director of Food Services took a moment to hit the emergency gas turn off valves before disappearing, behind fire doors, with the rest of the staff. The stairwell, in the west end of the building was clear, and staff started climbing steps to reach the first floor main entrance.

The firefighters darted toward the back of the nursing home and opened the door. Smoke billowed from the open exit, but there were no flames in sight. A volunteer on the search and rescue squad reported the origin of the smoke to be a utility closet, in the downstairs hallway, located near the back door. Fronted by double doors, the closet held cases of toilet paper, paper towels and cleaning fluids. A pair of firefighters passed the closet, and continued their search and rescue, while another pair stayed near the closet and readied the hose.

Carefully approaching the door, they crouched down in case fire briefly flared up when oxygen was introduced into the enclosed space. Smoldering fires could be as dangerous as actual flames, rendering their protective equipment essential as fire related deaths were often the result of inhaling carbon monoxide or combustible toxins, such as cyanide. Hoses ready, the firemen found the utility closet locked. After several unsuccessful attempts to gain entry, a Halligan bar was used to pry the door open. Cautious to avoid any back draft, the firefighters holding the hose sprayed the closet with water until all flames were doused. As the smoke began to clear, Scott peered inside and saw a body near the back of the utility closet. "Better call the chief, we have a dead civilian."

Working diligently to make certain there were no flames, they left the scene untouched to preserve any evidence present at the crime scene. The fire chief viewed the scene with the police chief, who immediately called the prosecutor's office and the medical examiner.

The fire, having been odd from the start, was officially deemed suspicious. A call for a firedog was sent out, to help them determine the cause and origin of the fire, and a test for propellants was added to the queue. Ventilation fans were hung throughout the ground floor, to rid the area of smoke. While waiting for the investigation to begin, the first responders replayed every moment of the mission in their mind, as they knew the prosecutor's interrogation would be thorough.

Chapter Thirty Four

Paolo floored the accelerator of his BMW and skidded along the icy road, back to the motel. "*Stronz*i, you didn't have to kill the woman!" Paolo screamed, slamming his fist on the steering wheel.

"She had an attitude," Roberto said, with blunt simplicity, spitting out the window in disgust. "The broad threatened to call the police if we didn't give her a check, pronto."

"All I needed was a name," Paolo shouted, his eyes in the rearview mirror.

"I have the name, Helen Coyle. She let it go the second she realized I was serious about killing her."

"Then why didn't you stop?"

"She already threatened us, saw our faces." He shrugged. "Greed brought her to the treasure and greed took her out."

"Everyone probably saw our faces. There are cameras, *stronzi*. We almost hit a minivan on the way out, and the police will be looking for this car within hours." Paolo fumed as he careened into the parking lot of the Starlight motel. "Get your gear and exchange our license plate with another car while we wipe the rooms. Since you're so smart, I'm sure you can do that within a minute... if not, I'll shoot you myself. *Capisci?*"

"Got it," Roberto mumbled, as he grabbed a screwdriver from the glove compartment and got to work.

Chapter Thirty Five

After hearing a few moments of Gemma's tearful revelation, detailing her consistent abuse from Paolo, Amy threw on her winter coat and scarf, and hurried out of the rectory. Gemma admitted Paolo's anonymous source, in Rocky Meadow, had been an aide named Susan, who worked at Mercy Manor and overheard a patient discussing the treasure.

Amy's fury intensified as Gemma completed her story then told of the similar circumstances of two other acquisitions, in the past year. Owners, who politely declined to sell or display their collections, were suddenly found hurt or dead within a matter of weeks. Gemma did not recognize Helen's name, and she did not know if Paolo had learned the information from Susan.

The roads were coated in a smattering of ice, but Amy drove hastily towards Mercy Manor to make sure Helen was safe. At least one known female was found dead, and she prayed it was not Helen. Hopefully, there were no other deaths.

Amy turned onto Brook Road, and immediately slowed down when she saw an array of flashing lights surrounding the building. Police cars were strategically parked to block the driveway, and a large group of people were gathered in the parking lot. Their faces were enveloped in horror. Amy could see patients huddled in their families' cars, to stay warm, until the situation was stabilized. A news van was setting up shop at the side of the road.

Amy rolled up to the officer near the driveway, who furiously waved his hand to motion her to continue down the road. She hesitated and shook her head. Scowling, he approached her car to verbally reprimand her. Sensing his purpose, she put the car in park, pulled her medical examiners shield and pressed it up to the window, before he said a word. When he nodded in understanding, Amy opened the window. "Dr. Amy Daniels, I'm the acting medical examiner. How do I get back there?"

"Credentials?"

Amy handed the officer her badge and accreditation, and glared at him while he scrutinized the information. Despite the fact the victim was deceased, Amy would be agitated until she knew the identity and cause of death. Amy expected the crime scene would not be disturbed until she arrived and examined the body, but in comparison to Boston medical standards, Rocky Meadow seemed to be a bit unhurried.

Once satisfied, the officer returned Amy's credentials and motioned to the officer in the patrol car to let her pass. The black and white pulled forward and allowed Amy to coast into the lot. Another officer directed her to the far corner, and Amy quickly found a space and parked.

Scanning the crowd, as she hopped out of her Audi, Amy spotted Katie and Willow, shivering in the cold. She pulled her forensic bag from the trunk, and caught the pair's attention. Willow ran over to greet her as they waited for Katie to catch up.

"Are you all right? What happened?" Amy asked, as she

looked at their worried faces.

"We have no idea," Willow said.

"Katie, are you okay?" Amy asked.

"I'm fine," Katie explained, with a worried sigh. "Father Victor pulled into the parking lot, just as a crazy driver was speeding out of here. We came so close to colliding, I was a bit shook up, so I needed a minute to calm down. By the time Willow and I got the soup and cookies together, fire alarms were blaring, and police started showing up in droves. People were running out of the building, and then the fire engines came. We've been standing out here ever since."

"You two must be freezing," Amy said.

"I hadn't really noticed until you mentioned it, dear. Do you have any more information?" Katie asked, looking up at Amy, with fear lingering in her eyes.

Amy tilted her head and considered how to tell them what she knew, without upsetting Willow. "I know someone is hurt, but I don't know who or how. I need to get down there, but I wanted to check on you. I don't think anyone is moving for a while, so why don't you go warm up in your car or you can use mine, if you need to." Amy held out her keys.

"Thank you, love," Katie said, with a genuine smile, waving off the keys. "We'll go back to the church van and see if we can find Father Victor. He went to help out a while ago, and we haven't seen him since."

"Ok, and while you get warm, try to remember every detail you can about the car that almost hit you. If this was arson, the person inside the car may be involved."

Willow remained pensive. "It was a New York license plate. One of those fancy gold and black ones."

"Great job, Willow. Anything else?" Amy asked, pulling her in for a hug.

"Father Victor would probably give you the best description of the car, but I know it was a sedan. A fancy one at that," Katie added.

"That's a great start," Amy said, picking up her bag. "I've got to get in there. When they start letting people leave, go back to the rectory. Michael is there with Ms. Montanari. Apparently, she believes she knows who's responsible for this disaster, so he's keeping her there until the police take her statement."

"How would she know about this?" Willow, wiser than her years, asked.

"Apparently, she feels the person responsible for the fire may have followed her to Vermont," Amy answered. "She was at the nursing home yesterday, before all of this unfolded, and is sure the culprit has been following her."

"Oh my," Katie said. "Then perhaps we shouldn't let her leave the retreat house at all, for her own protection."

"That's something for the police to decide," Amy said, over her shoulder, as she walked toward the building. "If I see Father Victor, I'll let him know you're waiting. Talk to you later. Stay safe."

"Come back for dinner, dear," Katie called after her.

Chapter Thirty Six

Marco Montanari listened to the low voice on the other end of the phone. His clenched jaw belied his strain. "Take care of her, *Arrivederci*." Ending the call, he turned toward the center of his boardroom and motioned for Luca to join him in the hallway. The young associate jumped from his leather chair, and darted across the room to meet him. Luca recognized the expression on Marco's face and immediately knew something was wrong with Gemma. After stepping into the hall, Mr. Montanari closed the wood framed glass door, to prevent any members of the board from overhearing their conversation.

"Luca, there has been another incident in America. Giancarlo called me, and Gemma called before that."

"Is she all right?" Luca asked, his face taut with concern.

"*Si,*" Mr. Montanari said as he smiled and placed his hand on Luca's shoulder. "But I fear Paolo will act on the threats he's been making to Gemma, if we don't put an end to this. I want you to leave for Rocky Meadow, Vermont, immediately. You are to find my daughter, and bring her home."

"Of course," Luca said as he felt his adrenaline rise. "My duties here?"

"They will be taken care of."

"*Grazie, Signore,*" Luca said, respectfully. "If you don't

mind, what happened? What do I need to know?"

"I've learned, from Giancarlo, Paolo sent her to Vermont to follow up on a report of a solid gold crucifix, hidden on the grounds of St. Francis Church. Paolo was informed by a medical aide, who overheard one of her elderly patients speak of it."

"The rumor is true then?" Luca asked, surprise evident in his voice.

"I do not know, Luca. Before Gemma could finish her inquiry, the nursing home was set on fire. Gemma overheard the medical examiner being called. Giancarlo was looking for Paolo and his men and he arrived at the nursing home as they raced away from the scene. A short time later, smoke was seen coming from the building. He's sure they are responsible."

"I'm horrified Paolo's greed jeopardized Gemma's life. Not to mention all the innocent people in the building," Luca said in disgust.

"Luca, go find my Gemma," Mr. Montanari commanded. "I'm sorry, our Gemma, and bring her home to *papa*. Giancarlo is making arrangements to find Paolo, and I will handle him personally. *Va,* I will take care of business."

"Yes sir, I will leave immediately. *Non sta in pena.* I won't rest until she's safe," Luca said, placing his hand on the man's shoulder.

"*Grazie Mille.* I will not forget this, Luca. I will call my pilot and have the jet waiting." In a burst of anxiety, Marco pulled Luca into an unexpected hug.

Chapter Thirty Seven

Amy approached the rear of the nursing home, carefully avoiding the hoses and equipment lining the path before her. Puddles were forming in various areas, some freezing, as the temperature dropped. Firemen walked back and forth, carrying squawking radios and oxygen tanks. The fire chief scribbled on a metal clipboard and looked up as Amy approached. "Whatever it is, not now, and if you're media, I'll have you arrested."

"Excuse me, I'm the acting medical examiner," Amy said, once again showing credentials. "You can't move forward until I examine the crime scene."

"You're the medical examiner?"

"That's correct," Amy said with authority. "Can you tell me anything before I go in there?"

The fire chief looked at Amy, studied her appearance and judged her ability to handle the case. After a few minutes, he shrugged and said, "The fire was in a utility closet, near the back entrance. Most likely arson. We forced the door, and extinguished the fire. Only one casualty. The body was found in the same closet."

"Can you tell me anything about the deceased?" Amy asked as her stomach clenched.

"Well, you're the expert, but the fire is suspicious, and it appears the victim was dead before it started. I don't think she died from thermal injuries or smoke inhalation."

"What position was she in?"

"She was lying between some brooms and cleaning equipment, against the back wall. Her legs were toward the center of the closet and sustained burn marks. The door was locked, from the outside."

"She was placed there before the fire?"

"That's what I think, but you'll have to do your exam to determine what happened postmortem."

"Chief, can you tell me anything personal about her? I received a report the victim was a woman. Do you know if she was a patient? Was she elderly?" Amy held her breath as she waited for the answer.

"Late forties. Probably an employee, by the uniform top she has on. Her face wasn't touched by the fire, so someone should be able to identify her. The police are upstairs doing a head count of patients and staff. At this point, it's all you and the prosecutor."

"Thank you, Chief," Amy was relieved Helen's description was not attributed to the body. At the same time, she felt guilty knowing the woman must have family who would be devastated upon hearing the news.

Several firemen stepped out of the back door. The Chief called one over, "Is it clear in there? The medical examiner wants to see the victim."

"Yes, the fire's completely out. We have ventilation going. There's a lot of water on the floor, so I'd be careful about slipping in those shoes, Ma'am."

Amy looked down at her feet, remembering she had traded her snow boots for pumps, in anticipation of the meeting with Gemma Montanari, earlier this morning.

"If you don't mind, I'll have one of my men take you in, and guide you through the fire damage," the Chief said.

"Thank you, I'd appreciate that," Amy said as she reached out to shake the Chief's hand.

Chapter Thirty Eight

Paolo stopped the car, at the edge of town, when he was low on gas. While he was busy at the pump, Roberto rummaged through the convenience store shelves for something suitable to eat. Knowing the police would be searching for them, Paolo had no idea where they would stay tonight, and they could not walk into a local restaurant for food.

Paolo had been in this situation before, and knew it was wise to stock up on supplies while they still had some time. Fresh sandwiches, greasy, overcooked hotdogs, and watered-down soft drinks would have to suffice for now. Paolo watched Roberto pay for the order and nonchalantly waltz out of the store, maneuvering around a stand of real estate magazines, sitting out front.

The pump clicked, informing Paolo the tank was full. He hastily replaced the nozzle, then grabbed a rag from the backseat and wiped his hands. In a moment of insight, Paolo walked to the real estate stand, and filled his arms with magazines.

"Hey boss," Roberto said. "Thinking of moving to Vermont? You must like trees and snow."

Paolo hopped in the car and dropped the stack on Roberto's lap. The angry gesture caused steaming coffee to spill over Roberto's legs. "Shut up. If you did what you were told, we wouldn't be in this mess. You may be sleeping under a tree tonight if we can't find somewhere safe."

"She was a threat," Roberto screamed as he tried to wipe coffee off his pants.

Swearing to himself, Paolo put the car in gear, and left the gas station.

Chapter Thirty Nine

After being escorted to the utility closet, Amy arranged for a plethora of photos to be taken of the crime scene, before the body was disturbed. Once completed, she neared the victim and performed a thorough visual exam.

The woman lay at the back of the closet, her head resting unnaturally against the wall. Limp as a rag doll, her lifeless arms rested in her lap. She faced the center of the closet, with her legs drawn up toward her torso. Amy noted the burned fabric of the victim's pants. The body's position was a tell-tale sign she had not struggled to escape her fiery cell. The burns were postmortem. Back in the morgue, Amy would be better equipped to determine the extent of her injuries, and cause of death.

After completing a visual exam, paper bags were placed around the victim's hands, so Amy could check for possible trace evidence or DNA, which would identify the murderer. If there had been a struggle, the victim may have scratched the killer. Nothing more could be done, until the body arrived at the morgue, for autopsy.

Amy inferred the Chief was most likely correct about the thermal injuries being postmortem, and signaled her team to take their final photos. Once the prosecutor's office granted clearance, she allowed the crime scene technicians to wrap the body, and commence transport to the Rocky Meadow General Hospital morgue.

Upstairs, Mercy Manor was cleared, and the front doors reopened to the patients and families waiting in the parking lot. The kitchen remained closed, but staff distributed snacks and bottles of water to patients and visitors. The electric to the first floor was in full working order, and nurses were returned to their stations to reestablish treatments, meds and routine.

Katie and Willow rushed into the rehab facility and found Father Victor, in the lobby, comforting an elderly patient with no family in sight. Together, they immediately checked Helen's room and found it empty. Unaware of where Helen was, or how long it would be before she was returned to her room, Katie tried to locate Helen's nurse, but the chaos had only begun to quiet down. Discouraged, the trio left Mercy Manor, leaving soup and cookies with the director of nursing, to offer to those who were most affected by the event.

The ride to the retreat house was eerily silent, as if discussing the harrowing event would make it seem more real. They arrived at the rectory in early afternoon, and noticed Gemma's car, along with a police cruiser, in the parking lot. Once in the foyer, they threw off their frosted coats and hung them on wall hooks. Willow retreated to the comfort of her bedroom, while Father Victor and Katie walked towards Michael's office. As they neared the room, Officer Jamie Brand pushed the door open, and stepped into the hall. Father Victor showed her to the front door, while Katie checked the office. Father Michael and Gemma both looked exhausted after enduring several hours of interrogation at the hands of Officer Brand.

"Oh my," Katie said as she walked into the room. "You two look as done in and exhausted as the rest of us."

"It's been a long day, Katie," Father Michael said. "How are things at Mercy Manor?"

"It was quieting down as we left. Dr. Amy still has a bit of work to do. I'm hoping she'll be able to join us for dinner," Katie said, checking her watch. "Speaking of which, I better get started if we want to eat before Christmas. I'll be back in a jiffy with some tea for the two of you. Ms. Montanari, all things considered, I assume you'll be staying for dinner."

"I have nowhere else to go. If you don't mind, that is," Gemma said, touched by their kindness.

"The more the merrier," Katie said with a smile, as Father Victor joined them in the office.

He eyed Michael and Gemma. "Everything okay in here?"

"Yes, we're a bit worn out from all this police business," Michael said, waiting for Katie to leave. When she did, he turned to Father Victor. "Did you learn anything else about what happened?"

"Nothing official, but when we turned into the parking lot, we were almost clipped by a car racing out of there. It was a black BMW with NY plates."

"I knew it must be Paolo," Gemma voice trembled.

"If you feel you are in danger, Ms. Montanari, you're more than welcome to stay in the retreat house, until this situation gets sorted out," Michael said. "We have plenty of rooms."

"Really?" Gemma asked with genuine surprise.

"Of course," Father Michael said. "Katie loves to fuss over company. We can't give you as much protection as the police, but you can be sure you'll be surrounded by warm, loving people here. We'll try to keep you safe."

"Where are your things?" Father Victor asked. "If you'd like, we can go with you to pick them up after dinner."

"The only place I could get a room was the Starlight Motel," Gemma said, somewhat embarrassed.

"The Starlight?" Father Victor immediately asked.

"Yes, why?" Gemma asked, confused by his reaction.

"Last night there were three men at Hasco's Bar and Grill. Tony Noce, the owner, is an ex-NYPD officer," Father Victor explained. "They looked suspicious and we overheard them say, 'Starlight Motel' and 'nursing home'."

"Oh no." Gemma began to shake again. "I had no idea they were staying there. I...I would've left."

"They may not be there anymore, but after dinner I'll ride over with you to collect your things. I'll call Tony to see if he can take a break and come with us."

"I would appreciate that very much," Gemma said, overcome with fear. She jumped when Katie pushed the door open with her foot.

"Here we are, a strong pot of tea for everyone. You'll have to help yourselves, so I can get back to making dinner."

"I can't wait, Katie," Father Victor said with a large smile. "I worked up a big appetite today. I may have even skipped a meal, with all the excitement."

"My stars," Katie said with a laugh. "And yet, you survived, Father."

"Not for long, Katie, not for long."

"Then you'd better come back to the kitchen and start peeling potatoes for me. If I have to do it all myself, you may be too weak to eat when it's ready."

Father Michael and Gemma relaxed, and sipped their tea, as they listened to Father Victor's jovial protests radiate down the hall.

Chapter Forty

Giancarlo continued to search for Paolo and his men. He drove back to the Starlight, and was not surprised to find the BMW gone. He swiped a key from the maid's cart, and thoroughly searched the rooms the men had checked into the night before. Their belongings were gone, but both rooms looked as if they had been evacuated in a hurry.

Next, he checked Gemma's room, and found her belongings untouched. Giancarlo decided to return to his room to formulate a search plan. As long as there was gold treasure to be found, he was sure Paolo and his men would not leave Vermont.

Entering his motel room, Giancarlo locked the door, and immediately called Mr. Montanari with an update. Giancarlo then learned Luca had already left for Vermont, and would arrive in several hours. After promising to meet Luca at the airport, Giancarlo hung up the phone. He rested his mind for several moments, then decided to stick with his original plan. Once he picked up Luca, they would come back to find Gemma and stay by her side. He had no doubt Paolo would be back for her.

Chapter Forty One

Upon completing her preliminary medical examiner report, Amy climbed to the main floor of Mercy Manor, to check on Helen. Considering the fact she had been assured all patients were safely accounted for, she was surprised to find Helen's bed neatly made and empty. Amy returned to the nurses' station, and located Elizabeth, who was trying to reorganize her work for the day. "Excuse me, I know it's been crazy, but I'm looking for my patient, Helen Coyle. Do you have any idea where she may be?"

Elizabeth, eyes lined with exhaustive shadows, looked at the doctor. "She should be in the dining room with the other patients. Did you look there?"

"No, I didn't," Amy admitted. "I know the kitchen was shut down, and I didn't think you were serving meals."

"Unfortunately, we don't have meals at the present," Elizabeth sighed. "We're using the dining room as a triage area, to make sure everyone is accounted for, meds are administered, and to provide group support. However, I just got word dinner should be here shortly. The kitchen staff at the hospital whipped up an extra two hundred meals to send over."

"That's extraordinary," Amy said with a smile. "What a great community effort."

"Yes, it is. In the meantime, our kitchen staff is still awaiting the 'all clear' from authorities," Elizabeth said, shrugging. "Thirty years of nursing, and I've never had a situation like this. The staff is in hysterics. They're saying an aide was killed."

"Really?" Amy asked, careful not to offer any information or make it known she was the acting medical examiner. "Do they have any idea who it was?"

"I heard it may be Susan Trevors," Elizabeth said, tearing up, strain evident on her face. "Who would do such a thing?"

Amy placed her hand on Elizabeth's shoulder. "I'm sure the police are looking into it. I don't think you have to be frightened."

"She wasn't the best employee, but that doesn't mean the other aides have to gossip about her. They said she hung around with a bad crowd, whatever that means," Elizabeth said with a shake of her head.

"I don't know what to say except, whoever did this, will be found," Amy said, comforting her. "Thank goodness everyone is safe. The best remedy is to get back to a sense of normalcy as soon as possible."

"Of course, you're right. Thank you. I guess I needed a moment."

"We usually need more than that after a potential crisis, such as this," Amy said. "This is scary stuff, but it's all over now. I'm going to find Helen and make sure she's comfortable. Are you okay for now?"

"Yes, I'm fine. I'd better get these medications given out," Elizabeth said with a small, nervous laugh. "I don't want patients getting upset. Some of them can be tough."

"I know what you mean," Amy said, with a knowing look.

"I'm sure everyone will feel better once they're fed and back to routine," Elizabeth said. "Thank you again for your kindness."

"You are most welcome," Amy said, as she started, once again, to look for Helen.

Chapter Forty Two

Driving down Route 4, Paolo found a run-down truck stop and pulled into a parking space. He turned off the engine and stretched his neck.

"What are we doing here?" Roberto asked, with a sideways glance.

"Where do you suggest we go?" Paolo asked as he spat out the window in disgust. "The motels are packed with skiers, and I'm sure we already have *polizia* searching for us, thanks to your stupidity."

Roberto looked out the window in silence. Vincenzo, sitting in the back, was getting restless and began rattling bags. "Hey, can I start eating some of this food?"

Paolo looked into the rearview mirror. "Why not? Pass something good up here."

The men handed the bag around and attacked their food. Paolo fished a paper-wrapped sandwich from the bag, and twisted open a bottle of soda. "This is ridiculous," he said as he leafed through the pages of a real estate magazine. "What town is this?"

"Rocky Meadow," Roberto said through a bite of an Italian hot dog. "Why?"

"I'm looking through this rag to see what cabins or houses are for rent."

"Are we gonna rent a cabin?" Roberto asked as peppers fell on his shirt.

"No, you *cretino*! I'm looking to see how long some of these places have been empty. There's gotta be one where we can hide out for a few days." Paolo tossed down his sandwich, and pulled his smart phone from his pocket. He entered a popular real estate link in the search bar, and entered the town and identification numbers from the magazine.

"Here's a couple of addresses that might work out." Not wanting to lose the information, he took a screen shot of four addresses before he flung the magazine, and shoved the rest of his sandwich in his mouth.

"What if there are people staying in them?" Roberto asked.

"Then we move on until we find one that's empty. The area is busy now. Other renters won't know if we're legitimate or not. Otherwise, we're sleeping in the car tonight." Paolo glared at Roberto. "We can thank Roberto for that."

"Whatever," Roberto mumbled toward the window.

Paolo collected his sandwich wrappers, used napkins, and soda bottle. Opening his window, he tossed them outside. The other men followed his example when they were done eating. Paolo added the four addresses to the GPS queue. "This may be your home tonight. If there's so much as a drop of grease on my backseat, you're dead," Paolo said as he started the car. Guiding the vehicle out of the lot, Paolo was already planning to ditch the car and purchase a new one, as soon as he got back to New York.

Chapter Forty Three

Amy stood at the entrance of the dining room, taking in the commotion before her. The small square tables, set with linen tablecloths, matching napkins, and silverware, were made to hold four patients, but were crowded with groups of five and six. Each resident sat at their assigned seat, waiting for their meal. Worried family members and aides surrounded the residents, helping wherever they could. Amy was saddened to see how many residents had no companions, Helen being one of them. Amy rushed to her table and pulled out a chair to sit next to her.

"Helen, thank goodness, we finally found you. Are you all right?"

"As good as can be expected," Helen said, amid a deep frown. She leaned over, toward Amy and whispered, "Get me out of here. I'll take my chances living alone. This place is going to kill me."

"Helen, you've only been here a couple of days. Your incision hasn't healed, and the staples haven't been removed yet." Amy explained. "Plus, you still have a long way to go in therapy."

Helen gave a sarcastic laugh. "Ha, I was in therapy when all hell broke loose. That aide left me sitting there an hour past the time I finished. Next thing you know, the fire alarm starts, and everyone goes crazy. Elizabeth comes running in to collect me, like I'm some sort of a runaway child."

Amy paused for a second before speaking. "You know she was there to protect you, don't you Helen?"

"I know that. Elizabeth is an awfully nice nurse. But when I see the other aide, she's getting an earful. I'm going to call the administrator when things settle down. Hopefully, she'll get fired."

Amy cringed at her words, fearing that discipline was not going to be an issue for the aide. "Helen, have you seen Susan since the fire? Anywhere? Even if she was just across the hall?"

"Of course I haven't seen her, but that's nothing new," Helen said in annoyance. "She probably ran out of here to save herself, and never came back."

Amy placed her hand on Helen's cheek in an attempt to calm her down. "You'll be fine. I heard the hospital is sending over tonight's meal. Everything will settle down soon, and I have a feeling you may get a new aide."

"That would be the only bright point in this dark day," Helen said, her shoulders and body beginning to slump, as fatigue kicked in and adrenaline faded. In a rare gesture, she took Amy's hand and held it for a minute, before she let it go. As her eyes misted over, she hung her head and said, "I thought this was it." She hesitated a second more before a tear rolled down her cheek. "I really thought I was going to die today, and I'm not ready."

Amy put her arm around Helen's shoulder and gave her a little hug. "Well, you were wrong. You're fine, and once your therapy is complete, you'll go back home and sleep in your own bed. At night, you can sit at the window and look at that beautiful view of the stars."

Helen looked up, her face streaked with tears. "Promise you'll try to get me home? You won't keep me here forever, will you?"

Amy looked at the fragile woman. "I swear I will do everything in my power to get you back home."

Helen reached out to Amy, and held her hand once again. "Everyone in my family is gone, and I've told myself a million times, I don't need people around me, because I've come this far with no family, no friends, no anything. I was never afraid to be alone, until today. I'm glad I found you. I can trust you."

"Thank you, Helen. I'll always try to be here for you. Plus, you have the whole St. Francis family. Katie and Willow brought you homemade soup and cookies today."

"I never got to see them," Helen said, her strength returning, as the moment of fragility passed. "I could use some lemon drop cookies right now."

"I have no doubt they'll be back with more, but until then, it looks like dinner has arrived," Amy said as double doors were opened by dietary staff pushing meal carts.

"Let's hope the food is an improvement over the usual sludge," Helen said as she straightened her tableware.

Laughing, Amy stood up, preparing to leave. "I'm sure it will be delicious, but just in case, I'll make sure to put in a word to Katie for you."

"I'm holding you to that. Let them know I'll be waiting," Helen managed with a smile.

"I most certainly will." Amy waved goodbye and walked toward the door, as Helen was being served her long awaited meal.

Chapter Forty Four

Paolo drove up the icy hill at a snail's pace, angry they had already driven past three of the addresses from the real estate book, with no success. All three places had snow-covered vehicles in the driveway, and smoke billowing from the chimneys. The men in the car were quiet, and Paolo could hear Vincenzo snoring softly in the back seat. "Okay, we're heading to the last place. For our sake, it had better be empty. Otherwise, it'll have to get cozy in here." Clamoring up the hill, they neared a two-story log cabin.

"This place looks nice," Roberto said as he eyed the beautiful cabin to his right.

"This isn't the one in the book, idiot," Paolo said, fatigue muting his anger. "This looks like a year round residence. The mailbox says 'Daniels'."

"I don't see any lights. Maybe they're away for the winter," Roberto said. "Can we check it out?"

"No, I don't want to be in there when someone shows up for dinner. Besides, there's a light on in the side window."

"Fine, but I'm getting tired," Roberto said.

"We're almost at the next address," Paolo said, glancing at the GPS. After ten minutes, they reached the top of Boulder Ridge, stopping at the first of three farmhouses in a row, to read the number on the mailbox. "Nope, not it," Paolo said. As he double-checked the

GPS, he did not notice Harold collecting firewood from his porch. "I think it's the one at the end."

Paolo edged past the Coyle farmhouse, and idled near the third driveway. They observed in silence for several moments, but there were no vehicle tracts in the snow covered driveway, or smoke coming from the chimney. Paolo angled into the driveway, and drove around to the back of the house. "Better to hide the car," he said as he turned off the ignition. "Although I'd be amazed if the police drove up here to find us. It's like being on the moon."

"Are we going in?" Roberto inquired as he sat straight in his seat.

"Yeah, let's try it," Paolo said. "Wake Vincenzo up and let's get in there as quickly as possible. Roberto, you go pick the lock. It's dark as hell out here, so I don't think anyone is going to see you."

"You got it," Roberto said, opening his car door. Walking toward the back of the house, he pulled a set of lock picks from his pocket.

Paolo yelled into the back seat. "C'mon, Vincenzo, get moving. Get the bags from the back, and be quiet about it."

Vincenzo murmured as he jumped from the car and grabbed the gear from the trunk.

Within minutes, using a tension wrench and pick, Roberto had the back door opened and stepped inside the house. He checked the first floor and found an empty refrigerator, a dusty thermostat, and a bare hearth. "No one's stayed in this house in a while."

"Good, look on that mantel and see if you can find some matches. Take the bags from Vincenzo, and get wood from the porch. Let's start a fire and warm the place up."

Roberto nodded as he stepped out the back door to meet Vincenzo.

"Leave the lights off," Paolo hissed into the darkness. "I don't want to take the chance of being seen. I'm going to scope out the rest of the house." Paolo walked away as Roberto began to prepare a fire.

Chapter Forty Five

Amy was welcomed into the retreat house as Katie set a steaming bowl of garlic mashed potatoes on the table. The conversation, usually amusing and joyful, was stifled that evening, by events of the day. Katie had managed to whip up a delicious pot roast, smothered with carrots and gravy, in addition to her homemade potatoes.

They began the meal with a prayer of thanks, and made sure to mention those who had been affected by the fire. After the prayer, Katie filled six ceramic bowls with piping hot chicken soup she had prepared earlier in the week. Gemma ate her first home-cooked meal in months, with polite awkwardness.

Feeling partially responsible for the fire at the nursing home, she was humbled by their invitation to dinner, and their efforts to make her feel safe and welcome. Amy was not at liberty to discuss details about the official investigation, so she remained quiet as the dinner conversation danced between winter weather and the impending holiday.

"I hear we'll be getting an Arctic blast next week," Father Michael said as he passed the biscuits across the table.

"It's cold enough," Katie said as she carefully ladled a second helping of hot soup for Father Victor. "Would anyone else like more soup or bread?"

A chorus of good natured dissension sounded at the table. "I want to save room for the pot roast," Amy said. "It smells heavenly."

Michael turned to Gemma. "You're in for a treat tonight, Gemma. Katie is a fantastic cook."

Gemma smiled at the group. "It smells wonderful. I can't thank you enough for welcoming me after everything that happened today."

"It's good to break bread together," Michael said as he looked over the table. "By the way, Katie, how are the Christmas dinner plans coming?"

"Very well," Katie said, taking a dainty sip of soup. "Willow has been such a help to me this year. We've set the menu, and word has gone out to the community, that everyone is welcome."

"We're planning on making more cookies tomorrow," Willow said gleefully. "I'm really starting to master Katie's chocolate chip recipe."

"Oh, the town has offered their bus to transport anyone who needs a ride," Father Victor said.

"The signup sheet for dinner guests and volunteers will be printed in the bulletin starting this week," Katie said. "And Sister Maggie did a lovely job with the giving tree. Each paper ornament holds a written request for someone in need, such as warm socks or a winter jacket. Gifts are already being left under the tree, and we've made sure to code the requests so no one feels embarrassed. It will be a wonderful holiday."

"You are all amazing," Amy said. Looking around the table, she made a mental note to grab several request ornaments and do some serious shopping. Amy never cared about the holiday for herself, but she was looking at it through different eyes now.

"We all make our contributions in different ways," Michael said smiling. "Your concerns are a bit more intense, which is why we like to see you relax and have a good meal on occasion."

"Thank you, from the bottom of my heart," Amy said.

"And mine, as well," Gemma chimed in.

"Enough talking, let's eat," Father Victor said, dipping a piece of bread into his chicken soup. Laughing, the rest of them proceeded to do the same.

When finished with dinner, they placed their utensils on their plates, and relaxed over a cup of cinnamon hazelnut coffee. Willow excused herself, and padded up to her room.

Father Victor turned to Gemma. "You've hardly touched your plate. You don't have to be afraid. Tony's on his way over, and we'll drive you to the Starlight motel. Katie will have a fresh room ready for you when we get back, right Katie?"

"Yes, that's right. Gemma, you can stay here until this nasty business straightens itself out."

"I appreciate everything you're doing for me," Gemma said with tears in her eyes.

"Now, don't go crying," Michael said. "You think that's a sacrifice? Amy and I promised to do the dishes to free up everyone's time."

Gemma dried her tears, among a bought of laughter, and smiled. Amy and Michael began to clear dishes off the table in neat stacks, as Father Victor ushered Gemma toward the foyer to gather

her coat and scarf. Bracing the cold, they raced across the icy path to Tony's idling SUV. Once the two were securely inside, Tony drove off toward town.

Wiping her hands on her apron, Katie heaved a large sigh and closed the door against the cold. She turned off the foyer light and returned to the kitchen. "Why don't you two go unwind? I'll get the dishes."

"Not on your life, Katie," Amy said as she filled the dishpan with hot sudsy water. "You know if I didn't eat here, I'd be home with stale toaster pastries. Dishes are the least I can do."

"Are you sure?" Katie asked while she watched Amy throw Michael a dishtowel.

"Absolutely," Amy said. "I used to love doing dishes. It's strange, but I find it soothing at times. Plus, the hot water helps keep those winter chills away."

"This way you can prepare Gemma's room and relax," Michael said. "She's bound to be exhausted when she returns. I'm sure a soft, warm bed, and clean fragrant sheets will be most appreciated. I promise I won't drop a dish."

"Well, if you're sure," Katie said, with a grin, as she untied her apron. "I'll move along then."

Turning back to the sink, Michael watched Amy place the dinner dishes in hot water. She washed the first plate, and after rinsing, placed it in the dish drain. She turned and looked at Michael. "So what happened with Gemma after I left?"

"Nothing dramatic. We waited for an officer to show up, but it took a while because they were all busy with the fire."

"That's for sure," Amy said as she continued to wash.

"It was strange, because the officer who came was the same female officer who whisked Willow away the day her grandmother died. I'm not sure if Willow saw her, because when she and Katie returned, Willow ran up to her room."

"Oh, she seemed okay at dinner," Amy said, pausing for thought. "Now that you mention it, she was rather quiet, except for that bit about the cookies. I feel bad for her. Someone her age shouldn't be exposed to this much crisis. She needs to be with young people, enjoying herself."

"I agree," Michael said, drying another plate and carefully placing it on the counter.

"I haven't found time to take her driving, but I will. I promise you that," Amy said, guiltily.

"I believe you," Michael said, plucking some silverware from the drain. "She believes in you, too."

"Thanks," Amy frowned as she turned toward Michael. "Now, I feel guiltier."

Michael chuckled as he placed the utensils in the proper slots of the drawer.

"So, back to my original question," Amy said, blowing her hair off her forehead. "What do you think of Gemma?"

"What do you mean?" Michael creased his brows.

"Do we trust her? Should we tell her anything about the crucifix?"

"Her fear of Paolo seems quite genuine, and she didn't ask to take or buy the crucifix. She simply wants to learn about it."

"She knows there'll be enough accolades negotiating a historic find like this," Amy said as she dunked another plate. "If we actually find it, and if you and the Archdiocese decide to share it with the world, she'll get plenty of positive press. A trained curator would derive enough gain from that alone. She doesn't need the actual crucifix."

"And that seems appropriate."

"Yes, it does," Amy agreed. "I can't blame her for being eager."

"So, what do we do?" Michael asked.

"Unless you can find something else in the archives, we're at a dead end," Amy said. "I can't think of anywhere else to look, or a way to open that door. Maybe Gemma has come across something like this in the past, and would be able to shed some light on the wells in the crypt."

"True, maybe we should discuss it with her. Either way, we need to sleep on it. It was an exhausting day, for everyone. Why don't we revisit this in the morning?"

"I can't tomorrow. I have to do the autopsy on the poor woman who died at the nursing home." Amy rinsed the sink clear. "I also want to speak to the police about Helen."

"Why?" Michael asked perplexed.

"I don't think there's any chance of Paolo returning to the nursing home today, between the prosecutor's office and the police, but I want to make sure Helen has some sort of protection."

"You're right," Michael said. "I never realized she may be in danger if those goons got her name. Ok, tomorrow will be a day off from treasure hunting. You do the autopsy and talk to the police. I'll continue looking through the archives. We'll give Gemma some time to relax and perhaps we can all sit down and talk after dinner tomorrow. What do you think?"

Drying her hands, Amy turned to Michael as he placed his towel on the counter. "That sounds like a great plan. Things always become clearer, for me, after I sleep, anyway."

Michael offered an encouraging smile and a strong hug. Within seconds, they heard Katie tip-toeing away from the kitchen doorway.

Chapter Forty Six

Tony veered his SUV into the poorly paved parking lot of the Starlight Motel. He cut the lights as he parked a few spaces away from Gemma's room. Surveying the parking lot for any sign of activity, he turned and cautioned both Gemma and Father Victor to wait in the car until he gave them the okay. Without hesitation, Gemma handed him the key-card to her room.

Tony slipped out of the SUV and carefully considered the dark, eerie silence that accompanied the harsh, cold air. He recognized an undercover officer sitting watch, in a Ford, several parking spaces away, and flicked a two finger salute in his direction.

Attempting to be aloof, he approached room 112, and slid the card through the chunky scanner lock. Rewarded with a small green flashing light, he rotated the handle until a soft click sounded, and then gently opened the door.

Blood pulsing, Tony stepped across the threshold, leaving the light switch untouched. The beam of his flashlight traversed the space, but nothing seemed to be disturbed. He advanced further into the room, and swung open the closet door to find a spattering of mold filled carpeting and extra pillows. The bathroom proved to be just as anticlimactic, allowing Tony to switch on the small mirror light and run back to fetch Gemma and Father Victor. He escorted them into the room, but warned them to keep the main lights off while Gemma packed her belongings.

Gemma carelessly tossed her clothes into her Louis Vuitton suitcase, then ran to collect her toiletries from the bathroom countertop. Father Victor unplugged her phone charger, and collected the half-finished mystery novel, which laid on the chipped end table.

Within minutes, Gemma and Father Victor rushed back to the car, with Tony following perceptively behind. They did not waste time loading the trunk, but rather piled the luggage around Gemma in the backseat. Once everything was tucked away, Tony hopped into the driver's seat and turned the ignition. Easing onto Route 4, he turned on his headlights.

After taking a few miles to calm down, Tony looked at Gemma in the rearview mirror. Exhausted, she was resting her head, on the suitcase next to her. "I know it was dark back there, but did you happen to recognize any of the cars?"

Snapped out of her reverie, Gemma looked up and swallowed. "No, not really. Paolo has a BMW, but he's sneaky. If he was watching my room, he would had hidden the car."

Tony continued to watch his rearview mirror. The car trailing them for the last five miles, peeled off at the entrance to High Mountain Lodge. Seeing only darkness in the mirror, Tony relaxed his shoulders and drove on to the retreat house.

Chapter Forty Seven

The tires of Tony's SUV skated on a patch of ice as he drove into the parking lot of the retreat house. After stepping out of the car, Tony opened Gemma's door, and began to unload the baggage surrounding her. Once she was free, Gemma wrestled one of her suitcases to the door, while Tony and Victor carried the rest. On the way, Tony grabbed Father Victor's attention. "Hey, when you're done, come back to the car. Let's go get a burger at the bar."

"You know me, I'd never skip a free meal," Victor laughed. "But what's really on your mind?"

"I thought we might do a little reconnaissance. Maybe those jerks will come back for dinner tonight. Worst case scenario, you get to eat the best burger in the world."

"In that case, I'll be right back."

After bringing his share of luggage to the door, Tony sat in the driver's seat and watched Father Victor lead Gemma into the foyer. After a few minutes, Father Victor emerged through the front door, jogged around the SUV, and neatly jumped into the passenger seat.

"Let's go. Mickey's working the bar tonight, which means I can fade into the background," Tony said as he put the car in gear. The ride to Hasco's Bar and Grill was opposite of the one from the motel, as Tony and Victor chatted the entire way.

Rushing in from the cold, Father Victor slid into an open booth, while Tony went to the kitchen to whip up two world famous Hasco cheeseburger platters, topped with fresh pickles, and homemade potato chips. When Tony finally slid into the booth, the two clinked their glasses of root beer, and plunged into their food. They ate and watched the crowd. Biting his last piece of burger, Tony tapped Victor on the arm to get his attention. "Don't look now, but Loafers just walked into the bar. He's got another guy with him."

Father Victor reached over to the next table for a bottle of ketchup and stole a subtle glance. "I don't recognize the new guy. Was he here the other night?"

"Not that I remember." They eyed the two men who grabbed a corner booth as soon as they were in the door. The men scrutinized the menu and placed a casual order. Tony knew they were surveying the room. He tossed his crumpled napkin back onto the plastic tray and said, "C'mon, let's get to the bottom of this."

Tony and Victor stood up, walked over to the other men's table and slipped into opposite sides of the booth, effectively blocking both men. Tony looked across the table at Giancarlo, Father Victor at Luca. After a moment of silence, Tony gave a bright smile and said, "Gentlemen, I'm the owner of this establishment, and want to personally welcome you to Hasco's."

"*Grazie,*" Giancarlo said with a stony face, as he contemplated his uninvited guests.

"Is this your first time to Vermont?" Father Victor asked, flashing a large smile.

"*Sì,*" Giancarlo said, but offered nothing more.

Discomfort lingered at the table for a few seconds before Tony spoke. "I saw you in here the other night. You seemed to be very interested in the three gentlemen, sitting across the room. I used to work with the New York Police Department, and I'm guessing you're some sort of security detail. I don't know what you're all doing here, but I thought we could work together."

"I do not know how we could help you," Giancarlo said dryly.

Father Victor leveled his gaze, then with a smirk added, "Gemma sends her regards."

Luca, though clearly interested in Father Victor's information, kept a practiced mask in place, as he turned toward him. "You know where my Gemma is?"

"Is she safe?" Giancarlo asked, then demanded. "We must speak to her, immediately."

"Whoa, not so fast," Tony said. "You haven't given us any information, gentlemen. When you tell us who you are, what you want, and who those other men are, we might be able to help you out."

Giancarlo and Luca studied each other with an unspoken communication. Giancarlo then turned toward Tony. "My name is Giancarlo. I work security detail for Marco Montanari, protecting his daughter, Gemma. This is Luca, a trusted associate, who has just arrived in Vermont. Our only concern is Gemma's safety, and her return to Italy."

"Now, that's more like it," Tony grinned. "And the other gentlemen you were watching. Who are they?"

"I do not know all their names," Giancarlo said.

"Let me help you," Tony said. "Paolo Sartori?"

"Yes, that is correct. The gentleman, who placed the order for the table, was Paolo. We believe he is a threat to Gemma."

"And we agree with you," Father Victor said. "Do you have any information about the nursing home fire? I almost collided with a BMW on the way there today."

"That was Paolo's car. I am almost certain they are responsible for the fire," Giancarlo said. "I followed them to the nursing home, but arrived too late to take action. I lost their trail with all the commotion."

"Where is Gemma?" Luca asked, getting agitated. "You said you would tell us, if we helped you."

"Gemma is safe," Father Victor said. "She is shaken up about Paolo, but she is safe."

"Take us to her," Giancarlo said. "I insist."

"I can't do that, gentlemen." Tony paused as the waitress arrived with their food and drink on a tray.

"Tony, what are you doing here?"

"Greeting our out-of-town guests," Tony said as he helped to pass their order. "Thanks, we'll take it from here. Oh, and the food and drinks are on the house for these fine gentlemen. No check."

"You got it," the waitress said as she tucked the tray under her right arm, blew a large bubble with her gum, and walked back towards the kitchen.

Tony returned his attention to the table. "I believe you are looking after Gemma's welfare, but I can't take you to her. If you don't mind, I'm gonna take your photo." Tony quickly raised his cell phone and snapped their pictures. "I'll show these to Gemma. If she agrees to meet with you, you'll get a call with the time and location. In the meantime, give me a phone number I can use."

Giancarlo wrote his cell number on the back of a napkin, and passed it to Tony. "Gemma will not know my name or face. Tell her the name Giancarlo. She should call her father and confirm with him. She will know Luca. I will be expecting a call, Mr. Tony….?"

Tony filled in the blank. "Noce, Tony Noce. Well, it's late gentlemen, so this won't be happening tonight, but do enjoy the food and get a good night's sleep. I expect you'll hear from us in the morning."

"I certainly hope so, Mr. Noce," Giancarlo warned. "Or I will find you."

"Duly noted," Tony said as he and Father Victor squeezed out of the booth.

Chapter Forty Eight

Amy rolled over and indulged in the blissful warmth and comfort of her bed, before coming to full consciousness, Saturday morning. Aware she had some flexibility in her schedule, she wrapped her favorite quilt around her. She opened her eyes to the row of windows before her, through which she could see the captivating lake, sprinkled with snow, which lay at the base of the mountain, below her cabin. The sun was beginning to peak through the gray snow-filled clouds, framed by blue sky. The view was breathtaking. Her morning schedule looming in her mind, Amy closed her eyes for five more minutes of rest.

With a defeated groan, she pushed back her quilt, and swung her bare feet onto the frigid wood floor. Within twenty minutes, Amy was freshly showered, bundled, and pouring hot coffee into her thermos. Reminding herself she would be in the morgue, Amy deliberately filled a second thermos. She knew her lab attendant, Alex Diggs, was already taking photographs of the deceased and preparing the body for autopsy. Placing the carafe in the sink, Amy added cream to each thermos, grabbed her things, and proceeded to the hospital.

Passing through the emergency room, Amy spied Ernie sitting at the central desk. She waved as she approached. "Hey, Ernie."

"Hi, yourself. What has you in here on a Saturday?"

"I have to do a post this morning on the woman they found at the nursing home."

"Yes, the unfortunate victim," Ernie said. "Yesterday was crazy. I started disaster planning. I didn't know if we'd have firemen with smoke inhalation or burn patients, but I was prepping for the worse."

"Thankfully, the damage and injuries were kept to a minimum," Amy said with a sigh. "It was a frightening experience for many people. Things can change in an instant."

"So true. In the meantime, you've had a few calls from the prosecutor's office. I guess they're eager for your results. One newspaper called looking for information, and you should also know that Lou Applebaum is doing rounds today." Ernie tried to hide his grin.

"All the more reason for me to get down to the morgue," Amy said as she grabbed her purse from the counter. "Nothing else came in overnight? No immediate issues?"

"Just the typical colds and falls," Ernie said, shrugging his shoulders. "You're all clear."

"Good. Let's hope it stays that way. See you later, Ernie." Amy said as she headed to the elevator.

Chapter Forty Nine

Katie buzzed around the kitchen while she zealously flipped pancakes, and set the holiday china on the table. Within minutes, everyone found their way into the kitchen, anxious for a strong cup of coffee and a short stack with maple syrup and bacon. Before Morning Prayer, Father Victor pulled Michael aside to fill him in on the events from Hasco's. "Tony's planning to come to the retreat house this morning, to have Gemma look at the photos of those men. If she wants to meet with them, we'll arrange a public place. Sound okay to you?"

"That's fine with me," Michael said. "If they truly are a security detail, we might as well have them stay here with Gemma, until this is all over with. I don't think Katie would mind a few more guests, especially with Christmas so near."

"Let's see what happens," Father Victor said.

The two priests joined the group at the table, and after a heartfelt prayer, dove into Katie's breakfast. Within minutes, Tony was rapping on the front door, eager to get a taste of Katie's cooking.

"Oh my, what a lively crowd this morning," Katie crooned as she continued to serve breakfast. The enthusiastic crowd chatted as Katie's serving platters were sent around the table, emptying as they passed. "Gemma, what can I get for you, dear? You must be hungry.

You didn't have much last night."

"Thank you," Gemma said. "May I have another piece of toast and more coffee?"

"Of course, let me know if you want more eggs or ham. Remember, this is Vermont. You might need a bit more of a start."

Gemma laughed as she spread some of Katie's homemade jam on her bread.

"How did you sleep, dear?"

"Oh, Katie. That was the softest bed I've ever slept in," Gemma said as she sipped her coffee, savoring the taste of Katie's special dark roast Vermont blend. "I thought I'd be too nervous, but I fell asleep the instant my head touched the pillow. And it smelled wonderful. Was that lavender?"

"Why, yes it was, with a few drops of almond oil mixed in. They say it's great for anxiety."

"Whatever it was, it worked wonders."

"Well, I hope it has a carryover effect," Tony said as he plopped into the only open chair, next to Father Victor.

"That doesn't sound pleasant, Tony," Katie said. "At least, have something to eat before you bear bad news."

Tony laughed resonantly between bits of maple bacon. "Oh, my wonderful Katie. How can I entice you to leave this place and cook for me at Hasco's? This is delicious."

"For the love of Pete," Katie said, as she crossed herself. "You're just as bad as Father Victor over there." She scoffed, as the men bumped fists in appreciation of their stomachs.

"Your meals are irresistible, Katie," Father Victor said. "I'd go to the ends of the earth for your cooking."

"Then, why aren't I cooking at that beautiful would-be soup kitchen right now? We were so close," Katie said dejectedly.

Father Michael took a sip of his coffee and chimed in to spare Victor the hot seat. "Katie, you said yourself, the Lord has his plans, even if we don't agree with them. Usually, it means he has a better one in mind."

"Yes, Father, I did say that. So, I'll just stop talking, have faith, and see what happens," Katie admonished herself.

"My poor Katie," Father Michael said as he put down his napkin. "So what are you up to today?"

"Once we clean up, Willow, Sister Maggie and I are going to take another run to Mercy Manor this morning, aren't we dear?" Katie said as she turned to Willow for support.

"Yup," Willow said. "We're bringing more soup and cookies to pass around while Sister Maggie checks in on a few parishioners. Helen is waiting for some lemon drops. Katie's cookie reputation has spread around the nursing home, so now everyone wants some."

"That's great news. You're irrevocably appreciated despite what happened, and even worse, what could have happened," Father Michael said.

"Well, thank the Lord it didn't," Katie said.

"Amen, to that," Father Michael said.

Michael addressed the large breakfast group, "As for the rest of us, I believe we need to have a little meeting in the library." His suggestion was met with unspoken understanding.

Chapter Fifty

Entering the bleak morgue, Amy waved to Alex with as much optimism as she could muster.

"Hi, Dr. Daniels. I have everything ready for you," Alex said. "I took the x-rays and the body is in position on the steel table."

"Thanks, Alex. I'm going to run to the locker room and change. I'll be right back." After throwing on her greens, Amy pulled on a white overcoat, and cinched up her hair. She took a quick glance in the mirror before returning to the main suite of the morgue.

"Are you ready, Doc?" Alex asked politely.

"Yes, but let's review what we know," Amy said. "Have you had any experience with the forensic pathology of thermal injuries?"

"Not so much," Alex shrugged.

"Still want to learn or possibly go into forensics?"

"Yes, I'm looking at schools now," Alex nodded.

"Okay, so today will be your first lesson," Amy said. "Before we even touch the body, I want to make sure you got all the x-rays."

"Sure did," Alex said proudly.

"Total body radiographs, including dental survey?"

"Yes Doc," Alex confirmed with a wide smile.

"Okay, great start," Amy said, clearly pleased. "In thermal injury from fire, we check the victim's blood for quantification of carboxyhemoglobin, and check for cyanide levels, as well as a regular screen for toxins."

"Ok, got it," Alex said.

"If blood isn't available, what else can you test to determine levels?" Amy asked, gently pimping Alex for information.

"The second best tissue choice for detecting carboxyhemoglobin, is skeletal muscle," Alex answered.

"Very good," Amy said as she leaned on the counter. "And what does all that tell you?"

"If the level is greater than fifty percent, it's likely the patient died from carbon monoxide poisoning, although people with cardiac disease or the elderly, can die with lower levels in their bloodstream."

"Correct," Amy said. "We're moving on Mr. Diggs. Did you collect all the victim's clothing?"

"It's being tested for accelerants as we speak," Alex said. "You said thermal injuries from fire. What other burns have you dealt with?"

"In Boston trauma, we saw everything. People came into the hospital with lightning strikes, chemical burns, radiation burns, electrocution, but the worst was abuse. I hated seeing kids who were scalded or burned with irons or cigarettes. Adults came in that way, as well," Amy said in quiet disbelief, reliving her days in trauma.

"That must have been rough," Alex said.

"It was, it truly was," Amy said quietly. "Pathology is not an easy job, so keep that in mind. Okay, let's get to work. The first thing we need to do is positively identify the body."

"No leads so far. Nothing on or around the body," Alex said.

"Ok, when we get the dental charts and x-rays, we'll use them to identify the patient as well as external markings. The police are using a facial photo for family identification."

"Sounds like a plan," Alex said, nodding his head.

Amy approached the autopsy table, and Alex helped her into her gown, mask, surgical cap and gloves. She reached up and turned on the overhead microphone. *"This is Dr. Amy Daniels, dictating the external exam of Jane Doe, Case Number 416892. Victim brought to Rocky Meadow General Hospital after being found in burning utility closet at Mercy Manor Nursing Home. Victim is a Caucasian female, approximately forty-four years of age, weight is one hundred fifty two lbs., and height is sixty seven inches. There is evidence of partial, as well as full thickness burns to the epidermis of the lower legs with superficial skin slippage. Exam of the left lower skin of the abdomen reveals a tattoo of two black roses, approximately three cm. by three cm. in size. Scars are noted on both breasts, indicating history of plastic surgery in the past. There is no evidence of cherry red lividity, or contractures. Epidural hematomas are present, as well as small skin splits on lower legs, near burns."*

Amy reached up and turned off the microphone. "Alex, were you able to get fingerprints?"

"Yes, printed and sent to the prosecutor's office."

"Great, I didn't think it would be a problem since the burns appear to be limited to her lower legs, but take note of the possibility of there being no fingerprints on charred bodies in the future." Alex nodded his understanding. "Okay, let's open her up and check the viscera. We'll check the x-rays for fire fractures, and most importantly, her trachea and lungs for soot. Now tell me why soot is important."

Alex swallowed and thought for a moment. "The only way for a victim to have soot in her lungs would be if she had been breathing during a fire. No soot would mean she was dead before the fire."

"That's right, Alex. It also means most of the injuries we've described were made postmortem. Sometimes, you can tell the difference between a postmortem heat-related artifact and an antemortem injury, by color and texture. You can also differentiate by the direction of injury in the muscle fibers. Since the upper body wasn't burned, muscle injuries located there were probably made during a struggle or related to her cause of death."

"This is fascinating," Alex said. "Thanks for taking the time to explain to me."

"You seem to know most of it already, but you'll remember this autopsy, when you get your degree in pathology," Amy said, with a smile. "Okay, let's finish the rest of the exam." Amy reached up, turned the microphone on and finished dictating the external exam.

Afterwards, they opened the body cavity and removed the organs, and checked each for disease and trauma after its weight was recorded. Next, the pair examined soft tissue to search for evidence of damage. It took several hours to examine the entire body, after which Amy turned off the microphone for the final time. "We're done here." Amy stepped back, took off her gloves, and lowered her mask. "Alex, would you like to close?"

"You know I would," he readily agreed as he pulled up his mask and checked his gloves.

"You got it," Amy said, stretching her back. "Once we have all the evidence and drug screens back, we can declare the cause of death. I'm going to the locker room. Please do a thorough job and thank you, Alex. You're a great assistant and I'm sure you'll make an excellent pathologist."

"That means a lot, Dr. Daniels." Alex smiled as Amy left the autopsy suite.

Chapter Fifty One

Stoking the budding fire in the library, Father Michael settled around a wooden conference table with Father Victor, Gemma and Tony. The men briefly recounted their meeting at Hasco's, before Tony unlocked his smart phone, and showed Gemma the photos of the two gentlemen. "Do you recognize these men?"

Gemma scrutinized the first photo. "I don't know this man, but he looks vaguely familiar. I have seen him in the city."

"He said his name is Giancarlo," Tony explained. "He was hired by your father to watch over you." Tony watched Gemma's reaction carefully and was glad to see surprise ignite in her face. Tony wanted to inform Gemma of their presence, but also to gauge her involvement in the activities taking place in Rocky Meadow. "He said you wouldn't know him, and suggested you call your father for more information. I can text you this photo so your father can confirm his identity."

"Yes, of course," Gemma said, clearly flustered.

Sliding to the next photo on his phone, Tony tilted the screen so Gemma could see it clearly. She recognized the second man instantly. "That is Luca. He works very closely with my father."

"This man is also in Vermont," Tony said.

"Luca is here?" Gemma asked, surprise intermingled with excitement registering on her face. "Are you sure?"

"I took this last night," Tony said. "He seemed quite concerned about you. He wanted to see you immediately."

Gemma could not hide the smile on her face. "Luca was worried about me?"

"Quite a bit," Tony explained. "In order to keep you safe, we didn't tell them you were at St. Francis. We wanted to be sure you recognized them."

"I've known Luca since I was a girl, but I haven't seen him for many years." A flush crept up Gemma's cheeks.

"He seems very special to you," Father Michael noted.

"I had feelings for Luca when he started working with my father," Gemma explained. "But I believe he thought of me as a silly school girl at the time."

"Well, he insists on seeing you, as soon as possible," Tony said. "If that's okay with you."

"Of course," Gemma said, smoothing her hair nervously. "Now? I need a few moments to freshen up."

Tony had a silent conversation with the two priests before turning back to Gemma. "Why don't you call your father and confirm these two men are who they say they are? If everything checks out, we'll call them and arrange a time to meet in the back room of Hasco's," Tony said, searching the faces of Father Victor and Michael for approval.

"Sounds good," Father Victor said.

"I agree," Father Michael said.

"Me too," Gemma said as she rose from her chair. "Please excuse me? I'll go make that call."

"Take your time," Father Michael said, smiling as he held the door open. He closed the door gently behind her, and let a moment pass to make sure she had left the hall. Turning back from the door, Michael caught the eyes of the two men. "I think it's time I bring you up to speed about this treasure."

Chapter Fifty Two

Amy stepped into the dreary corner office of the expansive morgue, and plopped into her worn leather desk chair. She glared at the mound of papers to sign, charts to review and reports to read, as the flashing red light on her office phone informed her of the impending litany of messages, she had yet to confront. She promptly returned calls, to the police department and prosecutor's office, while eagerly erasing messages from the media, consciously avoiding any opportunity to compromise the investigation.

Knowing the results of her dictation and lab testing would take several days to return, she immersed herself in the pile of autopsy reports from the week before. As Amy signed the final paperwork for a cardiac arrest victim, and the boy who had died in a skiing accident, she rediscovered the surface of her desk, and relished in the sweet sensation of progress.

"Knock, knock," Lou Applebaum cheerfully called from the door.

Amy visibly jumped at the sound of his voice. "Jeez, Lou. I didn't hear you come in."

"I could tell. It's a good thing I'm not the living dead, otherwise, you'd be a sitting duck," Lou chided.

"These reports are incredibly detailed at times," Amy said, realizing the brazen scent of his expensive cologne.

"I'm sure they are. Ernie told me you were down here doing the post of the nursing home death. I didn't see you in the hospital yesterday."

"Unfortunately, my day off turned into an investigation surrounding the circumstances of Jane Doe's death, which is why I have to spend the whole day in the morgue. There's a lot of pressure from the prosecutor's office, and I've already had calls from the police and fire departments. Which reminds me, I still have to speak with the nursing home's legal team and insurance company. And don't get me started on the media. This case is complicated, to say the least."

"I wish I had some reassuring words, but it's just terrible," Lou said, smiling sympathetically.

"Tell me about it," Amy said. "I want to retire and take up professional hiking."

"I hear you," Lou said. "Don't forget, you mentioned we could grab a bite at the Cider Mill on Monday. I know you're busy, but you'll probably need a breather by then."

Amy rubbed her temples and searched for a way to break her promise. Since she offered no resistance, Lou assumed she agreed with him. "I'll come by your office around twelve and pull you out of here. Regardless of how bad it is, a hearty lunch, with an eligible doctor, will perk you right up."

"Sounds like a plan." Amy blushed. "Thank you."

"My pleasure," Lou said in bashful excitement. Glancing at her desk, he shook his head. "That pile is mountainous. You're putting Everest to shame. You should head home for a nap before this paperwork messes with your head. Maybe you can start fresh on Monday."

Laughing, Amy nodded in agreement. "I have a few more things to do before collapsing on my couch, but thanks for dropping in, Lou."

"Hang in there, Amy," Lou said, his expressive smile showing his genuine concern for the woman behind the desk.

Chapter Fifty Three

Paolo tossed old newspaper onto the logs in the fireplace, and set them aflame by poking the hearth ashes with a stick. The fire blazed intensely for several minutes, but rapidly faded.

"You can't do it that way," Roberto mumbled from the corner of the room.

"What?" Paolo spun toward the man.

"You have to put the paper under little sticks, and then add bigger sticks, until the fire grows," Roberto laughed. "Or you could use flammable cleansers."

"I'll set a piece of furniture on fire, if I have to." Paolo angrily tossed a small log into the fireplace. "It's freezing in here, and it's all your fault."

"I second that," Vincenzo called from under the sheet used to keep the loveseat clean. Breathing in a cloud of dust, he began to cough in spasms, which did not cease until he got off the couch and approached the back door.

"C'mon, get up. It's afternoon already," Paolo said disgustedly. "Let's go grab something to eat."

"We should stop for supplies," Roberto said. "Some lighter fluid and flashlights."

"As long as you do exactly what you're told," Paolo snapped. "We don't need any more attention drawn to us. I'm not going to jail."

"Neither am I," Roberto said.

"Then you should have stopped when I told you to."

"I'm not going to explain it again, Paolo. The aide was a liability."

"This gold treasure better be worth my while, otherwise, you'll be explaining your reasoning to the end of my gun pressed up to your skull," Paolo said, through clenched teeth.

"Whatever you say," Roberto scoffed, shoving the screen as he walked out the back door towards the car.

Chapter Fifty Four

Amy and Michael had been in the library for over an hour, perusing the stack of documents Michael pulled aside, amid distracted glances at the fireplace. "Did you find any new information today?" Amy asked, tossing down a pile of yellowed papers in defeat.

"No, but I didn't have time to go through them all," Michael said. "Last night at Hasco's, Tony and Father Victor came across two men looking for Gemma. One of them, Giancarlo, was there last Thursday as well. This morning, we met with Gemma to see if she knew them."

"Oh right, I remember Victor mentioning that over dinner," Amy said, nodding her head.

"They talked with the men to get some information, and then showed Gemma their photos this morning. She didn't recognize Giancarlo, but it turns out he had been hired by Gemma's father to look after her."

"Really? That's devious. Gemma didn't mind when she found out?"

"Apparently not. From what I understand, Paolo has become an ever increasing threat. Both were becoming quite worried, but Gemma kept her fears to herself, while Mr. Montanari hired Giancarlo. At least, we finally have it all out on the table."

"Wow, you're actively counseling, while saving a damsel in distress," Amy teased.

"Wait, there's more," Michael said with a mischievous smile.

"Like what?" Amy asked excitingly.

"The other man, Luca, is Mr. Montanari's closest associate. However, it seems that Luca and Gemma have always had an unrequited relationship between them."

"You're kidding?" Amy shook her head in disbelief.

"Tony had Gemma call her father, to confirm the men's identities, which she did. So we all met at Hasco's and reunited them."

"How did it go?" Amy asked, overcome with curiosity.

"Wonderful," Michael said. "Gemma was happy to see them. She flew into Luca's arms."

"I can't imagine how relieved she was to see a familiar face. It must be hard to be in a strange place, in fear of an abusive man, with no family or support system."

"And rightfully so," Michael said. "We all sat and talked for a while, but Tony, Victor and I made sure to slip away, so they could have some time to catch up."

"That was very kind of you," Amy said.

"It was the right thing to do," Michael said. "As a matter of fact, the two men will be moving into the retreat house tomorrow, to keep an eye on Gemma until everything dies down. They suspect Paolo will go after her, in route to the treasure."

"I imagine so," Amy said. "No one has found Paolo and his men?"

"Not yet. The police are still looking, and the nursing home is on alert."

"Yes, I spoke with the police chief today," Amy said. "I shared my concerns about Helen, without giving him too much information about the treasure. He told me there'll be extra police presence at the nursing home until this is resolved."

"That's good," Michael said. "Katie told me there was more security when they went to visit today."

"Good. How did that go?"

"Very well, according to Katie. The residents were cheery. The kitchen was fully operational, and that local band, The Grain, had volunteered to perform at Mercy Manor twice a week, until the New Year."

"That's wonderful, Michael."

"How was your day?" He asked, noting the strain on her face.

"Stressful," Amy said truthfully. "I completed the autopsy, followed by a mountain of calls and paperwork."

"Ouch," Michael said. "Am I allowed to ask about the autopsy?"

"You're bound to silence?"

"Of course, but I wouldn't break the trust of a friend, in any event," Michael said, slightly amused.

"Of course, I can never be too careful," Amy said. "I haven't gotten the results of the lab back, but I'm fairly certain our Jane Doe is Susan Trevors. She was strangled, and whoever did it, tried to hide the body in the closet, and set the fire to conceal evidence."

"Wow," Michael said. "Maybe it's a good thing we hid Gemma."

"I think so," Amy sighed. "I haven't had any calls from anyone close to Susan. I'm not sure if she had friends or family."

"It would be sad to think so," Michael said gently.

"That's exactly what would've happened if it had been Helen in that fire," Amy pointed out. "No family, no known friends. Not everyone has someone to depend on, and if it weren't for you, and my little St. Francis family..." Amy stopped speaking, her eyes tearing up.

"Don't cry," Michael said, turning to pull her close. "I'm here for you. Everyone is here for you."

"I hope you realize how much I cherish knowing that," Amy said, looking up at Michael.

As he reached out to brush her hair away from her cheek, Amy was pulled into the gaze of Michael's blazing blue eyes and felt her breath catch. He took in her face, her tear-filled eyes, her trembling lips and incredible loneliness. Feeling her face flame, Amy quickly looked down and pulled away.

"I'd better be going," Amy said, avoiding eye contact as she spoke.

"Do you have to?"

"I think it would be best," Amy said. "Please thank Katie for me. I'm sure dinner will be great."

"But what about Gemma, our game plan?"

"I need some rest," Amy said, moving to lift her purse. "If we can't find anything in the archives, perhaps we can ask her about the wells. She's a trained curator, so maybe she's seen something like that before."

She flung open the library door, and walked to the foyer with Michael following closely behind. She threw on her jacket and scarf, and in the interest of time, stuffed her hat and gloves into her pockets, before moving to the door. Michael reached for her arm as she turned the knob. "Do you have to leave?"

Turning to face him, she said, "I don't want to, but I think it would be best for everyone." She hesitated on the snow covered porch for a tantalizing second, and then ran down the steps, crunching day-old snow in her wake.

Chapter Fifty Five

Paolo sat silently, enveloped in darkness, and watched as a young woman ran to her car, from the bright glow of the retreat house door. After leaving the farmhouse, he and his men found a store, twenty five miles away, where they stocked up on food and supplies to get them through the next day. On their way, he quickly drove by the Starlight Motel. He circled the parking lot, but immediately pulled away when he noticed the absence of Gemma's car.

Remembering her plan, he scoured the phone book in search of the only Catholic Church in the area, and plugged the address into his GPS. He pulled into the retreat house parking lot, and parked in the back corner. He felt a rush of adrenaline upon recognizing Gemma's car. They had been watching for thirty minutes, the details of the grounds now engrained in their memory, when they saw Amy run out to her car and drive off.

"Was that Gemma?" Roberto asked, squinting in the night.

"No," Paulo said, shaking his head. "That was some other woman. I think I have a plan."

Roberto watched as a grin spread across Paolo's face. "What? What are you thinking?"

"Get out your nicest clothes, Vincenzo. You'll be attending tomorrow morning's mass," Paolo said, his grin becoming a hideously twisted smile.

Chapter Fifty Six

Welcome to the parish of St. Francis. Today we celebrate the second Sunday of Advent. Our main celebrant will be Father Michael Lauretta, assisted by Father Victor Cerulli. Our entrance hymn is "O Come, O Come, Emmanuel". Please stand.

Amy picked up the hymnal and distractedly turned to page 246. As the choir began their melodious rendition of the entrance hymn, she dutifully followed along with the words, and watched the procession. First was the crucifer, who was an altar boy, carrying the cross. He was flanked by two altar servers holding candles, known as candle bearers. Behind them walked a Eucharistic minister, then a deacon, holding the Book of Gospels, high in the air. Next came Father Victor, as concelebrant, and finally Father Michael, as principle celebrant. Both priests were fully dressed in chasuble and alb. Amy continued to watch, as the group processed to the altar and took their places.

Michael spotted her from his chair and smiled, pleased she had decided to attend mass. Amy felt her heart in her throat, seeing Michael, on the altar, and thinking back to the night before. She had been upset and emotional, at the thought of so many lonely patients in the world, but she was starting to realize it was her own fear coming to light.

The thought of all the lonely patients she had encountered

over the years, intensified her worst fear, the one she had buried deep within, when her sister was killed. The same fear she cried herself to sleep with, after her parents died. It seemed everyone she loved either left or passed away.

Being a well-respected trauma surgeon, she never allowed anyone to get close to her, emotionally or physically. She constantly dealt with death and trauma on her table. She saw the emotionally raw wound it left on family and loved ones. Who was she trying to spare by not allowing a relationship that could inflict such pain, herself or the person she got close to? But how much joy did she miss in life by that restraint?

This last year, being with Michael, Katie, Willow and Father Victor, had changed her outlook. Previously, her job had prevented her from interacting with her family in the way she had wanted to, and once her parents were gone she became an introvert, refusing to open her heart to anyone. But now, after one year in Vermont, she realized joy and love, in the midst of death and fear, was possible, and she wanted more.

She almost willingly opened her heart, but for the wrong man. He was bound by spiritual obligation, but in her desolation, her moral responsibility had failed her. How stupid could she be? Michael was most likely pleased last night, realizing she was finally having a breakthrough. Ever the psychologist, ever the friend. Sadly, he did not realize the extent of the feelings she was developing for him, feelings for a man she could never be near. He had been working, as a psychologist, since she arrived in Vermont, and the ice surrounding her feelings was finally beginning to crack. Now that

Amy was feeling again, she needed to pull away.

She tenderly looked at Willow, seated beside her. Without any forethought, she reached over and squeezed her hand. Willow turned and smiled at her. Such a sweet, innocent, but sad face. What a strange little group they had become. Each experiencing loss of a loved one in a different way. Yet, they unknowingly banded together, and found joy and happiness. She did not want to lose that. For the first time, she did not want to run. Leaving her new friends would be more emotionally painful, than trying to protect her feelings, by abandoning the relationship.

Amy looked at the altar. She watched Michael's handsome face, his wavy black hair and beautiful blue eyes, and her heart clenched. She decided to never admit her true feelings for him. She did not want to jeopardize his career and faith over something she allowed to grow in her mind, something that may have only been the result of her isolation from human comfort.

Thankfully, her lunch with Lou was planned for the next day. Although not exactly eager to go, she made a conscious decision to make the best of it, and spend more time with Lou. Who was she to reject the attempts of an eligible man who cared for her? Lou was a kind and gentle man, who had not yet touched Amy's heart, but had the potential to be a great friend, or maybe even more. She had to at least try to connect with another man, to protect Michael from herself.

Chapter Fifty Seven

Paolo and Roberto dropped Vincenzo off at the bustling morning mass, and instructed him to memorize the layout of the church, so they could break in later and look for the treasure. Vincenzo sat in a back pew, clearly unaccustomed to Catholic mass. He shifted side to side, as he watched the procession, tried to follow the readings, and mumbled to simulate responses to the prayers. Before the mass began, Vincenzo spotted Gemma in the second pew. Having seen her only once, while with Paolo, he used the photo in his phone to confirm it was her, and noted she sat with the woman who had run out of the rectory last night. Feeling a buzz in his pocket, Vincenzo grabbed his cell and read the text message.

What's going on?

He attempted to remain unseen by other parishioners as he typed his response.

Gemma is here, the priest is still talking.

After a few seconds, a reply came back.

Watch her closely. .

Vincenzo quickly entered his answer.

OK.

He received another text.

Stay in church after mass. Light a candle, hide out as long as you can. We're leaving. Be back later.

Vincenzo read the text and scowled, until a wicker basket was thrust, under his nose. Looking inside, he saw dollar bills and envelopes snuggled in the bottom. Vincenzo looked up at the pole bearer who smiled, and realizing no envelope would be forthcoming, removed the basket from the pew. Once he was gone, Vincenzo responded to the text.

OK - hurry back.

Paolo and Roberto slumped in the BMW, hidden from sight, in a parking lot filled to capacity. Starting the car once again to blast the heat for a few minutes, Paolo recognized Gemma's car parked in the same spot as last night. "That's Gemma's car," he said, pointing it out to Roberto.

"Maybe she's staying here," Roberto said.

"Damn," Paolo swore. In an attempt to control his anger and distract himself, he pulled his smart phone from his pocket, and started pushing buttons. "I don't believe this."

"What's wrong?" Roberto asked, looking over at the driver's seat.

"I've been watching the reports on the local news," Paolo said. "They've been showing video of the nursing home for the last forty-eight hours, and they just announced the police are looking for a BMW with New York license plates. Someone saw us. Probably the van we almost hit, when we left the parking lot." Paolo closed his eyes and took a deep breath.

Roberto shook off Paolo's anger and asked, "So what's our plan here?"

"We know we're in the right spot," Paolo answered.

"Gemma is hanging around, so they must be working together."

"What are we going to do about it?"

"Once mass is over, there'll be people all over this lot," Paolo said. "You and I are taking off, so the car isn't spotted. We have to ditch the BMW and grab something else. Hopefully, Vincenzo can follow Gemma and spot some clues."

"Then what?"

"We come back in a couple hours, go in the church, and have a look around ourselves. We better find something soon, because our trail is getting hotter by the minute." Paolo turned to Roberto, his jaw clenched. "If I go to jail because of you, you're dead. You get that? You're dead."

Roberto looked at Paolo through narrowed eyelids, but kept his mouth closed. He turned his attention to the parking lot, to abate his frustration.

Paolo slid his hands over the gun in his waist band, believing for a moment, the time had come to use it. Sense beckoning in his mind, Paolo reasoned a crowded church parking lot was not the right place to take care of business. Besides, he would still need Roberto for a little while longer.

Snapping into focus, he noticed the flood of people clamoring down the church steps. The priests were perched at the top, shaking hands with parishioners. Avoiding unwanted attention, Paolo shifted the car into drive and disappeared into the parade of cars, filing out of the parking lot.

Chapter Fifty Eight

The choir broke into the recessional hymn, signaling the end of mass. The group on the altar processed to the back of the church with each row of parishioners falling in behind after kneeling and crossing themselves. Amy, Willow, Katie and Gemma stayed in their pew to wait for Michael and Victor to return, and hang up their vestments. As the altar boys began to blow out candles, the choir members collected their music and searched for their coats and gloves. Deeply troubled parishioners said extra prayers before leaving their pews to light extra candles, allowing Amy more time to realize she did not recognize anyone from the parish.

After a few minutes, Michael and Father Victor walked up the main aisle, laughing delightedly, and pausing when they reached the women's pew.

"Well, don't you two look like trouble?" Katie said, looking at them shrewdly, while buttoning her wool coat, and pulling on her fancy gloves.

"Katie," Father Victor said. "We're in a joyous mood after celebrating such a wonderful mass. At this point, a cup of your fine coffee would be the next best thing to heaven."

"And banana bread," Father Michael chimed in. "A big piece of warm banana bread."

Katie could not hold back her smile any longer. "You're

both like school boys, you know that?" Picking up her purse, she turned to Willow. "Come back to the rectory with me, dear. We've got a lot of planning to do. First, we need to make coffee and banana bread. Then we've got to organize our final list for cooking, shopping and decorating the rectory for Christmas."

"Can I take another shot at that shortbread recipe?" Willow asked.

"Of course. We'll never have enough cookies. Especially the way these two eat them," Katie said, tilting her head in the priests' direction. "We only have two weeks left to get everything done." Hiding a smile, Katie slid out of the pew, and pulled Willow through the side door, toward the rectory.

"I'd better get changed and help them out," Father Victor said, turning toward Michael. "Tony is bringing Luca and Giancarlo over this afternoon, and I'm not sure Katie has their rooms ready. Anyone else want to come?"

Father Michael surveyed Gemma and Amy before he answered Victor. "No, I think we'll stay here for a few moments. Tell Katie, we'll be over to the rectory as soon as we can."

"You got it. I'll see you all there," Father Victor said with a nod, as he walked toward the sacristy and whistled as he went.

Amy glanced toward Michael, her eyes questioning his decision.

"I'd like to take a few minutes to change out of my vestments. Then, if you don't mind, we'd like to show you something, in the church. Amy and I are stumped. We thought your expertise may offer us some understanding," Michael said to

Gemma.

"Anything I can do to help," Gemma said.

"Great. Give me a minute to change." He walked off toward the sacristy, and called out to Victor to hold the door.

"Why don't we have a seat while we're waiting?" Amy said to Gemma.

Smoothing her coat under her, Gemma sat down in the pew as Amy followed suit. Complete silence lingered between them, until Michael returned several minutes later, and joined them. "Did you tell her?" Michael asked, his eyes searching Amy's, until she turned her face.

"I haven't said anything, Michael. It's up to you to explain," Amy said quietly.

"Is this about the treasure?" Gemma implored of Father Michael. "Does it exist?"

"We don't know," Michael said. "We were told a treasure is hidden here in the church. That was the conversation overheard by the nursing home aide. Amy and I followed some of the clues given to us, but so far we have nothing to show for it. We did find something strange, and thought you may be able to help explain whether it's significant. It's actually in the crypt. We'd like to show you, if you don't mind."

"I'd love to take a look," Gemma said excitedly.

"Great, then let's go," Michael said as they stood and prepared to leave the pew.

None of them noticed the man lighting a prayer candle nearby, and had no idea the empty church allowed Vincenzo to hear their every word.

Chapter Fifty Nine

Michael led the group toward the transept, and stopped in front of the table, against the wall, weighed down by the statue of St. Francis of Assisi. Offering a short prayer, he slid the table aside, while Amy cradled the saint's replica like a newborn child. Gemma stood in awe, watching as the two opened a door that was virtually invisible, just moments ago.

It was late morning, and they were hoping the ground windows would allow enough natural light for them to see without a flashlight. As a precaution, Michael picked up one of the heavier prayer candles and carried it with him.

"If it's okay, I'll go first, to make sure we can see the steps," Michael said as he cautiously started down. Thankfully, the room was more illuminated than it had been when he and Amy explored the crypt at nightfall. The three inched their way to the bottom of the stairwell, the sound of each footstep ricocheting off the stone walls. The echo was so loud no one heard an additional footfall follow them down the stairs.

Gemma was stunned when the four small arches, fronted by black wrought iron gates, appeared in front of the group. She eagerly inspected each tiny room, as well as the benches siting in the middle of the main chamber. "We have crypts like this in the Monticello Cathedral, but I never expected to find one in Vermont. Are all the burial chambers full?"

"No, only half of them," Michael replied, placing the prayer candle on the bench. "This room is not well known in the area. We've kept it closed to the public."

"Perhaps you should rethink that decision," Gemma said. "The people buried here are to be honored, or they would never have been given such a prominent burial place. I can't imagine the history behind all of this."

"Funny you should say that," Michael said. "We've been researching hundreds of documents in the church archives, and we've found several references to a certain symbol." Michael walked to the other end of the room and pointed out the mark etched into the wall. "Does this look familiar to you?"

Gemma examined the symbol for mere seconds. "This could be the Savoy arms, topped with the Savoy Crown. The royal crown of Piedmont-Sardinia was destroyed by French Revolutionary forces. The Iron Crown of Lombardy, also known as the Crown of Italy, contains a nail, used in the crucifixion of Christ.

It's hard to tell, as it is a mere etching in marble. If we had the design details, and the colors, I could do more research. They used symbols like this, displayed on tapestry, when they went on crusades or important missions, to announce their identity."

Michael and Amy exchanged silent glances.

"This figure could indicate a resting place, or the direction in which to look for a treasure," Gemma continued excitedly. "Have you found any more symbols?"

Michael was the first to speak. "We've found something, but

we don't know what it is."

"Can you show me, please?" Gemma pleaded.

"Of course," Michael said. "We trust you'll keep this information completely private, until I've had time to discuss it with the Bishop, and decide what to do."

"Absolutely. Please let me see," Gemma said in earnest anticipation.

"Right this way," Michael said.

As they traveled further through the short hall of the mausoleum, their voices faded to the dismay of Vincenzo, who was still perched on the stairwell, attempting to hear their conversation without being seen. He dared to go no further and risk being lost in the crypt.

Michael and Amy pointed Gemma toward the stately wall before them. As Gemma examined the second etching, Amy explained their confusion. "The trail stops here, and we have good reason to believe the path continues on the other side of this wall. We thought these strange wells, in the floor, may somehow open a passage."

They squatted around the wells, Michael bringing the candle low, to cast light over the area. "There's an oily substance in each well, but we don't understand its purpose."

Within seconds, Gemma jumped up. "Move the candle away, quickly."

Michael complied and stood. "Why? What's wrong?"

"I think these may be oil-locks, but I'm not sure," Gemma said.

"What are oil locks?" Michael asked.

"They may open your doorway, but they could also be a trap," Gemma explained. "In the nineteenth century, we obviously didn't have safes with keys and locks, as we do now. I've heard of an oil-lock being used when a treasure was hidden behind a stone door." Gemma took a minute to catch her breath. "Let me explain. There are three wells filled with oil, or flammable liquid. By lighting the well on fire, a mechanism burns, which releases the blockage that is holding the door closed. If it works, the stone wall will open enough to allow you to slip through."

"That's fascinating," Michael said. "Should we try it?"

"No," Gemma yelled. "Not so quickly. The trick is, only one well will open the door. Lighting either of the wrong wells will cause an explosion, and the walls above us could possibly cave in. I've never actually seen something like this, but we have to figure out which is the correct well. Are you sure you don't have any documents to give you the answer?"

Michael shook his head. "I'm not sure. There are thousands of documents in the church archives. I've never had a reason to go back to those from the original construction of the church, until now. Dr. Amy and I started looking at a few of them, but a complete search could take years."

"And there's no guarantee an answer would eventually be found," Amy said. "Have you ever heard of an Italian carver by the name of Nicolo Pietra?"

"Why yes, he was credited with carving some of the greatest Italian works of granite and marble, in the nineteenth century. He has quite a historic reputation as one of the original carvers in Italy."

"We've come across his name in some of the documents, and believe the Archdiocese may have hired him to help build St. Francis," Amy said.

"He would definitely have had the talent and wisdom to fashion a hiding place such as this one," Gemma said, smiling in awe.

Amy turned to Michael. "So what do we do next?"

"I have no idea, except to go back to the archives," Michael shrugged.

"I propose we do some research," Gemma said. "Give me a day to find out all I can about Nicolo Pietra and rumors of this treasure. I have a few contacts who might be of assistance."

"Gemma, it's imperative you don't announce what's going on here," Michael said, concern in his voice. "And what about Luca taking you back to your father?"

"I understand completely, but I'll be able to do this in secrecy. Giancarlo and Luca will be able to wait a few days. They know I'm safe, and I feel better knowing they'll be with me from now on. Could we come back down here tomorrow?"

Michael thought about the next day's schedule. "Unfortunately not. We have a lot of programs being held in the church, and I think Sister Maggie may be leading a Christmas concert tomorrow night. Aside from the fact I should be there to support the parish, I wouldn't want to risk innocent lives in the event of an explosion."

"When would be the next possible time to come then?"

Gemma asked anxiously.

Michael looked at Amy. "I'm not doing anything unless you're with us. This is your find as much as anyone else's. What do you think?"

Pausing for a second, Amy said, "I'm not available until Tuesday night. Mondays are always hectic in the hospital, and I have plenty of calls to return about the autopsy. The prosecutor's office is waging a full investigation, and I don't want the church dragged into all that."

"Yes, I agree with you completely," Michael said.

"Okay, Tuesday evening then," Gemma confirmed. "That will give me a few strong days of research. I can't wait to get started."

"In the meantime, I'll look through the archive documents as much as possible," Michael said.

"And I'll fend off the authorities and the media," Amy said as she turned to Gemma. "Please remember not to discuss this with anyone."

Gemma readily agreed.

Michael stretched his shoulders. "Let's get back up to the church before Katie comes looking for us. Then we'd really be in trouble."

Laughing, they walked back toward the main room of the crypt. The echo of their laughter prompted Vincenzo to run up the stairs on his toes, and slide out of the doorway. Hiding behind a nativity display, he watched as the three emerged, moments later. Michael closed the door and returned the table and statue.

In the midst of an exciting discussion about their find, the group walked toward the delicious breakfast which awaited them, in the rectory, while Vincenzo said a mock prayer, in thanks for their utter naivety.

Chapter Sixty

Milling about until the three left the church, Vincenzo blended into a small group of lingering parishioners, his presence seeming completely natural. Once he walked out of the church, he grabbed his cell phone and dialed Roberto's number. After several rings, the line connected. "Where are you? I'm out front and you won't believe what I found out," Vincenzo hissed into the phone.

"We're almost there," Roberto said. "Look for a silver Nissan, and be ready to jump in the car." The line went dead.

Vincenzo stepped off the curb into the parking lot and assessed the cold, gray scene set before him. Within minutes, he spied a silver car glide into the parking lot, but held his approach until he recognized Paolo at the wheel. When the car stopped, Vincenzo opened the back door, and hopped inside. Within seconds, Paolo shifted the car into drive and started for the main road.

"Whose car is this?" Vincenzo asked, probing the back seat.

"Who knows?" Roberto turned to look at him. "We ditched the BMW to throw off the cops, and boosted this one from a nearby strip mall."

"Shut up you two," Paolo ordered. "Vincenzo, what did you discover?"

"A lot," he responded plainly. "After mass, the priest, Gemma and another woman went into an underground crypt. They were looking at some symbols on the wall. I followed them, but couldn't get close enough to see anything. Anyway, Gemma told them there may be a booby trap, but she thinks it's where the treasure is hidden."

"And?" Paolo asked. "Is that it?"

"No," Vincenzo shook his head. "They said they can't go down there tomorrow, because of some holiday program at the church."

"Damn. That means we can't either," Paolo said in disgust. "What else?"

"They're going to look into the church archives, and Gemma's sources, for more information. They're planning on going back down Tuesday night."

"Vincenzo, do you know exactly how to get down there?"

"It's pretty easy once you get inside the church, and I don't think they lock it during the day. A lot of people are bringing stuff in for the holidays."

"Good," Paolo said with a nod as he turned up the road which led to the farmhouse. "Tuesday, we'll go to church during dinner and have a look down there ourselves. If we can't find it, we hide out until they get down there."

An air of frustration enveloped the silver Nissan, as it passed Helen's house and continued to the end of the road. Harold stopped adjusting his window decorations to watch the car settle into the driveway behind the vacant farmhouse.

Chapter Sixty One

The cold dawn of Monday morning blossomed long after Amy arrived at the hospital. The emergency room was quiet, so she snuck down to her office in the morgue, to face the mass of papers on her desk. After a few moments of careless organization, she picked up her coffee and simply stared at the painted cinderblock wall before her. Not having slept well, if at all, she willed the caffeine to take over, while she thought back to Sunday.

Katie's majestic breakfast had been short-lived, as Amy, Michael, and Gemma needed to inspect as many archived documents as possible, all to no avail. Amy felt added stress, trying very hard not to be alone with Michael. She went out of her way to make frequent visits to the kitchen to help Katie and Willow. She was certain Michael sensed her discomfort, especially after he attempted to have a private conversation, which she cut short, and then left the room to stretch her legs. Sensing she was not ready to discuss what happened, Michael remained distant and aloof for the remainder of the day.

At dinner, Amy excused herself and returned to her cold, lonely house, only to be constantly burdened by fleeting thoughts of Michael. She made a mental note to check if Boston still needed someone to fill the trauma suite after the holidays, but then realized she would have to wait until her position as medical examiner at

Rocky Meadow General was taken. She couldn't help but laugh at the realization she had come to Vermont to escape her grief in Boston, and now she was willing to run back there to escape her discomfort. Perhaps, she needed to seek formal counseling again.

A persistent ringing drew her from her thoughts. She was forced to use a landline in her basement morgue office as cell phones were not allowed. After several rings, she picked up the receiver. "Dr. Daniels, may I help you?"

"Good morning, Dr. Daniels. We have an outside call for you. May I put it through?"

"Of course," Amy said, dread filled her chest as she anticipated the flood of calls regarding the nursing home aide autopsy.

"Dr. Daniels is on the line. Please go ahead, sir."

"Hello?"

"This is Dr. Daniels. Can I help you?" Amy listened to the technician from the specialty lab, relay the verbal results of the drug screen, for Susan Trevors. She thanked him for his timely report and hung up. Now, the only items pending were her transcribed dictation and Susan's x-ray reports.

Amy spent the next two hours alternating between being placed "on hold", and informing the prosecutor's office, as well as the local police and fire chief, that Susan had most likely died from strangulation, and the fire had probably been set to cover up evidence. The prosecutor's office would need her complete report for the investigation and court proceedings when the murderer was caught.

Absorbed in her work, the morning passed quickly. Around noon, she looked up only after hearing a knock on the door. "Hey, you better slow down. There's steam coming from your ears," Lou chided, smiling as he waltzed into the room, wearing a designer suit and crisp silk tie. "Ready for lunch?"

Amy paused for a second before she smiled. "I need a few minutes, Lou."

"At least I got you to smile. This case must be difficult."

"Actually, the autopsy was fairly straight forward. I imagine finding the actors is going to be another matter," Amy said, with a shrug of her shoulders. "Thankfully, the autopsy is where I get off the train. The prosecutor's office will take it from here."

"Good, then you won't be distracted during lunch. I hear the Cider Mill is pretty good."

"I wouldn't know. I've never been there, but I'm definitely looking forward to it," Amy said, her beaming smile masking the heaviness in her heart.

"So am I," Lou said, ecstatic Amy had finally returned his interest. "So am I."

Throwing on her slimming wool coat, Amy tossed her purse over her shoulder and turned out the lights. "Shall we?"

Chapter Sixty Two

Safely belted into Lou's SUV, they drove over the sanded snowy roads toward The Cider Mill. Lou couldn't hide his excitement, as he made small talk, in an attempt to get Amy to relax. "I've been looking forward to this, for quite a long time."

"I'm sorry, Lou, but you know my schedule has been crazy since I moved to Vermont."

"Yes, and for your information, the nurses are still convinced that you're working for the government, in some capacity. They haven't decided which agency yet," Lou said, chuckling as he drove.

"I can only imagine. It's not my fault there's been one dilemma after another since I moved here. I have no idea how I got involved in most of it."

"So you say," Lou chuckled as the scent of his expensive cologne filled the car. "The only thing I can say is, before you arrived in Vermont, Rocky Meadow General was a sleepy little place with no excitement. There have been at least four murders in the last year, and you've been involved with every one of them. Sure you don't want to share?"

"You're funny," Amy laughed as she looked out the window. "I have nothing to say."

"Because you can't or you won't?" Lou pressed.

"You know the old saying, Lou. If I tell you, I'll have to kill you." Amy genuinely laughed at the mere thought of being undercover.

"Okay, I believe you," Lou said as he glided his car into the parking lot of The Cider Mill.

"Thanks, I appreciate it." Amy unbuckled her seat belt. "I've heard a lot of good things about this place."

"It is a great spot," Lou agreed. "Very crowded on the weekends with tourists, but it should be tolerable on a Monday." Lou held the refashioned barn doors open for Amy, at which point the scent of cinnamon, apples and squash soup encircled her.

"Something smells divine." Amy took the seat Lou pulled out for her at an intimate table by the snow-frosted window.

"Doesn't it though? They originally served tea and coffee, but added soups and basic sandwiches, several months ago. Since then, the place has been packed."

"Looks like they made the right choice. What do you recommend?" Amy asked as she looked at a laminated menu, decorated with a historical theme.

"Let me see." Lou scanned the card. "Today's soups are squash and roasted tomato, so I'll probably pair the tomato with a half chicken salad sandwich."

"Sounds delicious, except I'll take it with grilled cheese." Amy smiled as she put the card down. "How does this work? Does a waitress come over, or do we go up to the counter?"

"We have to go up, but I think I can handle it. Tomato and grilled cheese. And to drink?"

"I think I'll have one of those Mocha Cappuccinos everyone

raves about," Amy said with a nod. "Thank you, sir."

"My pleasure," Lou said, as he bowed slightly. "I'll be right back,"

While he waited on a fairly long line, Amy took a moment to look around. The old mill had been converted into an adorable bookstore. Scattered about the room were covered tables which displayed best sellers, classics, used books and magazines. Each genre had a dedicated section.

As advertised, there were plenty of electric outlets for patrons to use their laptops, while they sipped their drinks. An area to the back of the large room was set aside for educational display cases and was changed with the seasons. The Cider Mill boasted many different specialty teas, as well as the best coffee bar in the region, and it enjoyed phenomenal reviews in several magazines.

Amy turned back to see Lou arrive at the table with their drinks. As he placed them carefully on the table, he said, "They'll bring the soup and sandwiches over, when they're ready."

"This place is fantastic. I don't know why I haven't been here before," Amy said in amazement.

"It's been open about a year, but I think it's really just becoming a sensation."

Amy noted the posters and asked, "What's in the back of the room?"

"I'm not sure, but they usually have small exhibits which relate to places of interest in Vermont. Let's see," Lou said, as he read the sign on the wall, near the exhibit. "It looks like this month is dedicated to the history of Vermont's granite quarries."

"Really?" Amy released an appreciative sigh after she took a sip of her coffee. "Okay, everyone is correct. The Mocha Cappuccino is to die for, seriously."

Lou flashed his heart-stopping smile and laughed at her expression, but was interrupted before he could make a witty comment by the delivery of their food. Gingerly placing the crocks of soup and sandwiches on the table, the counter clerk told them to 'enjoy', before rushing back to the wooden counter.

"This smells great," he said, shaking out his napkin, and placing it over the trouser leg of his suit. To avoid stains, he had already positioned his new silk tie, to the side.

The two enjoyed the casual atmosphere of the bookstore and had a riveting discussion about the latest cardiology study, snow and local gossip, only stopping when the clerk returned to clear their empty dishes. Amy took another sip of her coffee and smiled. "Thank you for lunch. It was wonderful, as was the company."

"I agree completely," Lou said, reaching across the table and covering Amy's hand with his. "It's been months since we had dinner, and I've been patiently waiting until you were ready. I hope we can get together again, very soon."

Amy's stomach clenched as she maintained her smile, and tried to change the topic. "How have your parents been? I know you've been busy with them."

"They seem to be better," Lou said. "Thanks for asking. I'll be with them for the holidays. They've both moved into the assisted living facility now, and they like it there. They're not overwhelmed with taking care of the house, and the facility offers them a decent sort of social life, probably more active than mine."

"That's only because you haven't pursued one," Amy pointed out. "There are several nurses, in the cardiac care unit alone, who would drop everything to go out with you."

"Maybe, but I'm waiting for the right woman to be available," Lou said with a sly smile. "But she's been busy the last couple of months."

It took a second for Amy to pick up Lou's hint, and when she did, she put her coffee down and patted his hand. "Lou, I really enjoy being with you, but I need to take things slowly for now. Do you understand?"

"Whatever you want. You're the boss." Lou looked intently into her eyes, while he covered her hand with his.

"In that case, I'd love to go look at some books and the historical display." Amy finished her coffee and collected her things.

"Of course," Lou said as he stood up and waited for her to lead.

Chapter Sixty Three

Father Michael shifted in his desk chair and restacked the pile of papers before him for the hundredth time. After celebrating morning mass, he enjoyed his coffee and hoped to spend a good part of the day perusing more of the archives, but his mind was stuck on Amy. They needed to reconnect. Despite being drawn to one another, both had taken moral and ethical vows. He did not understand why the feeling was there, but it was.

Amy already had trust issues and he did not want to make them worse. Michael had his own issues and knew the importance of not feeling abandoned and alone. He too, was lonely and thoroughly enjoyed Amy's company, but they were both professionals, bound by similar rules of confidentiality, honesty and compassion.

She felt she could not depend on anyone in her life, and suffered from feelings of loss. No wonder she was so protective over Willow. They were both drowning in the stress of life's issues, and clinging to the same small raft, in a wind-blown sea. It was not wrong to have a friend, a companion, a partner to navigate the complexities in life. Michael knew he could not cross any lines, but for him, they were starting to blur. He was aware of the risk and had counseled many other priests on the very same issue, but sometimes things simply happened.

Chapter Sixty Four

Amy and Lou made their way to the back of the Cider Mill and stopped to read the flap of various books on the way. Once they reached the historical display, Amy walked around the exhibit and read the cards affixed to each section to avoid awkward conversation with Lou.

From what she gleaned, stone began to be quarried in the late 1700's, with some references dating as far back as the 1600's. Colonial settlers cut into granite outcroppings of the surrounding hills to make lintels for their homes. The stone was also used for fence posts, doorsteps, and sidewalks for the town.

Quarrying grew rapidly after 1838. Vermont boasted the largest underground quarry in the world, as well as a deep quarry of almost six hundred feet. In the late 1800's, thousands of immigrants from Italy, Ireland, Scotland, England, and Norway began to remove stone to be used in architecture, as well as in the carving of statues and tombstones. Even the Jefferson Memorial, in Washington, DC, was made from Vermont marble, one of the state's three official rocks. The remaining two, granite and slate were quarried for gravestones, but also school chalkboards, as well as slate roofs.

The hierarchy of stone workers was formed by cutters, who were responsible for cutting and removing the stone, masons for laying blocks for foundations and buildings, and carvers, who were considered formally trained artists, carving sculptures, and monuments, heavily influenced by the marble trade in Italy. With the introduction of railroads in the 1800's, the flourishing stone trade attracted a slew of immigrant workers. American companies took the initiative and began to recruit their own Italian carvers and stone workers.

"This is more interesting than I thought." Amy spoke indirectly to Lou as she read the remainder of the card in front of her. "On to the next."

The next card described the Mount Rushmore National Memorial, a sculpture carved into the granite facade of Mount Rushmore near Keystone, South Dakota. The construction of the faces of Thomas Jefferson, George Washington, Theodore Roosevelt and Abraham Lincoln began October, 1927. Amy read the next card out loud. "Lou, listen to this. 'Did you know the figure of Thomas Jefferson was originally started on Washington's right side? After eighteen months of carving, the figure of Jefferson had to be blasted off the mountain and restarted on Washington's left side."

Lou listened intently and said, "I must admit, I didn't know that."

"See, you learn something new every day."

Amy read about modern stone artisans who cut, polished, and sculpted stone using pneumatic chisels, modern laser etchers, and computer-aided saws, rather than a simple mallet and chisel. Although techniques used since the days of Michelangelo still endured, many Vermont stone factories turned modern. They even offered self-guided quarry and factory tours, as well.

"This sounds interesting," Lou said, reading a brochure. "There's a Vermont Marble Trail, which is a driving tour along the marble corridor, running the length of western Vermont. Apparently, there are many examples of how the marble was used back then, as well as today. Would you like to take that drive one day?"

"Perhaps in the spring, when it would be warm enough to get out and explore," Amy hugged herself to keep warm from a small draft.

"It's a date," Lou grinned happily.

"Okay, only two more cases." Amy moved toward the end of the display. "This is interesting. They have some of the personal effects of the original stone carvers." Amy inched forward, admired the vintage chisels and read the names mentioned in the few salvaged journals. She froze when she saw the signature of Nicolo Pietra scribbled across the leather cover of the last journal.

Amy could not believe the answer to the treasure hunt could be displayed in a coffee shop, of all places. Perhaps Pietra explained how secret walls were carved, or the significance of oil wells. Amy realized she needed the journal, but what to do?

Slowly, she caressed the glass fronted display case, and was relieved to find there was no lock. All she had to do was slide the back panel open, retrieve the journal, and slightly rearrange the other books to cover the gap. As she continued to comment on the books, she started to cough. After a few seconds, her cough became more persistent.

Lou looked over at her in alarm. "Are you okay?"

"Sorry, it must be dusty back here. I probably could use

some water." Another cough erupted from her throat.

"C'mon, let's go get something for you to drink." Lou agreed.

Amy waved her hand in front of her face. "I don't want to go to the counter like this. Do you think you can get water and bring it back here?"

"Of course," Lou said. "Will you be okay?"

Amy nodded her head. "I'll be fine after I take a drink."

"If you say so. I'll be right back." Lou darted to the front counter to get some fresh water.

Amy briefly eyed her surroundings, and without hesitation, opened the panel, reached inside, and grabbed the hundred year old journal. Only the fragility of the yellowed pages slowed her, before she jammed the book into her oversized purse and haphazardly arranged the other journals. Her hand left the case as Lou ran back with her water.

Lou handed her the cup, and said, "Your face is turning red. Are you sure you're not having an allergic reaction to something?"

"No, I'm fine. Really, I am." Amy nodded her head, as she drank. Lou never saw her close the back panel of the display case with her other hand.

Chapter Sixty Five

"I can't believe I stole it," Amy said as she shook her head in disbelief. "I went against every rational thought I've ever had."

"Why?" Father Michael asked.

"Because it may be the only surviving document by Nicolo Pietra," Amy tried to argue her guilt away.

"Why didn't you ask?"

"Because I couldn't risk the chance they would refuse," Amy explained. "The journal is old. They may not want anyone touching it."

"So you made your own decision?"

"We're out of time, Michael. We're all going to the crypt tomorrow night, and if I requested permission, we might not have heard back for weeks. The Cider Mill may have had to ask the historical society, and then I'd have to explain why. Besides, didn't this little wrong serve the greater good? Doesn't the end justify the means? Is it wrong if your heart is in the right place?"

"I'm not going to validate that with an answer," Michael chided. He turned and walked away as his stomach clenched.

Amy sat on the floral printed loveseat in the library, misery seeping through her skin as she relived the day.

Lou and she had returned to the hospital where she finished her rounds, and spent the rest of the afternoon at Mercy Manor.

Helen's therapy was proving effective. Although Helen gained strength on a daily basis, Amy continued to push the elderly woman in a wheelchair, as they strolled through the facility.

Most of the residents fell into holiday routines of being serenaded by carolers as they ate their lunch, and made paper snowflakes to decorate the walls. Amy joined Helen for a Mercy Manor meatloaf dinner. Before she left the facility, Amy promised Helen she would return soon.

Amy's intention was to drive straight home and look through Pietra's journal over a hot cup of tea, but as she approached the covered-wooden bridge near the retreat house, she could not resist the warm, welcoming lights which reached out to her from the windows. Without thought, Amy turned the car to the right, drove over the bridge, and parked in front of the rectory. Michael, pleased to see her, welcomed her into the library. They enjoyed the warmth of the fire and sat at opposite ends of the couch as she explained how she came into possession of the journal.

"I was so excited and terribly guilty, all at the same time," Amy confessed.

"Spoken like a true Catholic," Michael laughed.

"Anyway, since I went through all the trouble, can we at least look through it?

"Absolutely," Michael said as he rose from the couch. "Pull up a chair. I'll clear a space and let's see what we can find."

Amy gingerly pulled the journal from her bag and placed it on the table, while Michael switched on a nearby lamp to give them a better view. Together, they flipped through the pages, in which

Nicolo Pietra detailed his early childhood, and apprenticeship as an artisan stone carver.

He was instrumental in the design of Papal statuary, in Italy, and garnered a prestigious reputation in a matter of several years. In 1870, he was asked by the church to consider traveling to America, to help design a large house of worship in Vermont. After soulful contemplation, he decided to accept the challenge. He had not married, had no children to worry about, and his fare and wages were all paid in advance. Nicolo closed his apartment, bid his family farewell, and set out for America.

"Look at this." Amy pointed to the next line.

'I passed the time on my voyage, detailing plans for the new church, although I never relaxed. I stayed in my cabin, taking meals in isolation, so I could guard my secret assignment, the sacred treasure.

Michael scanned the following lines carefully. "He doesn't say anything more about it in this passage."

"Okay, let's keep reading," Amy said, with bleary eyes. "It's got to be in here."

As the tension in the room rose, Katie pushed on the door, with a tray of vanilla tea and almond pignoli cookies in hand. "My stars, you two look like you're studying for a college exam. This should revive you a bit."

"Thank you, Katie," Father Michael said as he bit into an incredibly fresh cookie. "These are delicious."

"They are, but I can't take credit for them. Willow did most of the work. I can't believe how well she's taken to baking. Maybe she should tour one of those fancy culinary schools. She could take business courses, and between the two, make a name for herself."

"That's a great idea," Amy said. "Did you mention it to her?"

"No, she's very excited about the holiday right now. I didn't want to dampen her mood with talk about college. I swear that child has never celebrated a normal Christmas."

"It's sad to hear you say that," Amy said. "I'm trying to decide what to get her as a gift, but what do you give a poor little rich girl?"

Katie smiled at her. "The same thing you give her every time you see her. Love, friendship, security and support. She desires nothing more than that."

The lump in Amy's throat rendered her momentarily speechless.

"That's enough talking for now." Katie looked at the table strewn with the journal and archive papers. "You two need to go back to your work. I don't know exactly what you're up to, but it looks interesting."

"It is, Katie," Michael smiled. "It will be a fantastic achievement for St. Francis. That is, if we ever manage to find it."

"Well, continue on then." Katie paused at the door. "Let me know if you need anything."

"We will, I promise," Michael said with a grin.

Turning back to the journal, they continued to pour through the pages, learning more of the carver's story. "His penmanship was very good. I thought it would be more difficult to get through this,"

Amy said, scanning the pages. "I don't know if the historical society has made a digital transcription of these journals, but they really should. It's phenomenal reading."

"It sure gives us a different dimension than the history books," Michael noted.

The pair forged ahead, page after fragile page, until Michael stood up, stretched, and then added a couple of logs to the fire.

"Michael. I found it, here it is," Amy cried out. "It doesn't give a lot of detail, but listen to this."

April 23, 1878 - Today, I completed one of my greatest challenges and best work. I will not scribe all the details as I do not want a path to the treasure revealed by my hand. Suffice it to say, I completed the wall to the antechamber. It took the combined work of James Alex Coyle, myself and the Pastor to achieve success, but on this day, we are victorious.

The treasure will be safe, locked in its silk-lined chest for now. The main wall must be breached by the oil well. Once inside, all three parts of the treasure chest key must be located and screwed together. I have hidden the separate parts, behind additional stone puzzles, which will need to be deciphered for discovery.

I am most excited and proud of this work but cannot make it public for fear the treasure will be coveted for the wrong reasons. In case it is not recorded, I want to acknowledge, the RIGHT path is wrong, and MIDDLE ground is too common to be of any use. God Bless us all.

"We found it; I can't believe we found it. That's the answer to the oil well," Amy shouted. "He wrote of Helen's great grandfather and look here, he drew the same tiny symbol, on the bottom of the page."

"So what exactly do you think he's saying?" Michael asked. "What is he referring to? What if he is writing about the three parts of the key?"

"My guess is he's telling us to use the left oil well."

"Are you sure?"

"No, of course not," Amy said as she nervously chewed on the end of her pencil. "And I don't want the responsibility of telling you to choose the left, because if I'm wrong, there'll be an explosion in the church." Amy looked up at Michael and shrugged. "Where is Gemma? Maybe she can understand more of this."

"She's probably with Luca. He seems as enamored of her, as she is of him. They spent most of the day together, and haven't been separated since he moved in yesterday. I think she is well protected, and they've found their treasure already. It's too late to bother her now."

"Maybe she can read through the journal tomorrow, before we go into the crypt?"

"I'm sure she will. She's very excited about the treasure," Michael said. "Although, we don't know for sure it's the crucifix."

"I know," Amy agreed. "We'll never know until we actually find it. And that brings up another issue. What does he mean by stone puzzles? We may get through the wall, just to find another set of clues."

"We have to be patient and take one step at a time, but I'll be happy when we get through that wall."

"I know, and we're so close." Amy rubbed the back of her neck. "Michael, I'm leaving the journal with you, but promise me you'll sit with Gemma, if she reads it. I'm sure she is probably trustworthy, but let's face it, we're not positive."

"Agreed," Michael said.

"And the minute we're done, I'm returning the journal to the historical society, so I don't want any pages damaged or defaced."

"To assuage your guilt?"

"It's the best I can do, Michael. At least it's not for personal gain."

"True, that's true," he agreed as he nodded.

"Oh stop." Amy picked up her purse. "It's getting late. I need to leave. Tomorrow should prove to be an interesting day."

"Can you stay for a few more minutes? Maybe we can talk?" Michael asked as he placed his hand on her back.

Amy turned to face him, and searched his face before she spoke. "One day, we will talk. For now, let's step back and put things to rest for a while. Okay?"

"If you promise not to run," Michael said softly.

Amy's breath caught for a second. She looked into his eyes, and trembled as she whispered, "I promise."

Chapter Sixty Six

Amy had trouble concentrating in the hospital on Tuesday morning. Her mind was fixed on the journal. A historic discovery waited to be uncovered, at the risk of a dangerous explosion. Having cleared her desk in the morgue, she made her way upstairs.

It was exactly two weeks until Christmas Eve, and she did not want to see any additional cases come into the morgue, but she knew it was inevitable. There were always cases of 'holiday heart syndrome', an irregular heart rhythm, caused by high levels of stress, dehydration and excess drinking. It was just as likely after a vacation or major celebration, as it was at the holidays. Hopefully, there would be no cases and she could relax, for the next several weeks.

As the elevator doors opened, Amy made her way to the clinic, to help the staff examine patients with scheduled check-ups and minor illnesses. Amy relished having flexible responsibilities with her involvement in the morgue, clinic, and major surgical trauma calls, as it provided a much different dynamic than the intensity of daily trauma in Boston.

"Hey, you're looking lovely this morning."

Amy whirled to see Lou smiling appreciatively at her. "Hi, Lou," Amy said. "What are doing in my little clinic this morning?"

"I wanted to surprise you, but I've been talking to administration about moving forward with adding a cardiology component, to the clinic. I know you've been trying to add specialties for the last several months."

"Yes, that's right," Amy said, with a smile. "We can do so much with primary care, but some patients are really in need of affordable care, from all aspects of medicine."

"Hopefully, we'll be able to set up a regular schedule in the New Year."

"Thank you, thank you very much," Amy said, genuinely touched by his gesture.

"Hello, hello." Father Victor's voice boomed as he walked into the clinic.

"Wow, a regular party today," Amy said. "To what do we owe this pleasure?"

"I came looking for you, my dear," the priest said, with flourish. "I have finished my rounds here, and will be visiting Mercy Manor next. I was wondering if your schedule will allow you to accompany me?"

Amy laughed at his enthusiasm. "I'd love to go with you, but I need an hour to see a few patients, first. Are you able to wait?"

"But of course," Father Victor said. "I will distract myself in the hospital cafeteria, until you're ready." He moved closer to Amy and said, "Don't let Katie know that. She'd never let me live it down."

"Cross my heart," Amy said. "But in the event of an interrogation, I won't be able to resist."

"I don't blame you. Being questioned by Katie would scare the heck out of me. All right, good enough, I'll be back in an hour,"

Father Victor said, as he flashed Amy a kind smile before walking toward the elevator.

"He's funny," Lou said, watching him go.

"He's always cheerful, which is great when you visit patients in the hospital, especially around the holidays."

"I'd better let you go." Lou placed his hand on her upper arm. "You're on a tight schedule now."

"Thanks Lou," Amy said. "I really do appreciate your considering working in the clinic."

"Trust me, it will be my pleasure," Lou said as he leaned forward to place a quick kiss on Amy's cheek.

Amy felt her face flame as she turned and quickly moved toward a patient room. As Amy walked by, Kathy Wilson, the Clinic Program Director, blew a mock kiss at her, and suddenly Amy felt as if she were experiencing middle school, all over again.

Chapter Sixty Seven

Stepping out on the back porch, Paolo found Roberto leaning against the rail, smoking a cigarette. "What's up?"

"Absolutely nothing." Roberto watched his smoke rings fade in the cold Vermont sky.

"Are we all ready for today?"

"Guess so, but I don't know what to expect," Roberto said as he removed a piece of tobacco from in-between his teeth with his tongue. He turned his head and spat toward the ground. "I'd pack a tool bag, but I have almost nothing with me."

"Bring whatever you have," Paolo said. "We go to church around dinner. If we find the treasure, we'll grab it, and get the hell out. If not, we wait until they do it. Unfortunately, we won't be able to leave witnesses, so we take care of business and get out."

"Sounds like a plan," Roberto said. "I hate this place. I should've never left the city."

"Well, if the treasure is as big as I think, we won't need to pull another job for a long time," Paolo said.

"Let's hope so," Roberto said as he flicked ash off his cigarette.

"Speaking of witnesses, you know we need to keep this between you and me," Paolo said.

"I know," Roberto said. "But I like Vincenzo. He's been a

decent guy."

"Yeah, well he wouldn't be the first guy we've knocked off. Just make sure you do it before we leave Vermont. There are plenty of places to ditch the body. Maybe toss him off a cliff, or something. Hopefully, they won't find him until spring."

Roberto flashed fiery eyes at Paolo. "This is it, Paolo. I'll get it done, but don't cross me. You underestimate my desire, and ability, to kill you."

Paolo scoffed mockingly, and trudged back into the farmhouse.

Chapter Sixty Eight

Father Michael lifted a chair from the corner of the library, and positioned it at the main wooden table. "Please, make yourselves comfortable." Gemma and Luca sat down, side by side, after Father Michael placed the closed journal in front of them, and sat in the remaining leather chair. He cleared his throat and said, "Amy, ah, recently came into possession of this journal. We have seen several references to the Italian carver, Nicolo Pietra, and we feel confident this book is his personal account."

"Did you read it?" Gemma asked.

"Yes, we reviewed most of it and came up with a theory, but we don't have the same level of expertise you possess about Italian history or methods. We were hoping you could take some time to read it and formulate your own opinion, before we go to the crypt tonight."

"Of course," Gemma said as she looked toward Luca.

"I'll keep her company while she reads." Luca smiled as he placed his hand over hers. Gemma was obviously pleased with his attention and grinned widely.

"Thank you for this. If you don't mind, I'll be at my desk, clearing up some important paperwork," Father Michael said. "Any questions or problems, I'll be right over there."

Chapter Sixty Nine

Giancarlo sat at the bar, glass of red wine in hand as he watched Tony wipe the aged wood with a wrinkled, white dish towel. "Tony, how long have you owned this bar?"

"A couple of years now," Tony said, with a grin. "My partner's father left it to me after he died."

"Hmm," Giancarlo said, as he pressed the wine glass to his lips. "I can't say my son's partner would be the first person written into my will, if I even had one."

"Well, it's an interesting story." Tony leaned against the counter behind him and crossed his arms. "My partner was shot down in a bad bust. When I went to break it to his dad, we grieved together. We became great friends, and when he passed away a few years later, he left the bar to me."

"Do you miss it?" Giancarlo asked.

"Miss what?"

"You know, the excitement, the rush of being on the force?"

Tony thought for a moment and looked straight at Giancarlo. "I did at first. When my partner died, I kind of went off the deep end, asking myself if it was worth it. You know, why kill myself chasing a sea of scumbags that never cease to exist? I went wild, for a while, really roughing up the ones I caught. When the bar was left to me, I came up here to straighten the legal things out. I told my

Captain I was going, and he sort of suggested I take my time, you know, to think things through. Apparently, I was approaching the edge, and it was obvious to everyone, except me."

"And now?" Giancarlo pressed.

"Now?" Tony paused before he answered. "I'm glad I decided to stay. I see my share of interesting people, and I don't miss New York. We have a lot of visitors from the city vacation here. There's nothing left for me there, anyway. I have new roots here."

"I see," Giancarlo said as he nodded his head.

"What about you? What's your story?" Tony asked.

"Me?"

"Yes, you. Have long have you worked for Mr. Montanari?"

"I've worked with Marco for fifteen years. He's a brilliant man, an international entrepreneur, if you will." Giancarlo boasted a melancholy smile, as he emptied his glass in one purposeful sip.

"And how's that working out, for you?" Tony asked as he leaned forward and planted his arms on the bar as he waited for an answer.

"It works for me. Marco Montanari is a good man, his business is extremely reputable, and despite being wealthy, he treats his associates like equals." Giancarlo placed his wine glass on the freshly wiped bar.

"Can you, ah, retire, if you want to?" Tony probed.

"Of course," Giancarlo said through a stifled laugh. "I don't know what kind of movies you've been watching, Tony, but we work in textile trading, not an *organization,* if you know what I mean."

"I got ya, buddy," Tony said.

"One of these days I might just do that," Giancarlo said as he refocused the conversation. "Marco is one of my oldest friends who trusts and respects me enough to watch over his Gemma, the light of his life. Besides, I have a feeling once she returns to Italy, she'll have someone else to keep an eye on her."

"Ah, Luca."

"Plus, I'm not getting any younger," Giancarlo laughed and ran a hand through his slightly faded, black hair. "Perhaps it's time to retire, and buy a nice villa in Lake Como."

Tony laughed at the image. "Somehow, I don't see that happening yet. But, good luck to you, my friend." Tony looked up to see a frail elderly gentleman, walk in the bar. "Harold, what brings you into Hasco's?"

"Oh, I went to see Helen this morning, and I'm too tired to go home and cook," Harold said as he hitched himself onto a bar stool near Giancarlo.

"How's she doing?" Tony asked as he offered Harold a menu.

"Oh, she's doing just fine. That one's got a fire up her girdle," Harold smirked.

"I'm not sure I understand. Fire in her what?" Giancarlo asked, his face scrunched in confusion.

Tony could not contain himself and burst out laughing. "It means she's full of spit and fire, you know, she's a feisty woman, even though she's ninety-two years old."

"Oh, you mean to say she's a woman *piena di vita,* full of life." Giancarlo mused.

"Exactly. What can I get you Harold?" Tony asked, taking the pen from behind his ear.

"I'll have a nice beer on tap, and one of those thick cheeseburgers, with everything on it," Harold said, pushing the menu back over the bar.

"You got it." Tony placed the order before filling a tall glass from the tap and sliding it down to Harold.

He took a long swig and placed the glass back on the bar. "My God, that's good. I haven't had a cold beer in a long time. I've got to come here more often."

"We'd be happy to have you," Tony said kindly.

"Anyway, I made the mistake of asking Helen when she was coming home," Harold said, striking up conversation with the men. "Told her, I thought someone was cleaning out her house."

"I'm not sure I follow you," Tony said, puzzled.

"Well, about a week ago, I saw Dr. Amy and Father Michael up there," Harold began. "I figured they were checking on the house, 'cause God knows how the police left it, when they searched after Helen's accident."

"I think Helen asked them to retrieve some of her things," Tony explained.

"Yea, I figured," Harold said. "I still try to keep an eye on the place."

"That's kind of you," Tony said. "We need all the help we can get."

"Well, I'm glad I did, because this fancy BMW drove by, looked out of place in the snow, and I thought something bad happened. Figured it was a fancy lawyer or banker, 'cause pretty much everyone from around here knows enough to drive an SUV in the winter."

Giancarlo and Tony both jumped on Harold's words at the same time. "Harold, this is important, buddy. Did you see who got out of the car? What happened?"

"A couple of wise guys, if you ask me," Harold said. "But they went to the Benson place next door. That place has been empty for a couple of years now, probably even has rodents."

"Are they still there?" Tony asked.

"Pretty sure, at least they were, this morning," Harold said. "Maybe they're renting the place, but they're not there to ski, I'll tell you that."

"Why do you say that?" Tony asked.

"They parked the BMW in the back the first night. Next day, they leave in the BMW, but come back in a little silver Nissan. You'd think they would've used their brains and gotten an SUV. Thing is, I mention this to Helen, and she bites my head off, telling me to mind my business."

"Harold, we're glad you didn't," Tony said. "Listen, stay here and enjoy your burger and another beer, on the house."

"Why? What's going on?" Harold asked.

"Maybe nothing," Tony said, beckoning to Giancarlo as he grabbed his jacket. "But we're gonna take a ride up there and check it out. The police are looking for the guys who started the fire, and they put out a bulletin about a stolen silver Nissan. It's possible you saw them hiding at the Benson's."

"Think so?" Harold raised his eyebrows.

"Don't know, but stay here for an hour, okay buddy? Just in case it gets crazy up there," Tony said.

"You got it," Harold said. "This beer is worth it. I'll tell you that."

Tony ran through the kitchen to let Mickey know he was leaving. He grabbed his keys from under the bar before he and Giancarlo burst out of the back door, and into the parking lot.

"Should we call the police?" Giancarlo asked.

"Let's check it out first, then I'll give my buddy a call," Tony said, hopping in the driver's seat.

Chapter Seventy

"Which do you like better? Angels or stars?"

"What?" Katie asked, trying to understand the question.

"Which do you like better?" Willow asked as she held up the cookie cutters. "Angels or stars?"

"To eat, I prefer stars, with sprinkles. To watch over me, I prefer angels," Katie said with a smile.

"Do you believe in angels, Katie?" Willow asked, wiping cookie dough off her hands.

"Of course I believe in angels. Don't you?"

"I don't know," Willow said. "I don't feel like I've had a lot of angels around me."

"Well, that's where you'd be dead wrong, dear." Katie nodded her head for emphasis.

"But Katie."

"Don't but me," Katie said. "I know your life has been far from magical, but someone's been watching over you all along, and has finally brought you to the right place."

"I do love it here," Willow agreed.

"Angels don't always appear, wearing white flowing dresses, and sporting big wings," Katie said. "But I believe they're out there watching over us. God uses the best choice possible at the time. An angel may appear as a homeless man, a war vet, or a librarian. Most times, we don't even know it. Why, there may be times when God uses you as an angel, for someone else. That's why it's important not to judge people. They're out there, alright."

"I'll bet you've been an angel for a lot of people, Katie."

"Well, I don't know about that," she said, lifting a tray of sugar cookies out of the oven. "All I know is no one should ever be hungry in this world, so I'll set out to feed whoever asks. I don't care what they look like. Breaking bread with someone else brings us closer to them, and our Lord."

"You'll definitely have your own soup kitchen one day," Willow said as she smiled at Katie.

"Well, when and if I do, I hope you'll be willing to bake for me," Katie said, helping Willow place her star cut-outs on the next buttered tray.

"What will you name your soup kitchen?"

"Oh my, the thought never crossed my mind," Katie said, shrugging her shoulders.

"Well, think about it. What would you pick?"

Katie pushed her hair back with a floured hand, and left streaks of white from her nose to her ear. "Let's see. I think I'd want to call it, the 'St. Francis Soup Kitchen'."

"That sounds nice," Willow said. "You wouldn't use your own name?"

"Oh no, dear," Katie chuckled. "I'm simply doing the Lord's work. He sent me to St. Francis, so the credit stays there. Yes, that's it, 'St. Francis Soup Kitchen.'"

"I'm glad I have you, Katie. You're really special to me."

"And you are to me, Sweetheart. Now we'd better get this dinner ready. I don't know what they're up to, but I know they're planning all sorts of things in the basement tonight. Gives me goose bumps." Katie shivered as she spoke.

"I'd want to go down there, but I'll stay with you and finish these cookies."

"See, you're already an angel. Thank you." Katie turned as she and Willow shared a warm embrace.

Chapter Seventy One

Amy and Father Victor entered the lobby of Mercy Manor, the walls brightly decorated with multicolored chains and paper snowflakes. As it was near dinner, the residents were lined up, in wheelchairs, down the length of the corridor. The meal would be served in the next half hour, and it took that length of time to wheel all the residents into the dining room, and have their table places set for dinner.

Father Victor excused himself and set off to visit a few recently admitted parishioners, while Amy walked the length of the corridor, smiling at those who looked up at her. She found Helen in her room, in a chair before the window, longingly looking out over the falling snow. "Hi Helen, how are you today?"

Helen looked up and weakly smiled at Amy. "Hello Amy, I'm glad to see you. I'm fine, but I always feel exhausted when I get back from physical therapy. I wanted some peace and quiet, so I asked Elizabeth if I could wait here until dinner was ready.'

"Do you feel better now?"

"Yes, a little more rested," Helen said. "How are you?"

"I'm okay," Amy pulled a chair next to Helen's. "I wanted to check on you and make sure you're doing well."

"As well as can be expected, but I'll be better when I can go home," Helen said, weariness shadowed her face.

"I promised I would get you home as soon as possible, but you may have to tolerate an aide living with you until you're strong again," Amy said.

"As long as I get to go home," Helen said. "They gave me a new aide, and things are better here."

"I'm glad to hear that, Helen." Amy took a moment to look around the room, standing up to push all curtains aside to be certain they were alone. Reassured, she went back to her seat. "Helen, I wanted to let you know, we're going to look for the treasure tonight. Please don't tell anyone."

"My lips are sealed," Helen whispered, eyebrows arching in surprise. "But, I'd like to know what you find. Imagine, finding the treasure, after all these years."

"That's the point," Amy said. "I'm not sure what we'll find, but I'd feel better if you stayed near the nurse, or with a group of residents tonight. I don't think there's a problem, but I want you to be as safe as possible."

Helen was quiet for a moment as she studied Amy's face. "Were they after me?"

"Excuse me?"

"The men who started the fire? Everyone has been talking about it. I heard them say arson. Did it have to do with the treasure?"

Amy searched Helen's face. She was ninety-two years old and sharp as a tack, but Amy did not want to alarm her, rather, warn her in the event something did happen. "I'm not positive, but it's possible Susan overheard our conversation, and told someone else."

"Really?"

"Yes, I think so. I don't know if the men came looking for you, or were upset with Susan, but it's possible they killed her."

"My stars," Helen said as she held her hand to her chest.

"I don't think they would try anything else. Mercy Manor hired extra security guards for the facility. I thought you should know, and I want you to be on the lookout."

"Don't worry. If I see anyone strange, I'll scream my bloody head off," Helen said, anger flushing her face. "Mother always said, greed was the root of all evil."

"Don't get too worked up," Amy said. "Just be aware." Amy was squeezing Helen's hand when Elizabeth walked in to collect her for dinner. Without a detailed explanation, Amy indicated Helen should be watched closely, for the next twenty four hours. The nurse agreed to the order, sensed Helen's tension, and wheeled her toward the dining room.

Amy casually followed, and searched the halls for Father Victor. She spied him attacking a plate of cookies at the front desk, and approached with a questioning glance. He said a cheerful goodbye to a nearby patient, and joined Amy as she walked out of the lobby, to return to the retreat house.

Chapter Seventy Two

A little after four o'clock, the silver Nissan pulled into the church parking lot. Sunset came early during Vermont winters, and the entire area was already painted in cold darkness. Noticing few cars scattered around the lot, the men climbed out of the vehicle, and remained quiet to ensure they did not attract attention. Roberto had packed a thin bag with tools when he heard Vincenzo's description of the crypt. He retrieved them from the trunk, and carried them at his side.

Blending into the small succession of parishioners who were dropping off flowers and gifts, the men managed to enter the church unnoticed. They walked peacefully to the last pew, and sat down. Once adjusted to the silence of the church, Vincenzo discretely pointed to the location of the door, which led to the crypt. As the last parishioner walked past their pew, and flashed a merry smile before hurrying out the door, the men rose and Vincenzo guided them to the transept.

"It's over here." Vincenzo pointed to the table which held the statue of St. Francis of Assisi.

"It's blocked?" Paolo asked.

"They moved the table and opened the door," Vincenzo said. "Like this." He reached over and picked up the statue, handing it to Paolo, before quietly dragging the table away from the door. After returning the statue, Vincenzo was thrilled to find the door unlocked. With a small tug, the door opened, and he led Paolo and Roberto inside. The three men lined up on the stairwell, waiting for Roberto to illuminate the path before them with his flashlight.

"Vincenzo, follow Roberto down the stairs," Paolo said. With one arm out the door, Paolo inched the table closer, and settled for closing the door as snug as possible. He followed the stairwell until he met the other two men at the center of the cold, dark chamber.

"What is this place?" Roberto asked, a cold draft snaking over his shoulder.

"It's an underground mausoleum, a crypt," Vincenzo whispered. "There are four archways. Each one has a black gate in front of it, and behind the gate, there are three burial chambers."

"It's creepy," Roberto said, handing flashlights to the other two men.

"Are there any lights down here?" Paolo asked, feeling the cold marble walls.

"Not with a light switch." Vincenzo shook his head. "They did something the other day, but I didn't see how the priest got the lights on."

"You said they were talking about some symbol. Do you know where it is?" Paolo asked.

"No, only that's it's toward the back," Vincenzo said, pointing toward the little hall.

"Then let's get moving." Paolo said. With their flashlights, the men searched the walls, unable to distinguish any irregularities in the smooth marble. They tapped the wall with their fists to check for hollow stone. They pulled on each ornament attached to the wall, in hopes it would open a passage, yet found nothing.

"I give up," Roberto said, throwing his hands up in the air. "If it's here, we're not finding it."

"Vincenzo, you said they were definitely planning to come down here tonight?" Paolo asked.

"They said Tuesday night, but anything could change." Vincenzo shrugged as he looked toward Paolo in the dark. "What do you want to do?"

Paolo looked at his watch. "It's already six o'clock. Let's hang out for an hour and see if they show up. In the meantime, we have to find a place to hide when they get here. Are those black gates locked?"

Roberto walked up to the nearest gate and gave a small tug. The gate creaked as it opened. They tried the other gates, which also opened with a small amount of pressure.

"Okay, let's hang out for a while," Paolo said. "When we hear the door open, we'll head into the chamber over there. It should be dark enough and out of their way."

"Then what?" Roberto asked.

"Then we let them do whatever it is they need to do, to get the treasure. Once it's out in the open, it's ours."

"Think they'll put up a fight?" Roberto asked.

"Not if they have a gun to their head," Paolo said, grinning widely. "It's pretty dark and quiet down here. I doubt anyone would hear the gun go off once or twice."

Clearly flustered, Roberto stretched his hands behind his head, before sitting on the cold marble bench in the center of the room. "I don't know. I've got a bad feeling about this."

"I don't care how you're feeling, we're taking this treasure," Paolo yelled. "We've been holed up in this little town for six days. With the money from this job, we should be able to retire for good. Have all the bad feelings you want, we're not going anywhere."

Roberto held his hands up in resignation, as Vincenzo read the nameplates fastened beside the wrought iron gates. "Hey, they got priests buried down here."

"Yeah, well I don't want to join the club," Paolo said. "Don't touch anything. Go sit on the stairs and listen for voices or the door."

"You got it," Vincenzo said, shuffling over to the marble staircase. "I can't wait to get out of here."

Paolo and Roberto looked at each other with an almost imperceptible nod.

Chapter Seventy Three

"Everyone ready?" Father Michael asked, surveying the small group gathered in the foyer of the rectory. "Coats, flashlights, gloves, matches? Anything else you think we need?"

"I'll use my phone camera, if we find anything," Amy said.

"Are you sure you should be doing this?" Katie asked as concern clouded her face. "If the find is so important, shouldn't you have police with you?"

"Katie, we may find nothing," Michael began. "I'd really don't want to pull the police into this unless we absolutely have to, but we have Father Victor with us to be safe."

"Could you imagine if we find the treasure?" Gemma asked, excitedly. "Once word gets out, you'll have crowds for miles, tons of publicity, and this little town will be booming."

"I don't think we want that either," Katie said, frowning at the thought.

Willow stood next to Katie, an imploring look in her eyes. "Do you think I could go with them?"

Katie turned to her. "Not on your life, Sweetheart. After what happened at the nursing home, I don't want you out of my sight. I'm sorry, but I'll go crazy if someone gets hurt down there."

"I tend to agree," Amy said, looking at Willow. "If all goes well, and we find something fantastic, I'll come grab you myself to see it. For now, you should stay here until we know, for sure, it's safe."

"Speaking of which, you should lock all these doors, until we come back," Luca said. "Yes?"

"Yes. Lock everything. We'd better get going," Michael said, zipping his sweatshirt and tossing a small backpack with equipment over his shoulder.

"I'm starting to get nervous," Gemma said, prompting Luca to put his arm around her shoulders for a hug.

"Not to worry, *Tesoro*." Luca planted a kiss on her forehead.

"Let's go," Father Victor said, his hand resting eagerly on the front door handle. "Katie, lock this door the minute we leave. You might want to stay in the kitchen, perhaps cooking something, to make it seem like somebody's here."

"Oh, you'd better leave and in a hurry," Katie said, in mocked annoyance. She held the door open as the small group left and trudged through the snow, in an orderly mass, toward the church.

"The full moon is beautiful tonight," Amy said, looking up in the sky, as her boots crunched in the icy snow.

"That should help us, with the lighting in the crypt," Michael said.

"Crazy things happen during a full moon," Gemma said as she shuddered in her coat.

Scaling the icy steps, the group rushed through the church door, stamping snow off their boots in the vestibule. Puddles on marble were very slippery and they did not want to dirty the nave.

As they continued up the aisle, their wet boots created a squeaky echo which quieted, as they approached the table. "Did anyone touch this table since we left?" Michael asked. "It's not in front of the door."

Everyone shook their heads. "Are you sure you put it back after Sunday?" Amy asked.

"I'm sure I did," Michael said, but doubt crept into his voice. He pulled the wooden door open, and took a moment to look inside, but found nothing except darkness.

"It's dark down there," Father Victor said, feeling the cold draft come flying up the marble stairs. He handed out flashlights. "Let's light it up."

"Okay, let's go," Michael said, shining his beam on the stairs. "I'll start down first. Stay close together, and be careful on these steps." Michael took three steps down and stopped.

"What's wrong?" Amy said, in his ear.

"I don't know. I thought I heard something, but it's quiet now," Michael said with a small laugh. "I must be letting my nerves get to me."

"We should have come in the daylight," Father Victor said.

"We're so close," Gemma said. "We have to keep going."

"Let's do it," Michael said, continuing until he reached the crypt. One by one, the group congregated in the center of the room. The beam from their flashlights bounced across the marble walls.

"It's even more beautiful at night," Gemma exclaimed softly. "Have you had this place photographed? An exhibit with photos and history would be remarkable."

"As far as I'm concerned, the crypt is to stay out of the public eye for as long as possible," Michael said.

Gemma approached the black wrought iron gate which stood in front of them. Ten feet behind her, Paolo raised his finger to his lips, to remind the other two men to stay perfectly still. With hands on their guns, they readily watched the group's every move.

Gemma spun toward Michael. "You have fascinating history down here. I can't wait to tell the story to the world."

Paolo stood in the dark and tightened the grip on his gun, as he watched Luca place an arm around Gemma's shoulder. Paolo clenched his jaw, and anticipated blowing a hole in the arrogant bastard's head. Roberto touched his shoulder, which snapped Paolo back to attention.

"Why don't we get started?" Amy suggested, urging the group forward. "We don't know how long this will take."

"Let's get to the wells," Gemma said.

"Okay, they're over here, by the back wall," Michael said, leading the way. The group followed him, and stopped near the wall.

Father Victor knelt and pulled an LED battery operated camping lantern out of his bag. "This should help light things up a bit."

"Wow, you've really adjusted to Vermont living," Michael said, smiling at the other priest.

"Not really," Victor said, shrugging. "Katie packed the bag."

Once the nervous laughter died down, they looked at the wells and examined the wall once again. "We should get started," Michael said. He turned toward Gemma. "Tell me what to do."

"It's fairly straight forward," Gemma said. "Light a match, drop it into the well, and step back quickly. We should all stand back and get ready to run, if necessary."

"We agreed on the well?" Amy asked, searching everyone's face.

"Luca and I read through Nicolo's journal today. I think you are correct, and we should use the left well," Gemma said, turning towards Amy. "But if we're wrong, be ready to run."

Chapter Seventy Four

Tony's truck spewed icy slush to the side of the road, as he drove past Harold's house, and turned into Helen's driveway. "That's it," he said, pointing to the house on the right.

"Do you see the car?" Giancarlo asked, squinting towards the driveway.

"I can't see anything. It's too dark." Tony shook his head. "Harold said the guy who owns this house lives in Florida, and doesn't come up to do maintenance, so it's essentially always empty."

"How do you want to do this?" Giancarlo asked.

"Let's take a look around," Tony said, unbuckling his seat belt. "Maybe they aren't here, but it's worth a shot."

"Right behind you," Giancarlo said. Both men got out of the car and quietly closed the doors. Pulling their coats tighter, they quickly walked through the snow, toward the back of the house. With no car in sight, and the windows dark, they crept up the back stairs and slowly neared the door.

"The lock's been jimmied," Tony said, clicking a small flashlight in his left hand. He drew out his Glock and nodded to Giancarlo, who pushed the door open, without resistance. Tony moved his flashlight over the room. Aside from the scurrying of mice, the area was void of sound. The two men crossed the threshold and searched corners and halls without finding Paolo or his men. "Let's check the bedrooms, and get out of here if we come up empty."

"I assume they still have laws about 'breaking and entering' in America." Giancarlo chuckled as he followed Tony through the house.

"Last time I checked they did," Tony said. "But, I prefer to think of them more as suggestions." After searching the upstairs rooms, the pair ended up in the living room to make a game plan, while Tony ran his hand along the mantel. "They're not here now, but they were. This fireplace ash is fresh and there's lighter fluid. The sheets on the furniture are messed up and the mice were munching on these leftovers."

Picking up an empty bag of chips, Tony searched for evidence of Paolo and not drunken teenagers. "There's a receipt for three flashlights and rope. I'm sure Paolo was here." Scanning the room, Tony's flashlight beam fell upon a small table near the window. Giancarlo walked to the table, picked up several sheets of crumpled paper, and attempted to read them in the feeble glow of his flashlight.

"What does it say?" Tony asked, noting Giancarlo's expression.

"It's a handwritten map," Giancarlo said, shaking his head. "But I can't make it out. Tony, you have a look."

Tony walked over and studied the map for a few minutes. "Crap."

"What is it?" Giancarlo asked. "You recognize this place?"

"I think it's a map of St. Francis," Tony said, slowly taking in the crudely drawn landmarks. "They must be getting ready to hit the church. We'd better get down there and see what's going on."

"Right behind you," Giancarlo said as the two men hurried out of the house, the door slamming behind them.

Chapter Seventy Five

Michael looked at the small group gathered around him, tension lingered in the air. "Everyone get back to the center of the room. I'll put the match in and run over."

He waited for them to move away, and struck a large wooden match against the back of the matchbox. He dropped the small flame into the left oil well, and ran to join the group as they stared at the back wall, in eager anticipation. A flame began to flicker over the floor well and grew higher, a vibration pulsed under the stone.

"Something's happening," Amy said, grabbing Michael's arm for support. The rumble grew louder as stone began to fall from the ceiling. In pure astonishment, they watched as a marble panel slid open to reveal a small passageway in the wall.

"It worked, it actually worked." Gemma squealed in excitement. The others cautiously assessed the passage, as the rumbling stopped and the dust began to settle. "C'mon, let's look inside."

"Wait a moment." Father Victor picked up the lantern and leaned through the passage. The lamp cast a ray of light through the doorway and revealed another marble chamber. "It looks okay, let's go."

They systematically filed into the room, the air cold, damp and surprisingly fresh. At their left, Bible verses were chiseled into the stone and blackened, to render them easier to read. Along the right wall, hundreds of small marble squares were lined in rows. Directly in front of them, was a stone altar, placed in front of the opening to another passageway. Perched solemnly on the altar, was a treasure box, approximately four feet in length and three feet wide, bordered by suspended torches along the walls, waiting to be lit. "I can't believe it," Gemma said in wonderment.

"Let me take some photos to document this," Amy said, snapping continuous shots with her phone. "We should have brought a video camera with us."

"Maybe we can make it brighter," Father Victor said, lighting torches on each side of the chest, highlighting the entryway to the next passage.

"Gemma, you're trembling," Luca said. "Calm down."

"I can't wait," she said, turning to Father Michael. "It's your church. Please do the honors and open it, but hurry."

"Nobody is opening anything," Paolo yelled from behind them.

The group turned to see Paolo, flanked by Roberto and Vincenzo, each with a hand gun pointed in their direction.

"Paolo, how did you get down here?" Gemma said, fear and shock flooding her face.

"I followed you, my love," Paolo said. "Same as the last couple of jobs."

"Oh no, I knew it," Gemma said as Luca moved to protect her.

"Keep your hands to yourself, you cheeky son of a bitch,"

Paolo said, aiming his gun between Luca's eyes.

"No, Paolo don't," Gemma screamed, jumping in front of Luca. "Your bullet could set off an explosion down here and kill us all."

Paolo looked at Gemma. He reached out, grabbed her wrist and pulled her toward him aggressively. "As you wish, love. I'll just kill him later on."

"I'd like to see you try," Luca said, hands balled into fists.

"No," Gemma sobbed.

Paolo turned to Michael. "Open it," he said, waving the gun in the direction of the treasure chest. Michael did not move. "Open it or I start shooting," Paolo screamed.

Michael walked over to the chest and marveled at the heavy lid, draped in leather bindings, held together by sharp metal corners. Despite there being a lock, which required a special key, Michael tried to raise the lid, but without success. He turned to Paolo and said, "I don't have the key."

"Where is it?" Paolo roared, his face reddening.

"I don't know," Michael said, spreading his arms. "I don't have it."

"All of you, over there," Paolo said, waving his gun at the group. He herded them into the far back corner. "Roberto, Vincenzo, come take the chest. Now! We'll open it somewhere else."

"No, please," Gemma cried.

"Shut up," Paolo said as he watched Roberto and Vincenzo's failed attempts to pick up the chest.

"It must weigh a thousand pounds," Roberto said. "There's no way it's going anywhere. We'll have to open it right here."

Paolo shoved his gun under Gemma's neck. "Since you've been the one studying up on this treasure, my darling, you'd better open up the chest, unless you want the whole place to blow."

"Like I said, we need the key," Michael said, stepping in for the terrified woman. Paolo lifted his gun and fired, the bullet ricocheting off the wall between Michael and Amy. Everyone dropped to the ground. The piercing sound echoed through the chamber, as bits of marble flew through the air.

"Paolo, please stop," Gemma screamed, crying as she crouched against the wall.

"There's a way to open this chest and nobody is getting out of here until we do, if at all," Paolo growled, almost too quietly. "What would you have done next, if we didn't show up?" Eyes fixed on Michael, Paolo grabbed Amy by the throat, and pressed the gun to her temple. "Think quickly, Father."

"Paolo, let her go. I..uh..need her help. We can't figure this out, without her," Michael said, beads of nervous sweat collecting on his forehead.

"Make it quick," Paolo said, pushing Amy to the floor in front of the priest.

Michael immediately bent down to help Amy stand up. He held her tightly as they spoke. "The clue, what did the clue from James Coyle say?"

Amy thought for a few seconds, then recited the line from the journal.

"When the time comes for the wall to be breached, our predecessors will guide us. Only the humble will discover its passage and a righteous soul will find its key. God Bless us all."

"We said 'the humble' would be those who look down and saw the oil wells. What did they mean by, a 'righteous soul'?" Michael asked.

"A righteous soul is someone who is morally upright, without guilt or sin," Amy said awkwardly.

"That's a tall order in this society," Father Michael said. "I don't think that person exists."

"Well, they were referring to something specific," Amy said. "Do you think it has to do with the verses on the wall? Maybe they're a code of some sort and only a righteous soul would be able to figure it out."

"Let's give it a try," Michael said.

They cautiously stepped towards the wall and Father Victor held up one of the torches to cast light upon the verses.

"Ask, and it will be given to you; seek, and you will find; knock and the door will be opened to you."

"Those who trust in their riches will fall, but the righteous will thrive like a green leaf."

"Blessed are those who hunger and thirst for righteousness for they will be filled."

"Blessed are the pure in heart, for they will see God."

"Thou shalt not steal."

"What do you think it means?" Gemma asked, looking at the priests.

"The first verse, '*Ask, and it will be given to you;*' sounds like a clue. The verse is from Matthew 7:7," Father Michael said.

"It's interesting to find only the verses written on the wall, not their location in the Bible," Father Victor said. "That's unusual."

"Unless you stop chitchatting, you'll be able to ask the original carver," Paolo snarled. "We can have a theology class later. Find the key."

"We're working on it, sir," Father Victor said. "Unless, you have a better idea."

Paolo lifted the gun toward Victor, and mouthed the word, 'Pow.'"

"Maybe the marble squares on the opposite wall are involved," Amy said. "Why would they be there otherwise? Maybe they move or something."

"Okay, where do we start?" Michael asked.

"Well, you said that the first verse was Matthew 7:7. Is that right?" Amy asked.

"That's correct," Michael said.

"Okay, then a simple puzzle. We go to the seventh row and the seventh column and see what happens." Amy and Michael walked to the opposite wall, and counted the tiles. They pulled, pushed and prodded, with no result. "Let's twist it," Amy said.

Michael twisted the marble square to the right. "I don't know what's happening, but it's moving," Michael said, watching the tile spin. After a few turns, the tile lifted off in his hand. "It's a secret little opening, and there's a document inside." Michael reached in and removed the yellowed paper. He quickly scanned the words, while Father Victor held the torch over his head. "It's a letter about Nicolo Pietra bringing the treasure to America."

"Okay then, let's twist them all and get on with it," Paolo said.

"Wait," Gemma called out. "It could be a trap. The verses were written in a specific order, so we should search in a specific order."

"Fine, read later," Paolo said through clenched teeth. "Do the next verse."

"*Those who trust in their riches,*" Michael read aloud. "That verse is Proverbs 11:28. But is it eleven across and twenty eight down or the other way?"

"Guess you're gonna find out," Paolo said. "Try them both."

"Do eleven across first," Amy said.

Michael counted the tiles and when he reached eleven across and twenty eight down, he twisted the marble until it screwed off in his hand. He reached into the stone cove and retrieved a metal object. Pulling it out, he placed his hand under the lantern light. "It looks like the end of an old-fashioned key. See? This type of key came in three parts. The end has the pin and the bit with the wards cut into it. Now we need the other parts."

"Keep working," Paolo shouted. "If I knew any Bible verses, I'd waste you and find the rest of the parts myself."

"I guess that's why James Coyle wrote *only a righteous soul will find the key,*" Amy said. "Even if you found the room, you wouldn't have been able to find the key."

"Yeah and if I had been righteous, I'd be nowhere near as

rich as I am today. I'm getting tired of holding this gun."

Michael turned back to the wall. "Okay, what's the next verse?"

Father Victor ran his fingers across the next engraving. *"Blessed are those who hunger and thirst for righteousness.* That would be Matthew 5:6."

Michael again counted along the wall, twisted off the tile and reached into the exposed stone niche to find another metal token. "It's another piece of the key. Okay, let me see." Michael held both parts in his hand and was able to screw them together. "We have two parts."

The group was at odds. Elation and terror persisted and battled at each step.

"Victor, read the next verse," Michael said.

"Wait a minute," Amy said. "How do we know he's not going to shoot us once we have all three parts?"

"You don't," Paolo snickered. "But you can be sure I'll shoot one of you, right now, if you don't, so move it."

"The verse, what's the verse?"

Victor's eyes focused sharply on the wall. *"Blessed are the pure in heart, for they will see God."* That's Matthew 5:8.

"Okay, got it." As Michael began working the tile, Amy whispered to Gemma and Victor, in the dark corner. The group was filled with apprehension, as Michael removed the final metal piece. "Here it is. The bow of the key." Winding the key together, Michael held it up for Paolo to see.

"Give it to me," Paolo said as he reached toward Michael, his gun waving in his other hand.

"Stay where you are, Paolo," Giancarlo said. Paolo spun around to find a gun pointed at his head.

"What the hell is this?" Paolo asked, looking up. No one noticed Tony or Giancarlo's presence in the chamber, their arrival behind Roberto and Vincenzo an unexpected blessing.

"We'll take those guns, gentlemen. Move slowly or you won't ever move again." Tony and Giancarlo each moved behind one of the men, collecting their guns.

"That's it, time for people to die," Paolo said, turning his gun towards Giancarlo as the room burst into action. The group scattered, causing mass confusion. Father Victor brought the heavy torch down on Paolo's arm. As Paolo's gun flew across the room, Tony tackled Roberto to the floor. Vincenzo jumped on Victor, freeing Paolo to search for the gun. Luca grabbed Gemma and ran to the far side of the stone altar. Amy snatched the key from Michael's hand, as Gemma's agonizing scream momentarily stopped the world.

"The torch, look at the torch," Gemma shouted. Everyone turned to watch the torch roll toward the entrance, where it ignited the other two oil wells. Flames began to flare from the floor. "It's going to blow. We'll all be trapped."

Amy ran toward Gemma and pressed the key into her hand. "Quick, run out the back tunnel. I think it ends in the basement of the rectory. Hurry."

Gemma took off running and Luca followed. Amy turned to look for Michael, but instead found Paolo coming right at her, with Giancarlo on his tail. In a moment of panic, Amy screamed and followed Gemma down the dark passageway. Amy continued to run and Giancarlo chased Paolo in the same direction. In the chamber, Tony, Victor, and Michael continued to wrestle with Roberto and Vincenzo.

Amy had run about two hundred feet, even though she was unable to see in the dark tunnel. Extending her arms, she slowed down to keep from hitting the walls. Cobwebs collected on her face, as her feet skid across the dusty floor. Amy realized she had flown by other passageways, but kept going as straight as possible. She heard footsteps behind her, and men shouting at each other. Before she had time to register their voices, a large blast pushed her from behind, and flattened her to the floor of the tunnel. The walls shook. Stone erupted from the ceiling. The air became so thin, Amy could not catch her breath. A minute of silence passed, before her ears stopped ringing and she heard moans behind her. *Michael! Please God, don't let him die.* Coughing dust from her lungs, she raised herself from her hands and knees, and continued to run.

"When I get my hands on you, you're dead," Paolo barked from somewhere in the tunnel behind her.

"No you don't, you bastard," Giancarlo screamed.

Her mind still reeling from the explosion, Amy realized everyone was collecting themselves from the blast. *Had Michael escaped?* She ran faster now, as tears streamed down her face. Arriving at a small passageway, Amy scrambled up the flight of stone stairs directly in front of her, and burst through the opening, crashing headlong into Gemma. Brushing themselves off she said, "Gemma, are you okay? Where are we?"

"I don't know," Gemma said.

Amy twisted her head, seeing moonlight reflected on the other side of the small marble room. Adrenaline ignited her senses, she immediately recognized her surroundings. "We're in a mausoleum. It's the Coyle Mausoleum, in the cemetery." Amy was exhilarated upon remembering she and Michael were unable to lock the gate. "Gemma, run toward the moonlight and keep going." Gemma turned and ran out the front of the mausoleum. Amy desperately followed behind when her hair was yanked, sending her to the floor.

"Game over, bitch", Paolo screamed. He slammed her face into stone, and Amy's world went black.

Chapter Seventy Six

Gemma ran out the door of the mausoleum, clambering down the steps, and into the snow. Moonlight bathed the icy path, as she ran. Panting, Gemma looked back for a mere second and began to fall. While trying to regain her balance, her feet lost traction, causing her arms to swing wildly. Her body pitched forward, slamming into hard stone. Minutes passed before the woman stirred, regaining near consciousness after the shock.

Gemma tried to remember what happened, crying out as she moved. She felt a cold headstone next to her body. A cut on her face, leaked rivulets of blood, which pooled upon the snowy ground. One hand, caught underneath her body, clutched the key. The other was near her face, fingers sticky, and covered in blood.

She looked up, as shifting clouds revealed a full moon. The ground was cold beneath her. She wasn't ready to die. She had a good life, but there was more to do. Her eyes on the moon, she felt the pain begin to subside. Her body relaxed as a feeling of warmth and peace drifted over her. Maybe it would be all right? Or is this what it was like to die?

Had she realized dying wasn't painful, she would have ignored the anxiety which consumed her entire life. She squeezed the key in her hand and laughed. So close, she had been so close to the biggest discovery of her career. She knew it was never the money. It had always been the chase. As her mind floated toward inky darkness, the moon illuminated the gentle snow, as it innocently covered her trembling body.

Chapter Seventy Seven

Giancarlo burst through the opening to the mausoleum as Paolo was about to hit Amy a second time. Giancarlo lunged on top of Paolo, and they rolled off to the side in a violent heap, throwing punches and kicks through breathless verbal insults. "Mr. Montanari is waiting to talk to you."

"Let the old man try," Paolo said, throwing Giancarlo into the stone wall, before running out of the mausoleum. He slid on the icy stairs, and made his way through the silent cemetery. Paolo thought he saw Gemma running in the distance, and his desire for revenge surged through him. He was going to make her pay. Paolo would take the key from her dead frozen hand, and shove it in her father's face. Running down the graveyard path, Paolo was taken by surprise, when Giancarlo dove over the headstone next to him. They drifted across the snow, their momentum bringing them to a stop against a large granite headstone. Giancarlo punched Paolo in the kidney, and slammed his face into the snow. When Paolo stopped squirming, Giancarlo pulled his arms back and slipped plastic handcuffs around his wrists. Paolo screamed out, the side of his face burnt by the ice. Giancarlo jerked Paolo to his feet. "You and I are taking a little trip to Italy." The last thing Paolo noticed was the wording on the nearby headstone.

Nicolo Pietra

Here lies a good man

"Whatever a man sows, that he will also reap."

1830 – 1912

Chapter Seventy Eight

Luca tore through the passage, finally reaching Amy, as Paolo and Giancarlo escaped into the cemetery. As Luca helped her up, Paolo's scream rung out in the distance. "Are you okay?" Luca asked, concern in his eyes.

"I'll be fine," Amy said valiantly. While she rubbed the back of her head, a wave of nausea threatening to erupt.

"I need to find Gemma," he said anxiously.

"Please, I want to go with you," Amy said.

"Are you sure?"

"Yes, I'll be fine, let's go," Amy said. Together, they left the mausoleum. Luca held her as they made their way down the steps, and raced to the cemetery road. "Which way did she go?"

"Gemma? Gemma, answer me," Luca yelled, as loud as he could. They stopped for a second, to listen for an answer.

"Luca, you go that way and I'll start this way," Amy said. "She may have run all the way to the retreat house, but yell out if you see her."

"Okay," Luca said, as he started running through the snowy cemetery, calling Gemma's name.

Amy did the same on the left of the cemetery road, stopping repeatedly to see if she could hear Luca's voice. Realizing he was running to the right, Amy was about to take off again, when she heard a soft cry. "Gemma? Gemma is that you?" Amy yelled. "Where are you? Gemma, answer me."

Amy moved blindly towards the soft cry, and when the clouds shifted, she saw Gemma lying in the snow. She had hit a gravestone, a pool of blood had formed near her head. "Luca, she's over here," Amy yelled, as loudly as she could. "Come quickly, Gemma is hurt." Amy ran to get closer to the woman, while pulling her cell phone out of her pocket.

She dialed 911 and quickly explained the situation, dropping the phone to examine Gemma despite the dispatcher's insistence to stay on the line. "Gemma, stay with me. Can you hear me? It's Amy. Don't move." Amy ripped off her gloves and stuffed one against Gemma's forehead, applying pressure to the wound. She felt for a pulse in her neck and exhaled when she was rewarded with a steady beat. Amy ripped off her coat and placed it over Gemma while she continued to examine her.

"Is she all right?" Luca asked, falling to his knees behind her. Breathless, he removed his jacket and threw it on top of Amy's coat.

"She's moaning, but she has a good pulse," Amy said, wind blowing her hair into her eyes. "Don't move her head in case she has a spinal injury. I called the police and they're on the way."

Amy continued to check Gemma's breathing, as she moaned and became restless. Seeing a glint of moonlight on metal, Amy grabbed the key when it dropped from Gemma's hand onto the snow. Amy shoved it into her shirt pocket, as the sirens in the distance turned into wails.

"Luca, will you be all right here? I've got to go to the

parking lot and tell them where to find you."

"Of course, I won't leave her side. My darling Gemma. I'll never leave her again."

"Don't move her. They'll be here shortly." Amy jumped up and ran down the cemetery road, blood rushing to her head and causing her to gag. Her side ached, her head was spinning, and a massive headache formed between her eyes. When the emergency vehicles veered into the parking lot, Amy pointed them down the cemetery road as Katie ran out the front door of the retreat house with the police chief in tow.

Racing back towards the church, Amy flew across the threshold. *Michael, please be all right. Please don't die. I need you.* She continued to run, knowing the police were chasing her. She turned and motioned them to follow her as she made her way to the stairwell of the crypt. Shivering, she rushed down the stairs as quickly as she could, pain shooting through her body, and ran to the back wall of the crypt. Banging on the stone, she screamed, "Michael? Can you hear me? Michael, answer me. Victor? Can anyone hear me?"

Before the wall, was a pile of rubble, the opening almost completely sealed. Amy started to panic and screamed, "Michael. Answer me. Are you okay?" Her quavering voice turned to sobs, as she waited for an answer from behind the stone. Feeling the world slip away, she dropped her head into her hands. Hearing a muffled sound, she used whatever remaining energy she had to look up again.

Michael peered through the small opening, blood on his

cheek. "Hey, keep it down out there, you'll wake the dead."

Half sobbing, half laughing, Amy dropped to the ground as an officer wrapped a coat around her, and struggled to get her stabilized.

***

Several hours later, she sat on the marble bench, holding a steaming hot cup of coffee, sent down to the crypt by Katie. She refused to leave until they opened the room, and Michael was safe. While the officers called for equipment, Michael assured her Victor and Tony were safe as well. They were busy guarding their prisoners, Roberto and Vincenzo, who seemed to have taken quite a hit from the explosion. At least, that's what he told her.

The explosion had caused both the entrance, and a rear passageway to collapse, but the room itself was solid. In the middle of the room, sitting on the stone altar, virtually untouched, was the treasure chest.

Hearing a shout, Amy looked up and saw one of the policemen squeeze through the opening. Emergency medical technicians followed the officer. Anxiously, Amy squeezed in behind them. Michael held out his arms as she ran into them, dropped her head to his chest and sobbed. He stroked her hair, kissed the top of her head and calmed her.

"Everything is okay. We're okay. How about everyone else? I didn't want to shout through the door." Michael looked down at her, concern in his eyes.

For the next fifteen minutes, Amy recounted what had followed after their separation in the chamber. They were told by the emergency technician, Gemma had been taken to the hospital. Amy and Michael leaned their heads together, watching blankly as Roberto and Vincenzo were handcuffed and led out of the room. The police took photos and started reports, while Tony and Victor laughed and punched each other in the arm, like two school boys.

Michael squeezed Amy's shoulders and whispered in her hair. "We made it. We found the treasure and made history," Michael said chuckling. "Too bad we lost the key."

Amy turned to him with a large grin. "You mean this key?" She reached into her pocket, and pulled out the glimmering piece of metal.

"I don't believe it," Michael said, laughing as he looked up to the ceiling. "Do you want to open it?"

"No, you do it," Amy said, looking around. "It's probably the best time. We finally have a police presence."

Michael smiled and pulled Amy toward the altar. He waved Father Victor and Tony over as well. Together, they stood at the stone altar and unraveled the leather straps, as Amy handed Michael the key. He placed it in the lock, and with little resistance, turned until he heard the tumblers click. He moved the hatch out of the way and slowly opened the wooden lid with trembling hands. Victor grabbed the lantern and held it up. Before them, lying in purple silk, was a three foot golden crucifix. The edges were scalloped in fine gold, and the crucifix was set with rubies throughout. The gold gleamed, as the lantern light bounced off its beauty.

One of the officers, who now stood behind them, let out a low whistle. Michael turned to the officer and said, "You better get your partner to take photos of this, because no one's going to believe it."

Chapter Seventy Nine

Amy took a sip of her cinnamon flavored cappuccino, and sent a smile across the table. "This is the best Christmas Eve luncheon I've ever been to."

"The food was pretty darn good," Father Victor said, rubbing his belly.

"You're impossible." Katie pulled his dish away from him with a grin.

"It's not the food, although it was delicious," Amy said, looking at Father Victor, Katie, and Willow. "It's all of you."

"We're so happy to have you," Katie said, looking up as Father Michael walked into the room.

"Gemma sends her love." Michael sat down at the table with a large smile.

"How is she feeling?" Amy asked.

"Apparently better," Michael said, taking the cup Katie handed him. "She's thrilled to be back in Italy, and apparently they are spoiling her until she's fully well. Luca hasn't left her side."

"I'm so glad," Amy said. "I wasn't sure she'd be able to travel, with her head injury. Thank goodness the CT scan was negative."

"Speaking of head injuries, how are your headaches?" Michael asked, looking at Amy with concern.

"I haven't had a headache for two days now." Amy stared back at Michael. "Your black eye is gone. How is the neck spasm?"

"It's almost gone," Michael laughed. "Thank goodness I don't have to celebrate Christmas Eve mass with a shiner."

"Go on and laugh, you two," Katie admonished. "To think what could have happened down there. I'm glad I kept Willow with me."

"I'm glad too," Willow said, titling her head to the side. "Although the crucifix is so cool."

"Yes, it is," Michael said. "At least everyone is all right and together now."

"Did we ever find the letter from the crypt?" Father Victor asked.

"Just a few pages. It may have burned or been destroyed," Michael said. "The few papers I have are written by Nicolo Pietra and detail his journey from Italy with the crucifix. I can't be sure if he was sent by King Vittorio Emmanuel II. Anyway, he wrote of how, 'its presence in the new church,' caused quite a commotion. There were multiple attempts to steal it, as well as some negative reaction to having something so valuable, during a time of economic difficulty."

"So they hid it?" Father Victor asked.

"That's exactly what they did," Michael explained. "The attitude around the church improved greatly when it was gone. The church made an announcement the crucifix had been sent away, but the Pastor, Nicolo Pietra, and Helen's great grandfather, James Alex Coyle, secretly built the chamber under the church, to hide it. They left a few clues, so it wasn't lost forever. That's why Helen's family was bound to keep the journal. I believe she was the only one who had an actual record. Otherwise, the treasure would have been lost."

"If Amy hadn't found Nicolo's journal, we would've never figured it out," Michael said.

"By the way," Amy said, looking over at Katie with an arched eyebrow. "I heard the journal was returned to the display case, the day after the explosion. I panicked when I learned the historical society was contacted by the press to get more information for the article, but strangely, the journal was back in the display case."

Katie continued to be nonchalant. "Well, dear, it just so happened that Willow needed some driving practice. We were going to the Cider Mill anyway, to pick up a few Christmas gifts."

"I can't thank you enough, Katie, and Willow," Amy said, relief flowing through her body.

"You should have seen Katie," Willow laughed. "She slid the back panel open and put the journal inside, within seconds of one of the administrators running to the case to check for it. The media, or the historical society, had just called. I thought Katie was going to pass out."

"Poor Katie," Michael said, patting her hand. "You are unbelievable."

"Oh, please," Katie said, waving away their attention, while pretending to be angry at Willow. "It was nothing." The group laughed at the thought of Katie's secret mission.

"By the way, Michael and I placed a large evergreen wreath

on the Coyle Mausoleum, as well as Nicolo Pietra's headstone."
Amy smiled. "We stopped there to thank them for their help. It was
very shrewd of them, to connect a tunnel from the church to the
mausoleum. I told Helen about it and she was amazed. For a long
time, she hadn't been able to bring herself to visit the mausoleum."

"How is Helen?" Katie asked.

"She's doing well," Amy said with a laugh. "She's back to
her old self.   She was thrilled with the photos of the crucifix. I
promised to discharge her back to her home right after the holidays,
and she agreed to have a full time aide to help her."

"Will she be at the dinner tomorrow?" Willow asked.

"You can bet on that," Amy said, laughing into her cup.
"Father Victor promised to drive her and Harold."

"I told her I'd carry her if she couldn't walk and she got all
huffy with me," Victor said, feigning hurt.

The group laughed at Victor's rebuke. "I can't believe her
boyfriend is coming, that's awesome," Willow said excitedly. "I
wonder how Harold will react."

"I missed that part," Victor said. "What's happening?"

"Well, the nursing home fire was on national television, and
the story broke again when the crucifix was found," Amy explained.
"Helen's old boyfriend recognized her name and the church. Neither
one of them ever married. He just turned ninety four, and his niece
is bringing him to Vermont to see Helen and the crucifix. Helen's
been doing her therapy, twice a day, so she's nice and strong for his
visit."

"Good Lord," Victor said. "Let's hope she doesn't scare him

to death."

"What about poor Harold?" Katie asked as the rest of the group erupted in laughter.

"He'll be with her at dinner tomorrow, and I'm sure they'll always remain close friends," Amy said.

"My goodness," Father Victor said, shaking his head.

"In any event, I am thankful St. Francis is safe. We got the final inspection from the engineer. The church is stable, and ready for our Christmas Eve mass as well as our big dinner tomorrow."

"If we had that restaurant, we wouldn't have had to worry about the church dinner," Katie said. "We'd be able to offer a lot more than meals as well."

"Although, it was nice of Mr. Montanari to make such a big donation toward the food pantry," Willow said.

"Oh goodness, yes it was. We'll be able to provide quite a number of decent meals with his donation," Katie said, smiling at the thought.

"He was so grateful when Gemma told him how we helped her, he said it was the least he could do," Michael said.

Hearing the front bell, Victor jumped up to answer the door, and came back with Tony in tow.

"Sorry, I'm late," Tony said, pulling out a chair. "I was getting the bar set up for later. Christmas Eve is a big night at Hasco's."

"Oh dear," Katie said, shaking her head.

Tony turned to Amy. "Have you talked to the prosecutor's office? What's going on?"

Amy nodded her head as she sipped her coffee. "Yes, I did. Roberto and Vincenzo are being held and prosecuted for a number of crimes. They'll be in jail for a long time."

"Any word of Giancarlo or Paolo?" Victor asked.

"Not from the prosecutor's office," Tony said.

"What's that supposed to mean?"

"I know Giancarlo is in Italy," Tony said. "He's left me a message or two. He's thinking about retiring."

"And he didn't mention Paolo?" Victor asked.

"Not in his message," Tony said. "Although, I'm sure he didn't escape."

"Let's hope so," Amy said, sipping her coffee as she turned to Michael. "So what will happen to the crucifix?"

"For now, it will stay on display, in St. Francis," Michael said. "When things are settled, Gemma will act as curator, and we all get credited for the find. Thankfully, Mr. Montanari paid to have it encased in the bulletproof glass case and the Archdiocese is holding discussions about a permanent home."

"I inspected the case, and it's remarkable," Tony said. "I understand those display cabinets have a polycarbonate window which can stop a shotgun blast or a large caliber bullet. They use similar glass for some of the most important museum exhibits." The group nodded at the news. Tony did not tell them Giancarlo directed him to the tiny plaque, on the underside of the case which read, Donated *In Memory of Paolo Sartori.*

"Oh, Katie, I almost forgot," Victor said, slipping his hand inside his pocket. "There was a small package, near the front door, with your name on it."

"For me?" Katie asked. "Who in the world would leave a package for me?"

"Open it and find out," Willow said, leaning forward to get a better look.

Katie ripped open the brown paper and found a small gift, wrapped in gold paper with silver ribbons. "Good Lord, who sent this?" Katie asked. "There's no card."

"Open it Katie," Michael said, smiling at her wonderment.

Katie opened the gold paper and pulled out another small box. She opened the box and folded back the tissue paper. "It's a key," she said, turning it over in her hands.

"Is there a note?" Amy asked, leaning to get a better view.

Katie looked through the tissue and found a typed note, folded on the bottom. She picked it up and read aloud.

For Katie Novak, the new manager and chief of operations of the St. Francis Soup Kitchen. Inspections will be completed next week. Once approved, meals may commence starting in January and we look forward to working with you. Merry Christmas and the Happiest of New Years.

Katie read the address out loud and started crying when she realized it was the same address as the closed restaurant. She jumped up from her chair and ran over to Father Michael. She offered him a tight hug. "Thank you, thank you so much." Tears streamed down her face as she held the key up in the air.

"Katie, it wasn't me," Father Michael said, shaking his head. "I wish I could take the credit, but I don't know anything about it."

"Mr. Montanari?" Katie asked. "Did he buy the restaurant?"

"I highly doubt it, Katie," Michael said in all seriousness. "The construction started long before Gemma arrived in Vermont." Looking at the letter, he said, "There's a management company listed at the bottom, with instructions to call them regarding utilities and supplies."

"Well, I'm so excited, I don't care who owns it at the moment," Katie said, kissing the key and holding it to her heart. "It came from the Lord. I've prayed about it so much. I always fed the hungry when my husband and I worked the farm, and now I can start again. Thank you, thank you so much." She started waving them from the table, as she continued to cry. "Okay, up everyone. We have a lot to do before mass tonight, and I'd like to get the kitchen clean."

The group stood up from the table, giving her the private moment she desired, and started to go their separate ways. Michael turned to Amy. "Will you come to the library with me?"

"I'll be there in a minute, Michael. I'd like to talk to Willow first."

"Ok, I'll see you there," Michael said, walking out of the room.

Amy waved Willow over to the hall, and looked around to make sure they were alone. She hugged the girl tightly and smiled.

"What's wrong?" Willow asked worriedly.

"Nothing," Amy said. "I wanted you to know, I received legal papers to sign about my position on the Board of Directors of Willow Davis Enterprises."

"I thought they weren't going to send them until after the holidays," Willow said, her eyes opening in alarm. "Please, Katie must never know I own the restaurant. As much as she'll love having the soup kitchen, she'd feel funny if she knew it was me. When I saw she was going to lose the bid, I called my lawyer, Mr. Bradford, and begged him to do something. And he did, but I needed someone I trusted to be on the Board, so I gave him your name."

"I think you are the sweetest, most caring person in the world," Amy said, choking up as she hugged the girl again. "Your secret will be safe with me, and I will be happy to work with you."

"Thank you, Amy," Willow said, hugging her back. "I don't know what I would have done if you hadn't help me this year."

"You have no idea how you've helped me," Amy said as she gave her a final squeeze. "Okay, go get ready for church, and I'll be back in a few minutes." Amy watched as Willow ran off, and then made her way to the library. Michael was standing in front of the fire, warming his hands. He looked up and smiled, when she appeared in the doorway.

"The fire looks wonderful, Michael," Amy said, walking up next to him.

"We always try to *keep the home fires burning*," Michael said, placing his arm around her shoulders. "I wanted to give you a Christmas gift before mass."

"I didn't bring yours," Amy said, looking up at him.

"That's fine," Michael said, smiling as he lifted a beautiful present off the mantle, and handed it to her.

"It's heavy." Amy shook the square package.

"Go ahead and open it," Michael said, excitedly.

Amy slowly unwrapped the gift, ribbons first, and then the paper. She opened the box and drew out a beautiful snow globe. "It's breathtaking," Amy said, shaking the globe and watching the snow fall.

"It's a music box, too," Michael said as he reached over and flipped a small switch. The sweet tune of 'Silent Night,' drifted from the globe.

"Am I crazy or is that St. Francis?" Amy asked, smiling as she peered into the glass.

"Yes, it is. I had it made for you. There's the church and over there you can see our bench."

"It's wonderful," Amy said, tears rolling down her face as she continued to shake the globe and watch the snow fall.

"I want you to know, St. Francis will always be here for you," Michael whispered. "I will always be here for you. Things are a bit muddled right now, but we'll figure it out. You, me and our bench." Michael leaned forward and kissed her on the cheek. "Merry Christmas, Amy."

"Merry Christmas, Michael," she whispered. Amy stayed that way, wrapped tightly in his arms, in front of the fire, listening to tiny strains of 'Silent Night,' as they watched the Christmas snow fall softly to the ground.

CPSIA information can be obtained
at www.ICGtesting.com
Printed in the USA
LVOW10s1431291017
554201LV00010B/4:

F RAW
Rawlins, Linda
Sacred gold

1494 949006